Esperanza Romero
Feb 6, 1940 - Jan 1, 2021

I am grateful to have been loved by you.
Sad to have lost you.
Thankful for the impact you have made in my life.
May you rest in peace.
In my heart you will always be cherished.

Te Quero Mucho

About the Book

One night.
No names.
No numbers.
That is the deal we make.
After tonight, I'll never see him again, and I want to leave
town with zero regrets.

But, a year and a half later, I'm back with a secret I'm terrified
to tell.

Turns out the guy from that one reckless night is football
royalty. One of Sun Valley's infamous Devils.

I didn't tell him I was moving that night.
And, he isn't someone who handles rejection well.

Something I realize when I bump into him at my new school.
Sun Valley High. Home of the Devils.

And he decides to give me a lesson in why you never cross a
Devil.

ONE

Bibiana: The Summer Before
Junior Year

"**C**ome on, Bibi!" Monique whines before adding a coat of clear gloss over her full lips. "We're going to be late for the party. The one you insisted we go to tonight," she reminds me now as she toys with her hair. The dark brown box braids hang just past her shoulders. She glowers at me through the reflection in the mirror.

"I have nothing to wear!" Yes, now I'm whining, but sifting through my closet for something sexy—or, at the very least, something that doesn't scream "I go to a stuck-up private school"—is next to impossible. And being a Suncrest Saint— even if past tense—isn't something you advertise when mingling with the Sun Valley Devils. With any luck, we won't run into any of the true Devils tonight. That would cause all sorts of problems, especially since Monique's brother happens to be one of them.

He was in a car accident last week and is home recovering, so we should be in the clear. At least, I hope.

"Obviously." Monique reaches into her overnight bag. "That's why I brought you this." She pulls out a sleek, black, bodycon dress and tosses it my way.

I catch it and hold up the barely there dress, an immediate scowl on my face. "No way. I can't wear that," I tell her with a firm shake of my head.

Hand on her hip, she turns to me. "And why the hell not?"

"Because half the dress is missing, that's why," I hiss, careful to keep my voice down as I give the dress another once-over. Mom and her boyfriend—Miguel—are already in bed, and I don't want to wake either of them. Going out tonight isn't exactly approved. But you know the saying, "better to ask forgiveness than permission." Better yet, if Mom doesn't find out, then there's nothing to forgive in the first place.

In my hands, the dress looks no bigger than a t-shirt. A child-sized t-shirt. Yeah, no way am I wearing this.

Monique huffs out a breath. "At least try it on. What happened to you wanting to step out of your comfort zone today, huh? Weren't you the one who said you wanted to do something daring? Live on the edge?" Her brows lift in an expectant expression. "It's your last night in Sun Valley, Bibi."

Urgh, please don't remind me. "That doesn't mean I want to go out looking like a dime-store hooker," I tell her with a huff as a wave of sorrow crashes into me. Tonight is my last night in Sun Valley. Tomorrow, I'm moving. New town. New school. New life. In Richland, of all places. It sucks.

She rolls her eyes before turning away to finish her makeup in the full-length mirror that hangs from the back of my bedroom door. "Do I look like a dime-store hooker to you?" she asks over her shoulder.

"Obviously not," I snort. Monique is a goddess. Five-foot-eleven with rich brown skin, chestnut-colored eyes, and long braids pulled back into a half pony. She looks like Brandy Norwood from her Moesha days and I would kill to look half as good as she does. Her skin is flawless, and unlike me, she's managed to acquire curves in all the right places. I, on the other hand, am reed thin and straight as a bean pole. Mom swears I'll fill out eventually, but I doubt it. Not with my luck. At least I have boobs. Not much, but they're there.

"Glad we both agree. I'm wearing the exact same dress just in green. Try it on. You'll like it."

I roll my eyes but do as she says. It's not like I have a lot of options here. Most of my things are already packed. And even if they weren't, I still probably wouldn't have anything to wear. "Sexy" isn't really in my wardrobe vocabulary.

"Where did you get this from anyway?" I ask. "And how the heck did you manage to hide it from your mom?"

"Online. And I ordered it when she had a stupid floral shipment arrive for one of her charity things. There were so many delivery people in and out that day, she never noticed my lonely little Fashion Nova box."

"Sneaky," I tell her with a wink.

Monique and I have been best friends since middle school, which is how I know her parents would never approve of her wearing a dress like this. It's all about appearances for the Price family. They even took issue with our school-issued uniform skirts and had hers custom ordered three inches longer than standard. Though the hemline isn't the only thing about the dress they'd object to. They'd also balk at her wearing anything that wasn't designer and didn't cost a fortune. Can't wear the same clothes as the common folk.

Slipping the dress over my head, I smooth down the fabric and eye myself in the mirror.

"Damn, girl." Monique whistles. "You look stunning!"

I grimace. "This is...a lot." Though I can't pull my eyes away from my reflection. Monique is seven inches taller than me, so while her dress comes down just far enough to cover her butt, mine falls to mid-thigh. It's strapless and hugs my body like a second skin, giving the illusion of curves I know I don't have. But...wow.

Monique comes up behind me and pulls the clip from the back of my head, making my long, curly black hair fall around my face.

"This is perfect," she tells me. "It's sexy and screams for the love of God, please take my virginity."

I smack her arm but don't bother fighting my laugh. "I'm not trying to announce I want my virginity taken."

She tosses my hair clip on the bed and hands me a tube of bright red lipstick. "Doesn't change the fact that that is exactly what you're after. Come on, Bibi. This was your idea. Let's be rebels for once. We need this. A last hoorah before you abandon me."

I chew my bottom lip but accept the lipstick and move closer to the mirror to put it on. Squaring my shoulders, I remind myself that I'm leaving Sun Valley with zero regrets. I've spent the last sixteen years of my life being the good girl. The girl who never stepped out of line. Never caused a fuss. Never broke the rules.

I need to breathe. Even if it's only for one night.

At first, I was always on my best behavior because Mom was pregnant. She was older, the pregnancy unplanned, and it wasn't without complications. She needed help and support and I wanted to be there for her.

Then it was because my baby brother was sick. My parents had their hands full dealing with Afonso's condition. I didn't need to add to their plate by being reckless, and I didn't want to take attention away from Afonso. He was my baby brother. He was everything.

Then, right before his third birthday, he died. It gutted our family. Mom needed to grieve. No way would she have been able to handle me acting out on top of everything else. So, I continued to be the good girl. The rule follower. I can count on one hand the number of times my parents have ever needed to scold me.

Less than a year after Afonso passed, Dad left.

My family has been hit in the face with life again and again. There is never a good time to...I don't know...be a kid. To make mistakes. To act impulsively. Guilt worms its way through my chest reminding me now still isn't a good time. But then, when will it ever be? I'm sixteen years old. I want to be young and dumb. Not forever, but for a night. Just this one time. I want to make mistakes I can look back on. I want to know that I was wild and free. That I spread my wings and lived.

Afonso's been gone for three years now. Dad's been gone for two. It's been a whirlwind for Mom and I, but things have gotten better. Mom has a boyfriend. He's kinda weird but she smiles a lot more than she has in years, and I think she really loves him. He makes her happy. And I want her to be happy.

She's been through so much.

It's why I'm not complaining about the move. Well, not out loud at least. And why I stuffed back my tears and smiled ear to ear when she told me the good news. She deserves to be happy. I just...I want that for me, too.

"Okay. Let's go before I lose my nerve."

Monique's smile widens. "Eeeeee! This is going to be so much fun!"

I don't know if I share her enthusiasm, but I'm committed to this course nonetheless. For one night, I'm not going to be Bibiana Sousa—the good girl. I'm going to be the rebel. The wild child. A girl that goes with the flow, lets her hair down, and for once in her life, makes some freaking mistakes.

No one bats an eye as Monique and I stroll up to tonight's party house. I have no idea whose it is, but I also don't care. Suncrest Academy kids don't throw ragers like this, and by crashing a Sun Valley High party, we're less likely to run into anyone we know and have word get back to either of our parents.

"Come on, let's grab a drink." Monique hauls me through the front door and leads me in the obvious direction of the kitchen where a keg has been set up. Grabbing a red cup, she hands it to one of the guys manning the keg and he fills it for her, giving her an interested once-over.

"You here with anyone?" he asks, handing her the beer and tilting his head toward me in silent question. I shake my head, and wave off the offered alcohol, grabbing a water bottle from the open coolers instead. I know plenty of students who have zero issue with underage drinking but...I don't know...coming to the party to hook up with a guy seems risqué enough for me for one night. Drinking when I've just barely turned sixteen feels like I would be pushing it.

"Nope. Just my girl," Monique says, giving him a come-hither look as she takes a sip of her beer. The guys at Suncrest Academy don't give Monique a second glance. I'm pretty sure it's because they're intimidated by her. She's tall, a complete beast on the basketball court, and she has a spitfire personality. But it could also be because they're idiots. Actually, if I had to put money on it, it'd be because they're all idiots.

He tugs her close and she squeaks, though secretly I know she's thrilled by the attention. Like me, Monique is kept in a sheltered little box, rarely let out to play. We might say tonight is my night, but it's equally for her. We both need this escape from the constricting lives we lead, and Monique deserves to feel like the goddess she is.

"I'm gonna go mingle," I tell her, giving her the out she needs to have fun and not worry about me. She makes a face, about to argue, and I shake my head. "Have fun. You can't stick by my side all night, anyway. Remember?"

She rolls her eyes but smiles. "Fine. But find me if you need me, okay? And don't go home with anyone."

"Yes, Mom!" I snicker and turn around, following the sound of music coming from the back of the house.

I cut through the kitchen and dining room until I get to a set of double doors that leads to the back patio. A DJ booth has been set up. People are drinking and dancing, having a good time. I crack open my water bottle, taking a sip as I soak in the cool evening air, letting my gaze wander over the crowd. Everyone is clustered in these little groups as though natural cliques have formed and I kinda hate it. It's so high school.

I continue to scan the clusters when a guy on my far right grabs my attention. He's cute. My age with light blond hair and broad shoulders. He's laughing at something his friend says when our gazes connect. He stares for a second before lifting his cup as if to say hello. I smile. He smiles back. And then he goes back to talking. But every few seconds his eyes come back to me.

I linger where I stand for a moment, debating whether or not to head in his direction. It's obvious he's no longer listening to whatever his friends are saying. And he's not being shy about staring either. His perusal of my body lets me know he's interested but—

No.

Come on, Bibi. You can do this.

I take a deep breath. Be a rebel, I tell myself. I'm not going to just stand here like an idiot hoping he'll approach me. I'm going to be bold. I can do this.

I take a step forward when a voice behind me stops me in my tracks. "I wouldn't waste my time on Carson Bailey if I were you."

I whirl around, a scowl on my face as my eyes land on a boy hovering close behind me. "He has a small dick," he says, a savage grin on his face.

"Who said I was interested in his dick?" I ask, quirking a brow. And okay, yeah, maybe I am, but I don't have to admit it to this guy. Whoever the hell he is.

He snorts. "With a body like yours in a dress like that, you're looking for something, and it's not cookies at a bake sale. My money is on dick."

I roll my eyes. Jerk. "Maybe I just wanted to feel pretty."

He licks his lips, his eyes roving over my body in obvious appreciation. "Nah. You already know you're pretty. You want something else." His dark gaze is challenging as he boldly steps forward, our chests almost touching. A wave of heat floods through me at his proximity, and I take a second to drink him in. He's not just cute like the other guy. He's hot. He has dark brown hair and equally dark eyes that lift the smallest amount at the corners. He's Hispanic. Not Mexican, though. His jaw line is sharp. His brows angular. Not Brazilian like me either.

Honduran, maybe Guatemalan if I had to guess. Latin American for sure, there's a little too much indigenous in his features to be Spaniard but I don't bother asking to confirm.

Dressed in low-slung jeans and a form-fitting black shirt, it does nothing to hide his muscular body. He's most likely an athlete. No surprise there. He definitely has the confident swagger of one.

I force my feet to stay rooted as he towers over my tiny frame. He's much taller than me, maybe six feet. I have to tilt my head back to meet his stare, and a part of me itches to reach up on tiptoe and close the distance between our mouths, the blond boy all but forgotten thanks to his arrival.

My chest rises and falls with each of my breaths. My heart suddenly eager to beat out of my chest. I've never reacted to a boy like this. It's...intoxicating.

The corners of his lips quirk as if he knows exactly what I'm thinking and more surprising, he acts, closing the space between our lips, his mouth pressing firmly against mine. I gasp and he takes full advantage, his tongue exploring my mouth as the taste of sweet oranges and chili explodes across my tastebuds. I moan into his mouth, unable to stop my reaction to him. Man, can he kiss.

One of his hands grips my hip, the other tangles in my curly hair as he pulls me closer, our bodies pressed tight against one another and everything else around me disappears.

Hoots and hollers to get a room cut through the fog of desire and I pull back, breaking the kiss. He releases me with obvious reluctance, his hand still firmly on my hip and a stunned expression on his face.

I'm breathing heavy, my heart racing. That was...I don't know what the hell that was, but I've never been kissed like that. Never felt the need to clench my thighs together and curl my toes. Was it the same for him? I swallow hard and chew on my bottom lip. His gaze locks on my mouth and he licks his lips, my eyes tracking the movement. My hand reaches up almost as if it has a mind of its own, and my fingers curl into the fabric of his shirt needing to ground myself.

"You still want pretty boy over there?" he asks, tilting his head toward...what was his name?

I shake my head. Hell, no. I want him. This guy right here. If I'm going to lose my virginity to anyone, it should be him. Someone who makes me feel lightheaded after just one kiss.

"Good."

Without another word he reaches for my hand and tugs on me to follow as he weaves his way through the crowd, heading toward what I think is a pool house. "Where are we going?" I ask, my voice coming out a little breathless, my lips still tingling from our kiss.

"Somewhere quiet," he says over his shoulder and I notice he's clutching his side and there's a stiffness to his gate.

Is he okay?

I'm suddenly nervous. We're going somewhere quiet which is good. Right? It's what I want only I don't even know this guy. Then again, that is kind of the point of tonight. Only... God. Come on, Bibiana. Stop being such a worrier.

Reaching the pool house, he opens the door and we both slip inside. The room is dark, some outside light filtering in through the sheer curtains. He drags me toward a sofa and sits, a soft hiss escaping his lips before he tugs me down beside him.

"Are you alright?"

The room is silent except for our breathing. I sit stiffly beside him, my fingers still laced with his as my eyes adjust to the darkness. His thumb rubs lazy circles across the back of my hand, then he shifts to face me.

"Just a sports injury. No big deal."

I purse my lips. It's summer. Sports have ended for the year. I guess it's possible some practice over the summer months. I think football does maybe, but...

"Hey." He pulls me closer. "Come here."

He tugs me onto his lap, my thighs straddling his waist. His length presses against my core and I'm barely able to restrain myself from grinding against him.

He trails a finger along the side of my face, down my neck and settles it along the hollow of my throat. There's something strangely intimate about the caress. "What's your name?"

I hesitate.

"You holding back on me, mariposa?" I was right. Definitely Hispanic. His smile is both savage and sinful. There's this energy to him that draws me in, but it also terrifies me. This is supposed to be a one-night thing. Good memories and a fun time, but nothing more. No attachments. But there's something about him that tells me he's someone I'd find myself easily attached to. It's a good thing I'm only in Sun Valley for one more night. Wouldn't want to become one of what I'm sure are his many admirers.

"Hardly, just, why not keep this interesting?" I suggest as casually as possible.

He raises a brow, shadows cast across his face from the moonlight filtering through the room. "You don't wanna exchange names?" If anything, his grin widens.

I shake my head.

"What about phone numbers?" he asks, cocking his head to the side.

Another shake.

He chuckles. "Damn, mariposa. And here I thought I was the player."

If he only knew just how inexperienced I was. Stepping into the role I've set out for myself, I rock my hips against him and he hisses, his eyes glazing over with lust. "You're playing a dangerous game, mariposa."

"Why do you keep calling me a moth?" I ask, a breathy quality to my voice.

He leans forward, nipping at the column of my throat. "Not a moth. A butterfly," he murmurs. His hands find my hips and he presses me down against him, his hips thrusting upward to grind against my center. Electricity crackles between us. He tilts my chin, drawing my lips to his and fusing them together. Stars explode behind my closed lids and every rational thought in my mind floats away.

The more he kisses me, the drunker I am on his taste, and the more I want to throw caution to the wind. This feels good. Right. I don't even know him, but somehow, my body does. It craves him, silently begging for me.

His fingers dig into me, his erection hot between my legs. I weave my fingers through the short strands of his hair, pressing my chest against his, but it isn't enough. His kiss is drugging, pulling me deep into an abyss I have zero desire to escape. When his hands slip beneath the hem of my dress, tugging it over my ass and then my head, bearing me to his dark and hungry gaze, I offer no resistance.

His eyes grow hooded as he lasers in on my chest, a hand coming up to thumb over one taught nipple. I shiver and he grins. The satisfied smile of a boy who knows the effect he has on a girl. He leans forward, capturing my breast in his hot mouth, his teeth grazing my nipple as I rock against him. My body aching and desperate for more friction.

Between kisses, I tug off his shirt. Unbutton his jeans. It takes next to no time for the two of us to find ourselves naked, clawing at one another's skin and he wastes zero time in retrieving a condom from his discarded jeans pocket and rolling it on before pulling me down on top of him and lining himself up with my core.

A part of me wonders if I should say something. Let him know I'm a virgin. I've heard the stories. I know there is usually pain the first time. But I can't convince myself to ruin this moment. I want this. Unequivocally and desperately. I want this.

His cock nudges my entrance and I stiffen, bracing myself for what's to come. His hard, thick length pushes inside of me with slow and measured thrusts. I gasp at the sensations as he stretches me to my limits, to the point where pleasure merges with the sharp bite of pain.

"Fuck, you're tight," he hisses between clenched teeth.

My fingers dig into his shoulders as I seat myself on him. And when I feel that edge of resistance, that last layer of innocence I'm determined to stamp out, I don't let myself think about it. I suck in a breath, steel myself, and press my hips down until he's fully inside of me, pushing past the pain and focusing only on the pleasure.

He groans and slams his mouth against my own, consuming my cries and filling me up until I don't know where I end and where he begins. "Your name, mi pequeña mariposa?" he prompts when I pull back to catch my breath. My little butterfly.

I ignore the question, chasing his mouth instead and shifting my weight on his shaft. A breath hisses between his teeth, but he holds me steady. "You're a virgin."

It isn't a question, so I don't bother responding. Instead, I do the only thing I can—no, the only thing I need—and move.

I rise above him until only the tip of his shaft remains inside me before sinking back down with deliberate slowness.

He drops his head back on the sofa, his Adam's apple bobbing in his throat. "Fuck, what are you doing to me?" His voice is guttural, coated in desire and laced with hunger.

I repeat the movement twice more before he lifts me in his arms, standing to his full height, my legs wrapping around his waist. He walks us to a table, laying me back, our bodies never losing their connection.

"You're playing with fire," he cautions as he pulls out of me before flexing his hips and driving himself back in. Harder. Deeper. I writhe beneath him, uncertain if I'm desperate to get closer or trying to pull away.

My body is burning, my center slick with need as he thrusts into me again and again. Pressure builds inside of me making me needy and desperate for more. For all that he'll give. "Maybe I want to get burned."

He lifts one of my legs, drawing it up and over his shoulder as I hold the other tight, curled over his hip. His cock sinks deeper inside of me as he leans down, his mouth trailing wet kisses across my breasts, up my throat, and to my lips. He hits a deeper angle in this position. Every thrust and every pivot of his hips elicits new sensations.

The pressure inside of me continues to build until I'm spinning, unable to tell up from down. My visions blurs, stars explode behind my eyelids and my body jerks, jolts of pleasure spear through me without warning. He swallows down my cries until they become little more than whimpers and mewls, leaving me breathless and my body boneless.

My chest heaves. My body is slick with sweat and he's still rock-hard inside of me. There's something primal in the way he's looking at me right now. His hungry stare drinking in my sweat-slicked skin and thoroughly fucked gaze.

"You shouldn't have given me your innocence," he says, a fierce glint in his eyes. "I'm going to ruin you for any man who comes after me."

I bite my lower lip. Thank God I'm leaving tomorrow. This boy could easily become an addiction. This moment, these feelings, it's more than I imagined. More than I ever anticipated. And a hell of a lot more than I'm ready for. But to hell with it.

"Do your worst." I tell him.

His eyes flash. "Burn for me, mariposa. Burn."

TWO

Bibiana: 18 months later...

I'm anxious. More anxious than I should be. I try on half a dozen shirts, hating all of them before I settle on a basic, long-sleeved, black t-shirt and an oversized hoodie, resigned to the fact that today just isn't my day. None of my clothes look right on a body that doesn't feel like it's mine anymore. It's been nine months. And while I've managed to drop most of the weight, I'm still...different.

My breasts are larger. My hips wider. I'm soft in places that were once firm and I just...I exhale a loud breath. I've changed. And not just on the outside. Clothes can only hide so much. There are times like now when I feel like an imposter trapped inside my own body.

Luis chooses that moment to wake, and I silently curse myself for my little outburst. Rushing over to his crib that's positioned beside my bed, I lean down to pick him up, rocking him in my arms while making soft cooing sounds. A quick glance at the clock shows me I need to leave in fifteen minutes. If I'm late for my first day of school, so be it. Luis is more important, and I cherish these moments when it's only the two of us so much.

He's nine months old now, and my days of nursing my sweet little boy are numbered, especially with going back to school. I planned on getting my GED when we returned to Sun Valley, knowing Suncrest Academy would never take me back, but the public high school decided they'd accept my online alternative school credits. Surprisingly, I'm not as far behind as I thought, so I'll have the pleasure of attending Sun Valley High. *Yay.* Can you sense my sarcasm?

If I survive the last six months of senior year, I get to graduate. Mom thinks it'll be good for me. To find a sense of normalcy and be a teenager again. As if it's that easy. The thought of leaving Luis, even just for classes, is a hard pill to swallow. In such a short amount of time, this little boy has become my entire universe.

I sigh and hug him close as he nurses. These moments are special. I know that. And despite having his face memorized, I still get lost staring into his eyes and have to stifle a smile at how unlike me my own son looks. His eyes are a dark rich brown unlike my cerulean blue. His hair a softer shade of chestnut than my raven black. He even has his father's full lips and straight brows that make him look like he's scowling more often than not.

But he's precious, and he's mine.

A pang of regret hits me in the chest when I think of how he might never know his father, who might never have him to show him how to throw a football or work on a car. I want those things for my son. I want him to grow up with two parents who love him. He deserves the full package. But...I don't know who his father is. Not by name. And a physical description doesn't get you very far.

When I found out I was pregnant, I had no way of finding the boy I gave a piece of myself to. No way of letting him know he was about to become a dad. All I know about him is that he lived in Sun Valley. And when I told Mom as much after those two little pink lines appeared, she decided it was for the best to just forget all about him.

A thrum of nervous energy courses through me at the possibility of seeing him again. Every time I leave the house, I scan the faces of the people around me, hoping for a glimpse of the boy who inadvertently changed my life forever.

He said he'd ruin me for any man who came after him. He wasn't lying. Even after all this time, I still think back to that night. To the way he made me feel. Maybe I've built it up in my mind. I don't know. But what I do know is that he left a mark. I realized that even before I found out I was pregnant.

Luis finishes nursing and I make quick work of burping him and changing his diaper before picking out his outfit for the day—a pair of soft black cotton pants and a red onesie—and head to the kitchen where I know my mother is waiting for me.

She sees me as soon as I step into the room, and her smile brightens when she catches sight of Luis in my arms. "Oh, he's awake." She holds her arms out. "Come to Grandma, amorzinho," she coos. *My little love.* I can't help my smile. She used to call me that when I was a little girl.

Luis pulls away from her at first. He can be clingy when he first wakes up, but after a few more softly spoken words and some bribery in the form of a banana, he relents.

Handing him to her, I grab a *pão de queijo*—a baked cheese roll, just as a honk outside alerts me that my ride is here.

"There's breastmilk in the freezer and I have my phone on me. If he gets too fussy. I can always—"

"Go, Bibiana. We'll be fine," my mom tells me. I hesitate for a moment before the sound of the horn again jerks me into motion. I give Luis a kiss on the cheek, grab my breakfast, and head for the door. "Call me if—"

"Yes. I know, *minha filha*. I raised you, and you turned out fine. Stop worrying. Go. Have fun."

Fun isn't the word I would use to describe high school, but I keep my feelings to myself and hurry outside.

Jaejun Yu—Jae for short—is standing in my driveway beside a sleek, cherry red Acura TLX. He grins when he looks up from his phone and realizes I'm there before he rushes around to the passenger side to open my door.

"Thanks." I offer him a tight smile and slide into the passenger seat, tucking my backpack between my legs on the floor as he jogs around the car to get back in. I hate when he does that. I know he's being chivalrous or whatever, but it still feels weird. Like it means something more than it should.

"You all set?" he asks, a smile on his too-handsome face. He leans forward and tucks a strand of my curly black hair behind my ear, lingering a second longer than he should before settling back in his seat. "You look beautiful, Bibi."

I fight my grimace and mutter out a thank you as I buckle my seat belt.

Don't get me wrong, Jae is great. He's kind and handsome and he's always there to lend a helping hand like right now, taking me to school when he doesn't even go to Sun Valley High. He isn't even in high school. He graduated two years ago, so why he insists on driving me and wasting his time when I know he has classes at Suncrest U that he'll be late for baffles me.

I sound ungrateful. I should probably work on that. It's just that Jae tries really hard. All the time. We met at one of my mom's boyfriend's—Miguel's—work events and we sort of hit it off. But in the let's be best friend's way, not the I want to date you way. I thought we were on the same page, but the more and more we're around one another, I get the feeling that we're not.

I have no idea why he's even remotely interested in me. He's interning with Miguel's security firm while he finishes his degree, and he has his entire life laid out in front of him. Everything meticulously planned to ensure success.

He even has his own townhouse at twenty. He bought it when he was eighteen as an investment property shortly after graduation. Even as a teenager he had a plan. He's smart. Responsible. Has a good head on his shoulders and probably has health insurance.

Meanwhile, I'm an eighteen-year-old single mom with zero plans for my future beyond making it to graduation. I want to do something with my life, sure. But I'm still very much in survival mode here. I don't have the mental capacity to focus on anything or anyone beyond school and Luis and, let's be honest, he could do so much better than me.

Mom likes to nudge me in his direction every chance she gets, but...I sigh. I'm not ready for that.

Jae's an exotic kind of good-looking. Half Korean and half Italian, he has hazel eyes and dark brown hair worn long on top in a bun and shaved on the sides. He turns more than a few heads when he enters a room, and there is zero question as to why. His cheekbones are high and sharp, his jawline angular, and there's just something striking about him that makes it hard to look away.

But I don't have time for a relationship. And even if I did, I'm not sure I want one. No matter how much my mother pushes or how much I try to convince myself that I should give him a chance, I'm not ready to jump back on that particular horse. With my luck, the next person I sleep with will get me pregnant too. I snort. Okay, probably not thanks to the wonderful IUD I got after Luis was born, but still. Accidents happen and while I wouldn't trade Luis for anything in the world, my days of being reckless are over. No more unplanned pregnancies for me, thank you very much.

I haven't been with anyone since Luis's father. Pathetic, I know. I get one night of incredibly reckless sex only to become a spinster afterward. It's unfair. I grit my teeth and silently curse him. Thinking back on that night all this time later, my skin still prickles with heat, my body still desperate and longing for him. It's naive of me to think one day our paths will cross again. I know that. But it doesn't stop me from looking. The little girl inside of me still believes in fairy tales regardless of how stupid it sounds. I think a teeny, tiny piece of me will always wonder what would happen if I saw him again? If he knew about Luis?

It's not like I owe him my fidelity or anything but ... I don't know. A part of me feels like the idea of pursuing something with anyone else would be a betrayal.

It's been eighteen months since Monique and I crashed a Sun Valley Party, and unless he was a lot older than he looked and already graduated, there is a chance he still goes to Sun Valley High.

If he does, I'm going to find him. And if he doesn't, maybe I'll finally be able to put that night behind me.

THREE

Bibiana

H igh school is the same hell I remember it being, only somehow worse. At the academy, people at least smiled my way before they ignored me. It was like church where everyone is nice to your face for the sake of appearances. They keep their pettiness and bullshit for moments behind your back where you can't hear them.

Which is all fine. There, I had a solid friend group already in place. I knew who to trust. Who was a real friend, and who was fake and should be avoided. As a scholarship kid, I wasn't Miss Popular by any means, but I had Monique and that added a layer of protection. No one fucked with the Price family. If their money didn't intimidate you, Dominique Price, the town's football legend, star quarterback and self-proclaimed Devil would. It only took one time during freshman year for the entire school to realize that Dominique would always defend his sister's honor whether he attended

Suncrest Academy or not. And he did one hell of a job using his fists to accomplish that.

Here, there is no mock politeness and there is zero common courtesy in these hallways. I'm the new girl and everyone has already decided to hate me on sight. I'm greeted with looks of disgust or ignored entirely.

It's infuriating and not the reception I'd been hoping for, but there isn't anything I can do about it. The best I can hope for is to skate through and not cause any waves while drawing minimal attention to myself. The school's administration know I'm a breastfeeding mom. They've made some accommodations for me, and my teachers have been made aware that I'll sometimes arrive a few minutes late if I need to pump before class. Thankfully, the school is letting me duck into the nurse's office when I need to, so I don't have to resort to using the girl's bathroom.

I'd rather keep my single-mom status a secret if I can help it.

I'm not ashamed to be a mom. Luis is the best thing that ever happened to me. But I don't want to broadcast it to everyone in the school either. Teenagers are assholes. I would know. And I refuse to give anyone here ammunition against me.

I make it through my first two classes without incident and spend the second half of lunch—after pumping—alone in the library, which is surprisingly pleasant. There's something about being surrounded by worn books that I take a special sort of comfort in. I'm skimming through a fantasy novel when voices a few book stacks away draw my attention.

Setting the book back on the shelf, I edge closer, curious to see who's there. The library had been empty when I arrived. I wonder if maybe there are others like me who don't blend in with the crowd hiding out in here.

"Why are you doing this to me?" a girl's voice whines.

I peek my head around the shelves, spotting a blond with her arms folded across her chest. Her hair is a tangled mess of curls thrown into what I'm assuming is supposed to be a bun, but instead is a riot of crazy that she somehow manages to pull off. She's wearing red basketball shorts, white sneakers, a black Sun Valley High Red Devils t-shirt, and an annoyed expression directed at whoever it is she's talking to.

"Kasey, I'm just trying to be supportive," another girl says, though I can't quite make her out from my position.

"Liar. If you come to my game, the Devils will come and you know it."

A snort. "And that's a bad thing because..."

"Because they're assholes." A pause. "Okay, fine. Roman isn't as much of an asshole, but Emilio and Dominique totally are." Devils and Dominique can only mean one thing. The Sun Valley High mascot is a Devil but no one talks about just anyone like that.

"I don't see what the big deal is. Aaron goes to your games."

"He's my brother and he does actually want to support me. The Devils want to go hoping I mess up so they can make fun of me for it later." I pause at the mention of the Devils and consider what I know about Monique's older brother. Yeah, I could see him doing that. He can be a real asshole when he wants to be.

Despite going to Suncrest Academy, I know all about the Devils. Hell, even without for Monique I would know about them. They're legend in these parts. A group of four best friends. Three football gods and one skateboarding king. The Suncrest Academy Saints have always hated the Devils because when they showed up freshman year, the Saints began losing. Every single football game against the Devils from that year on has ended in defeat. As far as I know, the score is still the same.

"Oh, so for the same reason you go to their football games?"

Yep. Definitely those Devils.

"That's not the—"

Having stepped too close to one of the shelves, I accidentally knock over a few books. They make a loud clatter and the voices cut off from what they'd been saying. I silently curse as I rush to pick them up, kicking myself for not paying closer attention to what I was doing.

Footsteps grow closer just as I place the last book back on the shelf. I turn to head in the opposite direction as a voice calls out, "Hey!"

Shoot.

I spin around, hands raised and a grimace on my face. "I'm sorry. I didn't mean to eavesdrop. I just, uh..." I've got nothing. No valid reasons or excuses come out of my mouth as I stand there like an idiot faced with two girls I don't know. God, I hope they're not the catty type. I'm not prepared for an in-your-face confrontation on my first day back.

The blond I spotted initially looks annoyed but the other girl —a petite brunette with distinctly Hispanic features—eyes me curiously without any anger or annoyance in her gaze.

"You're new here, right? I don't think we've met before," she says, offering me a kind smile that takes me by surprise.

"Yeah, sort of." I tuck my hands into my back pockets. "I lived in Sun Valley growing up, but I went to Suncrest Academy before." I wince. Probably should have left that part out. There's no love lost between the two schools. "I moved and did an online school thing for a while. Now I'm back. And here I am." I cringe. "Sorry. I'm rambling. I do that when I meet new people. Just ignore me." Why can I not stop talking? Oh my god, Bibi, get it together.

She laughs off my awkwardness. "You didn't want to go back to the academy when you moved back?" she asks conversationally, and my shoulders relax.

"It wasn't really my choice, not that I'm upset or anything. Sun Valley High is great. Err, well, I hope it'll be great. I guess I can't really judge it after one day, but so far it seems fine." I shrug. "Suncrest Academy doesn't accept subpar credits in their program." I make air quotes when I mention subpar credits and the brunette chuckles. "If I want to graduate on time, I had to come here."

"Well, welcome." Her smile widens. "I'm Alejandra, but everyone just calls me Allie. I transferred in last semester."

I perk up at the mention that she's a transfer student too. "Really? Where from?"

She nods. "Yeah, really. I moved from Richland. This is Kasey." She indicates the girl beside her who offers me a halfhearted wave.

"Oh, I lived in Richland this past year in a half. Before moving back, I mean. It's nice." I am definitely ruining this first impression here. "So uh, are you both seniors?" Please let me have classes with one of these girls. I could seriously use someone who doesn't look at me like I'm ruining their day.

"I am," Allie says. "Kasey here is a freshy."

"Do not call me that. It's as bad as baby Henderson."

Allie laughs. "Ignore her. She's in a mood."

Kasey rolls her eyes. "I'm not in a mood." She folds her arms across her chest, and I fight back my laugh. She's pouting like Luis. Bottom lip jutted out and brows furrowed into a scowl.

"Sure," Allie drawls.

"Urgh. Whatever. Do your friendly chat thing with the new girl. I'm off to ruin Sarah's day." She turns on her heel and heads straight for the exit.

"And how exactly do you plan to do that?" Allie calls after her.

Kasey turns, walking backwards. "I caught Emilio making out with some random in the hallways after first period this morning. Sarah is going to lose it when she finds out." Her eyes glitter with mischief.

"Please tell me he's not still sleeping with that piranha?" Allie groans.

Kasey grins. "He's a Devil with lots and lots of sins. You let him fool you with that smile of his, Allie. You should work on that. Emilio is a player through and through. He'll sleep with anyone who has a rack and a nice pair of legs. Sarah knows it too."

"Then why are you about to start drama?"

She chuckles. "I just want to give her a little reminder that just because she's screwing a Devil, doesn't mean she's special."

Allie mutters out a curse before turning back to me. "Sorry about that. Sarah and Kasey have some history. She sorta screwed over Kasey's brother."

I shrug, not really sure what she has to apologize for. "Don't worry about it," I tell her, though I'm adding Kasey to my be cautious of list because she sounded way too excited to go and mess with whoever this Sarah girl is. "I'm not really following, anyway. Is this Emilio guy a friend or boyfriend or something?" I hope he's not her boyfriend. She seems nice and it would be really screwed up if he was hooking up with a bunch of other girls on the side while seeing her.

Allie laughs. "Just a friend. I don't think Emilio has a single boyfriend bone in his body. Monogamy and him don't mix. But that's probably a story for another day."

"I've got time," I say and I do. The bell won't ring for another ten minutes, and I like her. She's friendly and has this open and welcoming personality. I don't want to get ahead of myself, but she is totally friend material. Monique would love her.

She waves me toward one of the tables. "Come on, I should probably give you the lowdown on the Devils, anyway. If you don't get it from me, you'll get it from someone else and it's probably better you get it from me."

We take our seats and I pull out a small package of *Presuntinho*—Piraque crackers. Allie tosses her bag on the floor and I wave the package toward her. "Want one?" I ask.

She purses her lips before shrugging. "Why not." I hand over a cracker and she takes a bite. She chews slowly, her brows furrow before she swallows. "That's....interesting," she says, but takes another bite.

I nibble on my own and grin. "I take if you're new to ham-flavored crackers?"

"Yeah. You could say that. They're sort of weird but also kind of—"

"Addicting," I finish for her, leaning across the table to hand her another.

She nods and takes it. "They are. Anyway, what was I saying?"

"The Devils," I prompt, because any information about the guys who rule this school is sure to be useful.

"Right. So anyway, the school is run by the Devils. Three guys all the girls want and all the guys want to be."

"I thought there were four?" I ask, thinking back to the gossip I'd heard when I lived here before.

She scowls and thinks for a moment. "Oh! You're probably thinking of Aaron. Hmm..." Tapping her finger against her chin she thinks for a moment. "I guess he was a Devil. Before I arrived at least." A shrug. "He's not really one now. The guys kind of had a falling out. But they're working it out"— she doesn't bother hiding a mischievous grin that makes me think she plays some part in their working it out—"but no one really considers Aaron a Devil. He's too nice for all that."

"That's...good?" I say, not really sure how to respond to that. "Are the Devils all assholes or something?"

She chuckles. "I'm sorry. They're not all bad. The Devils, I mean. Roman, Dominique, and Emilio are great guys. They just take some getting used to. They're not really trusting, which can make them come off as standoffish. But once you get to know them, they're the sweetest guys. Aaron, too. And his outer shell, thankfully, isn't as hard to crack. You'd like him."

I raise a single brow and she laughs. "I'm not trying to play matchmaker or anything. Promise."

That's a relief. "So, if they're standoffish and you're a new girl too, how do you know them so well?"

Her cheeks turn a soft shade of pink. "I'm dating one."

"Not the one screwing the piranha, right? That's what you called her?"

Allie laughs, a deep chuckle that has the librarian shushing us from across the room. We both hunch down lower in our seats, effectively chastised. Allie's next words come out softer. "No. Not that one. I'm dating Roman Valdez. The one Kasey was talking about is Emilio Chavez and the piranha is Sarah Draven. She's a junior and a complete bitch. New girl to new girl, I would avoid her."

"Noted. Thanks for the heads up."

She nods.

"Do you speak Portuguese," I ask.

Brows furrowed, she shakes her head. "No, I'm Mexican, so Spanish."

I frown. "So, why call her a piranha, then?"

She shrugs. "She's like the fish. She hunts down men, has a pack of vicious girls with her at all times, and her mouth cuts like a blade when she opens it."

Ah. That does make sense. "Good description."

"Does it mean something else in Portuguese?" she asks, and I nod.

"Yeah. Slut."

Her lips smash together, and I can tell she's fighting to remain quiet as her shoulders shake with silent laughter. "I think I like your version better," she whisper-shouts when she finally gets control of herself.

Me too, I think to myself, though out loud I ask, "Anyone else I should steer clear of?"

Her features tighten and she nods. "Yeah. Silvia Parrish. She's a senior like us so you might have classes with her. She and some friends jumped me in the bathroom earlier this year. I wouldn't mess with her. I think the guys have effectively put her in the doghouse but still...I'd be careful."

"Oh, my god. You were jumped?"

"Shhhh.... Not so loud."

I cringe. "Sorry. But seriously? Why were you jumped?" That sort of thing would never fly at the academy. There are rules and consequences. No one there can afford to be suspended let alone expelled which is what would happen if you got into a physical altercation with another student.

She huffs out a breath. "It's another long story. But the Cliff Notes version is that she wanted my boyfriend. It's not really worth going into but seriously, steer clear. You can't trust her."

I swallow hard. What sort of school did I walk into this morning? Brawls in bathrooms is not something I signed up for.

"Don't worry, though. She won't try anything with you. At least I don't think she will. She hates me because I have the guy she wants, but unless you start dating a Devil, I think you're in the clear."

Relief washes through me. "No worries there. Not really one for dating guys right now."

"Girls?" she asks, and I choke on my cracker, coughing hard as I smack myself in the chest.

"What? No."

She raises both arms. "Hey, no judgment here. If you're into girls—"

I shake my head. "I'm not. I just...I don't date. I have a lot going on in my life, and boys are a complication I don't need."

She smirks. "I've heard that one before. But if you change your mind, let me know. It might be fun to play matchmaker, you know?"

Ha. I highly doubt that.

FOUR

Emilio

"Emilio. Hurry up. I'm not going to be late because of your ass," Aaron calls, heading toward our last class of the day.

"Bro, I'm cutting. If you're late, that shit is on you." As soon as the words leave my mouth, Roman and Dom—who'd been walking beside him—stop and turn toward me, scowls stamped across their faces.

"Why? Something up at home?" Roman asks, concern immediately coloring his voice.

I sigh, wishing I could take my words back. I'd lie, but these two fuckers are like brothers. Hell, I'm closer with them than I am with Roberto and Antonio, my actual blood brothers. Aaron, on the other hand, he's a work in progress. Definitely still a fucker. Dammit. I don't want to lie to their suddenly concerned faces.

"Shit is what it always is, but that's not why I'm cutting. I'm gonna kick it with Sarah. Smooth some shit over if you know what I mean?"

Aaron snorts. "Seriously? You're skipping for a piece of ass?"

My eyes narrow. "I wouldn't have to if your little sister minded her own damn business."

His brows furrow and he glances from me to the other guys, an unspoken question on his face. Aw, man. He really has no idea. He'll figure it out eventually.

Dom chooses to fill him in. "Kasey told Sarah he was getting some on the side." It isn't a lie. But she didn't have to throw me under the bus like that. Baby Henderson should be team Emilio. Or at least stay out of my fucking business. But no, Baby Henderson always has to stir the fucking pot.

Not that it should matter. Sarah knows what we're doing isn't exclusive, but I guess having it thrown in her face hurt her feelings, or some shit and now I have to deal with it.

Aaron's frown deepens. "Why would she do that?" The poor bastard actually sounds confused. His little sister has the wool pulled over his eyes, but she doesn't have the rest of us fooled. Baby Henderson is a hellion, and since she joined our crew—not that we had much of a say in it—she's made it her mission to stir the pot any way she can.

Usually, she reserves her antics for Dominique's benefit—those two are like gunpowder and a lit match when they're in the same room—but lately she's enjoyed fucking with me, too.

I don't like it.

"Because she's demon spawn," I mutter, turning to head for the exit. I need to make my escape before Allie catches sight of me or she'll drag my ass back to class come hell or high water. That girl is the mother hen I absolutely adore but do not fucking need right now. "I'll catch you boys later."

"Rubber up," Roman shouts after me. "You don't need to create any devil spawn anytime soon." Yeah, a definite "no" to that. The spawn, not the rubber. I always remember to wrap my shit.

I give him a two-fingered salute just as Allie turns the corner, some random right beside her.

"Peace, *carbón.*" My eyes linger on the unknown girl for a moment. There's something familiar about her. She's wearing snug fit jeans and a giant ass black hoodie. It hides most of her body, but for some damn reason I'm intrigued.

I pause, knowing I shouldn't. It's only going to get me in trouble, but she isn't someone I've seen Allie with before. Allie only ever kicks it with the Devils or Kasey, no one else at Sun Valley High can be trusted. Not after what went down earlier this year. Girls are catty fucking bitches and seeing some random next to her has me both curious and on alert. "Where do you think you're going?" Allie calls, noticing that my feet are still pulling me toward the exit and not in the direction of our class.

The girl beside her lifts her head and our eyes meet, recognition flaring through me. No fucking way. Her bright blue eyes widen and I know right away she recognizes me too. Isn't that a fucking plot twist for today?

I give her another once over, remembering her in a whole new light. Small waist. Flat stomach. Perfectly round tits. The way her hair felt wrapped around my fist. Her pussy convulsing on my cock.

I bite back a groan. Well, fuck me. I need to get laid. Pronto. My eyes narrow on the blast from my past before I shove my thoughts away and turn back toward Allie. No way am I giving this chick even a second of my time. Not after she fucking ghosted me like I was nothing. I refuse to let this girl think she has any sort of hold over me.

"Sorry, vanilla. I gotta run." I edge back closer toward the exit, the new girl still in my peripheral. Look away, dammit. Look away. Her eyes are wide as saucers and glued to me. Her mouth forming a small O. I shouldn't like the attention, her obvious surprise, but I do, and the distraction allows Allie to creep right up on me.

"Oh, no, you don't." She grabs my arm, looping hers through mine and turns me away from the doors I'd almost made it too. "You can't miss fourth. It's the one class we all have together and, my new friend has it too. Come say hi and don't be a jerk. I like her." The last is muttered under her breath.

She tugs me forward, but I keep my feet planted, looking down to meet her determined brown-eyed gaze. "I'll make it up to you. But, I really do need to go. I got someone waiting on me." I make sure to say it loud enough for the other girl to hear.

Allie scowls and turns back to her friend who's still staring, eyes wide and mouth parted. I'm not sure if I should be flattered or insulted that she's yet to tear her gaze off me. Is she remembering our night together in vivid detail like I am? Or maybe she's realizing who the fuck I am and what I can do to her if she steps out of line here. I can make her life her hell if I want to.

We fucked like rabbits that night. I buried myself inside her warm cunt three fucking times. Took her goddamn innocence. You'd think that would matter to a chick, but she acted like it was nothing. Gave as good as she got. No hesitation. No insecurities. Even on the last round when we ran out of condoms, she didn't bat an eye when I suggested I could pull out—something I never fucking do.

I don't know what I expected, but it wasn't passing out beside her with the chick wrapped in my arms only to wake up with her gone and the space on the couch cold beside me.

I swear for a whole week I wondered if I'd dreamt the entire thing up. I never saw her again, and no one knew who the hell she was when I described her. And now, she's here. Wide-eyed and hot as shit, even in that oversized hoodie she's trying to hide in.

I pull out of Allie's grip, giving Roman a nod. I don't have time for this. Thankfully, he understands my meaning and before Allie can move for me again, he wraps his arms around her and pulls her into an embrace. She melts in his arms. God, they're disgustingly cute together. And I speed walk out the door, hearing her muttered curse behind me, but she doesn't run after me again.

Thank god for small favors. I love Allie to death, don't get me wrong. But since she and Roman made things official, she's decided Dom and I are her latest pet projects, and I for one have no desire to be reformed from my savage ways, nor do I have any plans to deal with the new problem staring at my retreating back right now. I can feel her eyes boring into me, but I refuse to give her the satisfaction of knowing just how much her being here is fucking with me.

It won't be long before she learns who I am and what it means to be a Devil.

I run a hand through my hair. Fuck. Who knows what will happen then. Will she turn into every other chick in this school determined to land me? And no, I'm not being arrogant. Every girl at Sun Valley High wants to date a Devil. Some for status, others for what they perceive to be an easy life if they can lock us down early.

Roman, Dominique, and I are football legends around these parts. Each of us with full ride scholarships to Suncrest U and a good chance at going pro in the future. It's why we get so much attention and why I make it a point of never dating exclusively. Women can't be trusted. They always have an ulterior motive.

Will she throw herself at me like the others? Regret leaving me in the pool house like she did? Ghosting me like the sex wasn't fucking magical and shit? I know we said no names. We sure as shit didn't exchange numbers. But I still expected to see the girl at some point.

I suck on my teeth. I know it was just as good for her as it was for me. No way is she unaffected after seeing me today. Hmm... I can work with that. Show her the mistake she made. What she passed up on. And then remind her why she'll never fucking have me.

Outside, Sarah is sitting on the hood of her Jetta. I head straight toward her, a shit-eating grin stamped on my face as a plan begins to form in my mind. The previous appeal of getting my dick wet isn't the same, my mind now full of other more intriguing possibilities. But I'm also not going to let this chick get in my head. I'll fuck my way through the entire school if I have to before I let that happen.

"Ready to blow this place?" I ask Sarah once I'm close. I'm committed to the course of action and I'm always one to follow through. Sure, seeing her with Allie may have thrown me for a loop. I won't deny I've thought about her a time or two this past year and a half. You would too if you'd had awesome sex with a hot chick only to never see her again. But here she is in the flesh. Hmmm...maybe if shit doesn't blow over with Sarah, I can work out a different arrangement. I mean, she'd been down for a casual fuck before.

No. That's what she wants. Wanted. I'm not giving it to her again. Letting her fucking use me. Nah. Her disappearing act deserves a little punishment. She needs to see what it's like to be left behind. Tossed aside like you don't fucking matter.

A plan starts forming in my mind.

If she and Allie are friends, Allie will have my balls for breaking the girl's heart. I consider this. Fuck it. It'll be worth it. She never should have ghosted me. I told her I'd ruin her for anyone else, and if I didn't accomplish that the first time around, I'll make it my mission here and now.

"I'm ready for you to do some groveling," Sarah retorts, arms folded across her chest, shoving her breasts up higher in her already too-tight green top. "I can't believe you made out with some random this morning."

My grin widens. "Baby, I don't grovel." I lift the hem of my shirt, exposing my cut abs that look amazing thank you very fucking much. "Women beg to be with this, not the other way around. Besides," I drop the hem of my shirt. "I didn't kiss Gwen. She kissed me. What was I supposed to do?"

She pouts. She thinks it's cute. It's not. But I let it slide, knowing she'll come around. Sarah knows the deal between us. She doesn't get to own me. I'm not hers, and this thing between us isn't exclusive. I don't do relationships. Never have. And I have no desire to in the near future. Maybe when I'm thirty. But hell, who knows, I might decide to be a badass bachelor forever.

"Urgh, do not say her name in my presence," she snaps.

Irritation flashes through me but I shove it aside and lower my voice to a growl. "You know you want to beg for me, baby girl."

Her eyes darken and I can see desire burning in her honey-colored gaze. She licks her lips but manages to hold herself in place. Funny. She thinks she's going to make me work for it.

Sarah wants something I refuse to give her. Commitment. And while I'm here, smoothing shit over with her, it's not because I actually give two fucks about losing her. This little arrangement between us is one of convenience. Shit gets too real at home sometimes and she's a hot little body to pass the time in. Nothing more. Nothing less. Well, maybe a little less, but I try not to be a complete asshole about it, which is why I'm here. I should get brownie points or something for that shit.

It's easier for me to cut fourth and give her a rare moment of my undivided attention than to find another piece to bury myself in. A new chick might get clingy. I don't have time for that. I've got a scholarship and football on my horizon. I'm not looking to chain myself to anyone. Then again...my mind flashes to the brief blast from my past before I focus back on the chick in front of me. Stop fucking thinking about her.

"What if I don't want to?" Sarah's lip juts out further and I lean toward her, nipping at it. She moans and arches toward me.

"Then I guess this—like all good things—will come to an end."

She wraps her arms around my neck, pressing her breasts against my chest. "I don't want it to end." Her voice is low and breathy. "But I hate that I have to share you."

I fight the urge to roll my eyes and decide to respond to the first part of her statement, ignoring the second. This is to fucking easy.

"Then you know what to do?"

The corners of her mouth curl into a seductive smile. "My place?"

I nod and accept her keys when she hands them to me. Like I said, too fucking easy.

FIVE

Bibiana

"Urgh. What is going on with him?" Allie says, but I'm barely paying attention to her because oh my god, that was him.

"Emilio." I whisper his name to myself, liking the way it sounds. Emilio Chavez is what she said his name was. Oh my God. Luis's dad is here. He's really here and he has a name. Well, obviously. He has a name. Everyone has a name.

A million thoughts are running through my mind. I can't seem to focus on any single one of them.

What do I do? Should I go after him? No. That would make me look like a crazy person. He recognized me though, right? At least, it looked like he did. Not that he stuck around. I'm not sure what I expected. It's been eighteen months and it was just a casual hook up. I mean, yes, it was memorable for me. I lost my virginity that night. That's kind a big deal. And even if I hadn't gotten pregnant, I wouldn't be able to forget being with him. We had sex three times. I didn't even know a guy could do that. I thought it was a one and done sort of thing, but Emilio certainly proved me wrong. And I didn't realize a girl could orgasm as many times as I did. I expected pain. Discomfort. Embarrassment. What I did not expect was...that. It sounds so dumb, but it was a dream. Magical.

As stupid as it sounds, slipping out early that morning to get home before Mom and Miguel woke up was physically painful.

He'd been asleep when I left, and I didn't bother to wake him. At the time, I told myself it was because I wanted to avoid an awkward goodbye. But if I'm honest with myself, I think I didn't wake him because I knew it would hurt even more to leave. He made me feel things I didn't realize I could feel, and that scared me.

But judging by his expression when he saw me, I'm just one in a long line of hookups for him. My shoulders slump and my stomach drops. Why does that realization hurt so much? I don't even know him. I knew what the deal was. And hell, I've been dealing with the consequences of that night ever since. Seeing him in the flesh shouldn't suddenly bring about these feelings of loneliness.

Allie's chatting with three boys in the hallway when suddenly she's snapping her fingers in my face, drawing my attention. "Earth to Bibiana. Where'd you go?"

I shake my head. "Sorry. What'd you say?"

Allie rolls her eyes but smiles before turning to the boy closest to her.

"Bibiana, this is my boyfriend, Roman." He inclines his head toward me, his way of saying hello. "This one is Aaron," she indicates the blond boy with the skateboard, "and this ray of sunshine is Dominique." I know she's kidding, because Dominique is definitely not a ray of sunshine. He's wearing the most brooding expression of the bunch, his eyes still trained on the door Emilio just exited out of. Allie elbows him in the stomach and he pretends to wince, rubbing his stomach, but I don't miss her smirk. She knows she didn't really hurt him.

"Ignore him. I swear he knows his manners. He just rarely shows them."

Roman tilts his head back and laughs, a deep chuckle that has Allie's smirk morphing into a wide smile. God, they're cute together. My heart gives a pathetic lurch. I want what they have. It looks so easy. They're so content. What if...no. I can't get ahead of myself here. It was just sex, Bibi. Stop trying to remember it as anything else. And besides, once you tell him about Luis, he still might want nothing to do with you.

Determination straightens my spine when I think of that. He doesn't have to like me. He doesn't owe me any sort of relationship or commitment just because we have a kid together. But he does owe Luis his attention and affections. I just hope he's the kind of guy who will step up once he realizes what we created together.

"You look…" Dom's voice pulls me from my thoughts. His head tilts to the side as he scrutinizes my face. "Familiar," he finishes. "How do I know you?"

Allie's eyes brighten. "You two know each other?" She bounces on her feet.

"Not really." I say with a shrug. I'm not sure if I should be answering her or him, so I go with the less intimidating option of the two. "I'm best friends with Monique. His sister. We used to go to school together."

"Oh! I haven't met her yet. Is she as stoic and broody as her brother?" She turns to him. "And why doesn't she go here?"

Dom grunts and I laugh. "She's Dominique's complete opposite," I tell her. "And she's a senior at Suncrest Academy. Dominique's parents only let him go here because of the football program."

Allie's eyes widen and she whirls on Dominique. "You have a twin!?" She squeals. "Why haven't I met her yet?"

All three guys shake their heads. "She's not my twin. She's my little sister and I haven't introduced you yet because look how well that worked out for us when you hooked up with baby Henderson. I do not need to add fuel to that fire."

Aaron and Roman both nod in agreement.

"If she's not your twin, then how—"

I answer for him. "Monique is smart. Like insanely smart. She skipped eighth grade. That's why they're both seniors. She could probably graduate early if she wanted to."

"Okay, this is great. You know Monique and I'm friends with Kasey. The four of us have to get together this weekend. It'll be so much fun. Girl's night!"

The guys groan in unison just as the bell rings, signaling that we're officially late to class. I should probably be a little concerned about that, but I'm too excited over the prospect of making new friends and finding my son's father to think about anything else.

"Come on. We'll sort out all the details after school. We better hurry or Mr. Chu is going to bite our heads off." I follow her to class, a small ball of warmth unfurling in my chest.

As the teacher drones on about this week's assignment, I slip my cell phone out from my pocket and fire off a text to my mom. It's only been a few hours, but I'm not used to being away from my little boy this long.

Me: How is he?

Mom: Perfect.

She includes a picture of Luis sleeping in her arms and I smile, running a finger across the screen before opening a new text conversation and pulling up Monique's number. There is no way this can wait.

Me: He's here.

Three dots appear almost instantly because of course she isn't paying attention in class. Like she even needs to.

Monique: Oh my God! Did you tell him?

I roll my eyes. Is she serious? You don't just see a guy for the first time in close to two years and drop a baby in his lap day one.

Me: No. I didn't get the chance to talk to him, but at least now I know he's here.

Me: Also, I ran into your brother.

I leave out the part about her brother being friends with Luis's dad. Knowing Monique, she wouldn't be able to stop herself from grilling Dominique about him and I don't want word of Luis getting to Emilio from anyone but me.

Monique: Was he an asshole?

I snort. Heads turn my way and I bite my lip, sinking down lower in my seat.

Me: No. He's friends with this girl, Allie. She introduced us. I think you'd like her.

Monique: Don't get any ideas about replacing me B.

I roll my eyes and smile.

Me: Not possible. But she wants to hangout this weekend. Us three and a girl named Kasey. You in?

I hope she says yes. Now that I know Allie and Kasey are friends with Emilio, I have every intention of feeling them out and getting every detail I can about him. He one hundred percent has every right to know he has a son, but that little boy is my everything, and I owe it to him to make sure that whoever I bring into his life isn't going to walk right back out of it either.

Monique: Yes! I need to meet this chick.

Me: Allie?

Monique: No. Kasey. Dom gripes about her ALL THE TIME. Anyone who can rile my brother up like that is someone I need to know.

Me: LOL. Okay. I'll tell Allie you're in. TTYL.

I shove my phone back in my pocket just as the teacher walks by my desk, placing a sheet of paper on the surface. "Pop quiz. Let's see what you know and how behind you all are. I like to see what I'm working with. Fair warning, Christmas break is over, and I don't tolerate slackers in my classroom," he says, and the collective room groans.

The rest of class goes by in silence as we all work on the math quiz. I finish before the bell rings and take a few extra minutes to go over my work until I'm satisfied with all of my answers. I need to finish strong this year. I might not know what I plan to do after graduation, but I want college to be an option. Monique is going to Suncrest U. And I don't know... maybe I can work out a way to go there too. It wouldn't be full time. Not with Luis. But it would be something and I'm okay with college taking a little bit longer. I'll do whatever I need to do in order to make sure Luis gets the life he deserves.

I wonder briefly what Emilio's plans are after high school. How his plans might affect my own. But before I get too stuck in my own head, I force myself to take a breath and relax. There's no point in worrying about any of that yet.

For now, I need to figure how to tell him about Luis, which sounds a hell of a lot easier than I know it will be. After that, I can worry about the rest.

SIX

Emilio

T his is one of the absolute worst fucks I've had in my life. I don't know what the deal is. Sarah is into it, but my dick certainly isn't. Her moans are loud and dramatic. And the excessive back scratching is starting to hurt. It's like she's auditioning for a B-rated porn flick.

"Yes. Yes. Oh. My. God. More. Emilio, Yes!" Her moan is obnoxiously loud.

I grit my teeth as she tightens her grip around my hips with her legs and I plow into her, trying to find a rhythm that will do something—anything—for me, but it's no fucking use. Her pussy convulses on my cock, her eyes all but rolling into the back of her head as she finds her release again.

Fuck.

How is she enjoying this? I made her come in the car before she dragged me up here, and she's clearly getting her rocks off a second time, but I'm not even close. I can't get into it. I should be focused on the naked girl beneath me, but instead, my mind wanders to her. To her full lips. Her striking blue eyes. The way she looked lying beside me before I fell asleep.

This was a mistake.

We've been screwing for close to twenty minutes. Sweat drips down my back and my release is literally nowhere in sight. I thrust into her harder. Deeper. I am not going to let her get in my fucking head.

Goddammit. What is wrong with me?

Fuck it. I've had enough. I groan loud and scrunch my eyes closed, faking that I've dropped my load, before I pull out and sag against Sarah's naked body. Thank fuck for condoms. Between that and my hand I should be able to hide my still evident hard on. How fucking embarrassing.

I roll to my side, grab my boxers off the floor and head to the attached bathroom, my hand over my dick as if I'm trying to keep the condom from slipping off. Sarah's breaths are heavy behind me as I close the door and sag against the wall.

I stare at my still erect cock and clench my jaw. "You and me are going to have words," I mutter. Bracing my hands on the countertop, I take a moment to catch my breath and will my cock to stand down. Does it? No. Why? Because my dick is a fucking dick. "Not cool, dude. See if you get action again anytime soon." He won't come in Sarah's cunt, and he's determined to leave me with a case of blue balls.

Fuck me right now. I lean back and fist myself, working my length up and down in an effort to find my own release. I can hear Sarah moving around in her room, but I block out the sounds as I think of the one chick I shouldn't be thinking of. Get it together, man. You're letting her fuck with your head. I tighten my grip, envisioning her tight little pussy. The soft mewls of pleasure she made. The way she clung to me like she couldn't bear to let go. That was seriously a good fucking night.

Out of nowhere, my orgasm slams into me. Fuck. I empty myself into my hand, my chest heaving as I meet my own startled reflection. That was unexpected. I'll have to try that fantasy more often.

Irritation thrums through me. She left. She walked away without a word and now I can't even get off without thinking of her. This is some seriously messed up shit.

Washing my hands, I take care of business, slip on my boxers and go back out to Sarah's room in search of my jeans. Ah. There they are. I start dressing, eager to get the hell out of here, when—still naked—Sarah makes a beeline for me. Her small perky tits bounce with her steps and she gives me a wanton look. What is she up to now?

She runs her manicured nails over my chest and leans up on tiptoe to kiss my neck. "That was fun," she says, her voice husky.

I force myself to remain still and face her. I do the polite thing and plant a kiss on her lips, giving her a sly grin.

"Always fun," I tell her. "But I gotta run. I'm supposed to meet Roman after school and"—I check the time on my phone—"school's already out. I'll catch you later," I say, not really meaning it. Coming here was supposed to smooth shit over between us so we could go back to our casual arrangement. An arrangement I'm no longer interested in maintaining.

Her face falls and I hesitate. Tilting her chin up I brush my thumb along her jaw.

"Why the long face, beautiful?" She brightens at the endearment but forces a petulant look on her face. One I can see right through.

"I thought we could, I don't know, hang out?" Her cheeks turn pink and I stifle a groan, forcing the easy and carefree smile to remain on my face. I need to end this. If the shitty fuck wasn't an indication, this whole wanting to hang out bit certainly is.

"Sarah," I draw her name out and tsk.

Her eyes water, and despite feeling like a piece of shit, I force myself to say the next words that come out of my mouth. "We're not a thing. We're friends with benefits—without the friend part."

She sniffles. "And if that's not enough for me?"

I look up the ceiling. We just went over this. "Then I'm out. I don't do complicated pussy." I grab the last of my clothes and head for the door.

"Stop."

I don't.

"Emilio Chavez, if you walk out that door you are never getting with me again," she threatens, as if that is enough to make me reconsider.

"Later, Sarah." This was a mistake. I should have stayed in class.

"Emilio, please."

I sigh, but keep walking, pulling out my phone to text Aaron.

"I drove you. You can't just leave."

Clearly, she doesn't know me if she thinks a thing as simple as a ride will slow me down.

Me: I'm going to your place.

Aaron: Why?

I roll my eyes. Come on, man. Get with the program.

Me: Shit with Sarah. I need a lift to Roman's.

Aaron: Fine. I'll drop everything I'm doing and be right over.

I grin. Fucker thinks he's funny.

Me: Sounds good, friend.

I shove my phone in my back pocket and cut across the lawn, grateful for once that he lives next door. If I wait on the porch for Aaron to show up, Sarah will just follow me and do the whole begging then yelling then begging again thing, so I make my way to the back gate and take a seat on one of the patio chairs.

Aaron's place is nice. He lives in one of those cookie-cutter gated communities where all the houses look the same and they have to deal with HOAs that tell you exactly how long your grass is allowed to be. His parents do well enough if memory serves. He went to private school for a while before he started kicking it with us. Then he convinced his parents to let him go to Sun Valley High so he could be with his friends.

That blew up in his face. Well, sort of. I guess it's working out now, what with Allie around. Henderson and Roman made some sort of deal I don't have all the details on. All I know is that he helped Roman win Allie back and Roman decided to drop the beef between them. Personally, I'm not that forgiving. He fucked up and we all got hurt because of it.

We might tolerate him these days, but I sure as shit don't trust him.

My phone dings and I glance down at the screen.

Aaron: Where you at?

Me: Backyard.

A few seconds later the back door opens, and Aaron walks outside. He's wearing his usual emo shit. Black pants. Black shirt. Black beanie pulled low over his blond hair. He looks like Justin Bieber had a baby with Machine Gun Kelley. No wonder the dude is still single. "You could use a little more color in your life," I tell him.

He frowns. "Are you on something?"

"Nope. That's your MO. Not mine," I say with a grin.

His scowl darkens.

"Really, man. You wanna go there right now?"

I shrug. Why not? I'm already having a shitty day. But Aaron decides to flip shit around. Smooth fucker.

"What happened to smoothing shit over with Sarah?" he asks, taking a seat in one of the chairs beside me.

"Decided the pussy wasn't worth the effort. She's getting too attached."

He snorts. "You've been staying the night at her place almost every night for the last month. What did you expect?"

"You've been tracking me?" I ask, remembering he's hooked up with her, too. "Jealous it was me in her bed instead of you?"

He snorts. "Hardly. I try not to repeat my mistakes. And no, fucker, I'm not tracking you. But you're not hard in the mornings when you do the walk of shame to your car early enough to get your sister to school."

I shrug, not meeting his eyes. I don't like that he knows how often I've been here. Aaron's not an idiot, and he demonstrates that even more with his next question.

"What's really going on, Emilio? Why don't you wanna be home?"

I jerk my gaze to his. "What the fuck is that supposed to mean?" It comes out angrier than I intended, but fuck, he's got no right prying into my business.

"It means, I'm not stupid. I know you have issues with your dad. Why haven't you said anything to Roman or Dominique?" Because Roman's got Allie now. I'm not about to crash in on their happy little life. And Dom... I shake my head. Dom's got his own problems. Neither one of them needs to worry about mine.

"It's not a big deal." I push to my feet.

"Stop fronting. What's going on?"

"Drop it," I snarl.

Aaron lifts both hands. "Fine, be an asshole. I was only trying to help."

"Right, well, the only help I need is a lift to Roman's. You going to help with that or not?"

He scowls, but nods. "Come on. But just so you know, screwing random girls isn't going to solve your problems. And getting involved with chicks like Sarah Draven is going to come back and bite you in the ass. I would know."

SEVEN

Bibiana

M y palms are sweaty. My knees weak. I don't know what to say to him. How to break the news or even start a conversation with the guy, so I do the smart thing and avoid him. Okay, it's also the cowardly thing to do, but it's not like I have a lot of options here. I only manage to make it two days before I'm faced with speaking to Emilio though, and like all the times before, as soon as I see him, it's like everything around me stops.

"Hey, beautiful," he says, taking me completely by surprise as he sits down at the lunch table. It takes me a second to realize he's not talking to me. His words are directed toward Allie, who is seated beside him, but hearing his voice has goosebumps breaking out across my skin. "Who's the new new chick?" he asks, his tone suggestive, but he's still not looking my way and it bothers me. It's not like we're strangers. He can say hello. Just as easily ask me for my name instead of asking Allie when I'm literally sitting right in front of him.

Roman smacks him upside the back of his head as he claims his seat on Allie's other side, but there's a smile on his lips that says he's not actually pissed. "Lay off Allie's new friend," he comments, not making eye contact, but this time I don't take it personally. Given all that I've learned about the Devils of Sun Valley High and how uncommon it is for anyone new to be welcomed into their inner circle, Roman's quiet acceptance of me is enough.

"This is Bibiana," Allie says. "Play nice."

"Bibiana. Hmm..." Emilio says my name as though testing its flavor. The corners of his mouth curl on either side, his expression almost savage as he finally deigns to look at me.

His chocolate brown eyes lock on mine and I freeze like a deer caught in headlights, unable to tear my gaze away as he rakes his bottom lip through his teeth, electricity crackling between us. Was it always like this? I think back to the night we met. The chemistry between us. I swallow hard because yeah, it felt just like this. An imaginary cord stretched taut between us.

Dominique drops his tray beside me, claiming the seat to my left while Kasey claims the seat to my right, pulling my attention away from Emilio and effectively shattering the moment.

Emilio turns to Dominique, ignoring me now as the two dive into a conversation about the upcoming game. Listening in, I learn the Devils made it to the playoffs. No surprise there. They finished their season undefeated, so making it all the way and going to state is their next objective.

Roman joins the conversation, leaving Allie, Kasey, Aaron, and I to talk amongst ourselves. I try to push Emilio from my mind, but every few minutes I can feel his eyes boring into me. His gaze like a physical caress, only when I turn to look at him, he jerks his attention away.

"Hello, Earth to Bibi," Allie calls, and I force my gaze away from him.

"What'd you say? Sorry, I got a little lost in my head."

She smiles. "Right. I was saying, what do you want to do this weekend? We're dragging Aaron along, too." My eyes flick to his as I consider her question.

"Uh..." Crap. Now isn't the time to tell them I have a son, but I can't very well go out on weekends with him either. I'm a mom, and yes, my mom watches him while I'm at school, but I don't like the idea of dumping Luis on her just so I can hang out with friends. I'm his mom. I'm the one who should be taking care of him. He's my responsibility.

I don't want to lose more time with him either, especially when I'm already not seeing him during the day most of the week. It's made him clingier then usual, and he's only going to be my baby a little while longer. Soon, he'll be a toddler. Then a little boy. The thought alone makes my chest ache. He's growing up too fast.

"Why don't we do something at my place?" I suggest. "Movies, junk food. Something casual?" I'll come up with a way to let them know about Luis between then and now. Hopefully it's not a deal breaker for our friendship. Monique loves Luis and Allie seems nice. With any luck, she'll love him too.

Allie's eyes brighten at my suggestion. "Yes! I love that idea. You guys in?" She looks between Kasey and Aaron.

"I'm in. What do you think, little sis?" Aaron asks, ruffling his sister's hair.

"Urgh, don't do that," she whines, smacking his hand away as if she's annoyed, but I don't miss her affectionate smile. "Yes. I'm in. I could use a low-drama night and some junk food."

"Perfect. I'll text you guys the address. Let's plan on, I don't know, seven-ish?"

Everyone nods just as the lunch bell rings and we all rise to drop our trays in the waste bin as we head to our next class. I lose track of the others in the crowd, not really worried since I'll see them again—save for Kasey—fourth period, when a hand wraps around my arm and pushes me into an open classroom door. I stumble forward before whirling around, hands fisted at my sides and ready, only to find Emilio behind me.

He closes the door, pressing the lock and leaning against it as he folds his arms over his chest and gives me a once-over before quirking a brow. "Pretending we don't know each other?" he asks, a sinful expression on his face. The bell rings again and I grit my teeth together. I'm already behind. I shouldn't miss any of my classes without a damn good reason, but Emilio doesn't look like he's going to just let me brush past him. He looks like someone who has something they need to get off their chest, though I can't imagine what it is— I'm supposed to be the one with something to share.

I swallow hard and take a few steps back, managing to put some much-needed distance between us. My heart is racing in my chest, my palms suddenly sweaty. "I'm not pretending," I tell him. "I just didn't know if I should mention—"

"That we fucked." The gravely quality of his voice grates along my senses. "That I buried my dick inside of you three times before you vanished. Poof. Like a ghost."

My brows furrow and I take another involuntary step back. He sounds angry, almost. But that can't be right. He has nothing to be angry about. At least, not yet.

Emilio pushes off the door and stalks toward me, that's the only way I can describe it. His eyes are bright, practically glowing, as he closes the distance between us, a predatory glint in his eyes.

"You running from me, mariposa?"

I swallow hard and manage to shake my head, that nickname eliciting a strange sort of emotion in my chest. Emilio leans into me, his breath fanning across my neck. My hands fly up on their own to clutch at the fabric of his shirt. I don't know if I plan to draw him in or push him away, but the steady thrum of his heartbeat beneath my palms grounds me.

"Good. Because if you run," he trails his nose down the side of my neck and nips at my shoulder with his teeth. "I'll have to give chase."

I shudder, my entire body responding to him, but I force myself to take a deep breath. This...isn't what I expected.

"I remember the way you taste," he whispers, tugging the neckline of my zip-up hoodie to the side and trailing kisses across my skin. "The way your pussy squeezed my cock when I buried myself inside you."

His vulgar words make my thighs tighten, even as a shiver of apprehension races down my spine. He draws back, a savage curl to his lips. "Do you remember?"

My stomach tangles in knots. Of course I remember. I remember every single moment of that night in vivid detail. Every kiss. Every touch. But I don't tell him any of that. I'm stuck standing here, words frozen in my mouth as he looks at me like he wants to devour me, but there's a cruel edge to his smile. One I don't know how to interpret. The boy I met eighteen months ago was wild. He had a devil-may-care attitude. And sure, I don't really know him, but first impressions do mean something. Emilio acted like he didn't have a care in the world. He was the kind of guy always looking to have a good time. Searching for his next thrill.

This Emilio is different.

He doesn't give me the chance to dwell on that. Instead, his lips press against mine, and suddenly I'm drowning in the taste of him. Sweet oranges and chili, just how I remembered him tasting. Each caress of his tongue awakens something dormant inside me. I lose myself to the sensations when his arms band around me as he lifts me from my feet, my legs wrapping around his waist of their own accord.

He carries me over to a desk and sets me down on the smooth surface. One of my hands curls around the edge for support while the others holds onto Emilio, afraid to let go. My heart races behind my rib cage. There are a million reasons why I need to stop this, the most prevalent one being that I still haven't told him about Luis. But I can't think. Can't get enough air to form the words I know need to be spoken.

His kiss is frantic. His grip possessive as he tilts my head, deepening our kiss and pressing his body closer into mine. Then I feel it. The hard length of him pressed firmly against my core. It reminds me that I haven't been with anyone else. Not since that night. Not ever. He was my first. And so far, my only.

The next thing I know, his fingers are unbuttoning my jeans and working their way into my panties. I tear my mouth from his and suck in a lungful of air. "What are you doing?" I gasp as his mouth latches on to the side of his neck, nipping and sucking at my skin in a way I know is sure to leave a mark.

His fingertips graze over my center, and I shudder in his arms. He chuckles, the sound smug and self-assured. "So fucking responsive. What does it look like I'm doing,

Bibiana?" The way he says my name makes my toes curls and short-circuits my brain. He manages to slide my jeans down my hips before I realize what's even happening. He unzips the front of my sweatshirt, but when his fingers curl beneath the hem of my shirt, reality sneaks back in, reminding me that I am not the same girl he slept with eighteen months ago. I've changed. My body has definitely changed. And I'm not ready for anyone, let alone the boy who haunts my dreams, to see it.

I stop his hand from tugging up my shirt but have zero clue as to where to redirect it when he makes that decision for me and squeezes my breast over the material of my top. I wince. It doesn't hurt but...gah...if I leak milk right now, I will be so mortified.

I need to put a stop to this entire thing. This, whatever it is, cannot happen right now but—oh my God. His finger rubs over my center, the thin material of my panties hardly a barrier as he presses a finger inside me.

I moan into his mouth. This is a stupid, horrible, insane thing to do right now, but I can't seem to make myself tell him to stop. And I have to accept the fact it's because I don't want him to.

EIGHT

Emilio

She lets out a sweet whimper when I cup her breast in my hand and squeeze it. They're larger than I remember. More than a handful, but fuck me if they're not perfect. Her eyes darken with need, if not a little apprehension. She's nervous. That should bother me, but it doesn't. Seeing her open desire feeds the beast inside me, so I give both of us what we want, slipping one finger inside her dripping cunt. Fuck me. My girl is ready, needy.

Wait. What? She is not my girl. Where did that thought even come from? Gritting my teeth, my cock strains against my zipper, desperate to thrust into her heat, but that's not on the menu today. This isn't about getting my dick wet. It's about proving a point.

A moan leaves her as I sink a second finger into her pussy. Fuck, she's so goddamn tight. I nip at her lips, small mewls of pleasure escaping as I work my fingers in and out, finger fucking her until she's writhing on the desk. Gasping my name.

"You like that, baby girl?" I ask, taking pleasure in watching her squirm. She doesn't answer, but she doesn't need to. Her heavy breaths, the rapid rise and fall of her chest is answer enough.

She wets her lips and the sight of her tongue peeking out does things to my head. Makes me want to devour her. Body, mind, and soul.

I tower over her, our mouths centimeters away from one another. I suck in the air she breathes, my free hand tangling in her thick, black hair before I crush my lips against hers in a punishing kiss. Her legs clench, her back arching as her breasts press against my chest. She's close.

I add in a third finger, stretching the walls of her pussy, making her take all that I can give. Next time, it'll be my cock buried inside her tight little body instead of my fingers.

The thought has me clenching my jaw, nostrils flaring. There isn't going to be a next time, I remind myself.

"Oh, God." She stiffens against me, her jeans dangling from one leg while the other wraps around my hip.

"Come for me, Bibiana," I grind out against her ear, savoring the way her name tastes on my tongue. My thumb finds her clit, circling the bundle of nerves and like glass, she shatters.

Her body goes taught. Her moan muffled by my lips as her orgasm tears through her.

I swallow her cries and suck on her bottom lip until her body relaxes, her shoulders slumping and her pleasure-drunk gaze finding mine.

I withdraw my fingers, adjusting the raging hard on in my jeans before bringing my hand to my lips and sucking her orgasm clean from my fingertips.

Her eyes widen in surprise. A blush heating her cheeks. I don't bother hiding my savage smile before gripping her jaw and forcing her to taste herself on my tongue. When she's breathless once more, I release her and turn to leave.

"W...where are you going?"

I don't answer. I don't turn around. I force myself to take step after step away from her so she knows exactly what it's like to have someone mark you, only to walk away and for you to be forgotten.

I skip third period but make sure I'm in fourth. Allie will have my ass if I skip our calculus class again. It's the one class Dom, Aaron, Rome, Allie, and I all have together, and I swear she treats it like it's a family meal. I head to the back of the class where Dom and Aaron are already seated and nod at both of them as I take my seat. Bibiana has fourth with us too, and it looks like this girl doesn't give one fuck about making a scene, because as soon as my ass hits the chair, she storms into class, cheeks tinged pink and eyes ablaze as she heads straight toward me, righteous anger etched into every line of her body. "What the hell was that?" she bites out, slamming her small hand against the top of my desk.

I might not have thought this through completely, but damn if she's not beautiful like this. I'll have to piss her off again sometime. Possibilities race through my mind and a slow smile curls the corners of my mouth. I look her up and down, silently cursing myself for not getting a glimpse when I had the chance of the tanned skin she hides beneath her oversized sweaters. "I don't know what you're talking about." I spread my legs and lean back in my seat, folding my arms across my chest. She stands there. Indignation written all over her face. "Did you need something?" I ask. "Class is about to start."

Her eyes brighter, a lick of fire rising to the surface as her gaze narrows on me. "I don't know what you're trying to do here, but you can't just..." she waves her arm in the air. "You can't do what you did and then walk away like that."

I cock my head to the side. "Why? You had zero problem fucking me and walking away. I thought this was our thing." The students around us snicker but neither of us look their way, too focused on glowering at one another instead.

Bibiana bares her teeth, leaning forward and pressing her face close to mine. I'm tempted to kiss her again. Capture her lips with mine and see how she reacts, but I manage to hold myself back. Barely. The pull between is strong. I don't fucking like it. She's not only under my skin. It's like she's burrowing her way into my goddamn soul. What is it about this girl?

I catalogue her features, taking in her bright blue eyes, her kiss-bitten lips, and her sexy-as-hell scowl, all the while ignoring Dominique's interested stare. The asshole's probably already envisioning my downfall at the hands of the tiny thing in front of me. He's a cruel bastard like that. Seriously though, he and baby Henderson deserve one another. And me, do I deserve her? I'm not sure if I've been given a gift or a curse with Bibiana's arrival.

"What is your problem? We had a one-night stand. Why are you acting like an asshole whose feelings are hurt when you knew the arrangement upfront?"

I scoff. "Baby girl, my feelings are far from hurt. You just seemed a little tense earlier. I figured I'd help you out."

She isn't buying it, but I don't fucking care. The entire room is looking our way. She doesn't know it yet, but her little outburst isn't going to do her any favors here. My jaw tightens. I don't know how to feel about that.

Roman and Allie walk in and like any other day they head straight for me and Dom claiming the seats nearest to us. "Is everything okay?" Allie asks.

I shrug. "Not sure. You should ask your new friend here."

Allie's shoulders drop and she gives me an exasperated look. "What did you do?"

Bibiana smirks. Cute. She's only known Allie a handful of days. Vanilla would never take her side over mine, but I let her think she's won. For the next thirty seconds, at least before I turn to Allie and look her right in the eye. I'll probably go to hell for this. Then again, I'm already a Devil. Hell's been a forgone conclusion for me. "I gave her an orgasm." I say loud enough that the entire class can hear. "Not sure what the problem is. She enjoyed it, but now she's complaining. Sorry, baby girl. I had to get to class. I know you have needs so if you behave, I'll consider helping you out again later." Her cheeks flush and fire licks her gaze.

"Screw you," she curses and turns, looking for a seat, but she isn't left with many options. She can either sit her pretty ass down where she's at, putting her beside Allie and directly in front of me, or she can go sit front and center at the head of the class.

Her nostrils flare and I watch as she considers what to do, her fingers curling into a tight fist at her side.

She does what I expect and claims the seat in front of me, her back ramrod straight and shoulders stiff. I lean across my desk, my mouth hovering behind her ear as I whisper, "That's right. Be a good girl and next time I'll get you off with my mouth instead of my fingers."

I watch in fascination as goosebumps break out across her skin.

"There isn't going to be a next time," she grinds out.

I laugh and lean back in my chair. I thought that too, but I've suddenly changed my mind. No longer content leaving her after just one round. An eye for an eye isn't enough. I don't want to get even. I need to be ahead. To win whatever twisted game it is we're playing.

This girl has me under her spell, and I refuse to be the only one who suffers for it. She deserves to be punished. I need that. Need to know I'm the one in control. I don't want to hurt her. Not physically.

I want to strip her down of her defenses and make her beg. I want to tease and taunt her until she can't take it anymore. And when she's finally had enough, I want to push her a little bit more. Show her just how much she can take. I don't know why I feel this way. But it's an insatiable need, and fuck it, I may hate myself for this later, but it doesn't change the fact that I'm drawn to this girl. And instead of doing the smart thing and keeping the fuck away, I'm going to bury myself in her until neither of us knows up from down. And I'm going to have a hell of a time doing it.

NINE

Bibiana

"Relax," Monique tells me.

I'm pacing in the living room and despite Luis being asleep in my arms, nervous energy makes it hard to stand still.

"It's not a big deal."

Easy for her to say. She isn't the one about to tell everyone she has a kid. A kid who happens to also belong to their friend, but I'll save that story for another day. Maybe. Hopefully. Urgh. I don't know. I tried all week to find the courage to tell Emilio about Luis but there was never a good time and then after the whole classroom incident, I don't know. I need to tell him but a part of me also doesn't want to.

He did what he did and then went about his business like it never even happened. And every time I turned around he was either hitting on a girl or making out with one in the hallways at school. It ... sucked.

I haven't been touched in a year and a half. Not that he knows that, but still. He doesn't get to do that. Make my body light up like the world is on fire, only to walk away and pretend like what happened between us isn't a big deal. Like it meant nothing. Because dammit it did. To me at least. Just the thought of him makes my blood boil. Where does he get off? He is such an asshole.

I don't understand him and trying to figure out what is going on in that head of his gives me a migraine. He watches me. Always out of the corners of his eyes like I won't notice but I do. He tracks my movements and more times than not it's like he's waiting for me to show up before he leans into another girl. Like he wants a reaction out of me but I refuse to give it to him. I'm not an idiot and I refuse to be pulled into this twisted game of his.

Ignoring me, the girls, it's all intentional. He wants me to react, though how, I'm still not sure. I have no claim on him. I can't be jealous. Well, I can be, because I clearly I am, but I have zero reason to be. He's not mine. I'm not even sure if I want him to be.

I don't know if the fact that he's doing this all on purpose is a relief or just pisses me off more. But at least I know I'm not the only one affected. Every time another guy that isn't one of the Devil's talks to me, Emilio's jaw tightens. It's a subtle reaction but it's there.

It's petty and immature of me but, I've taken to messing with him at lunch. Intentionally eating my food in a provocative manner. His eyes burn. His jaw clenches. But despite his suggestion two days ago, that next time he'll make me come with his mouth, he hasn't said a single word to me. I've been on the receiving end of heated stares and lingering looks, but that's it. No words. No smiles or openings for conversation. No way to casually say, "did I mention we have a son together?"

I hate it, and I love it, and I have no freaking idea what to do about it. Finding a way to tell Emilio about Luis was complicated enough to begin with. Now it's a cluster fuck of epic proportions.

The doorbell rings, startling me from my thoughts, and I rush to answer it, Luis propped on my hip, his head on my shoulder. I'm equal parts terrified and excited for Allie and Kasey to meet him. I haven't introduced him to anyone outside of family except for Monique, and she's my best friend so that doesn't count.

"Relax, B," Monique says as she joins me. "They're gonna love him."

I gave Allie a heads-up that I wanted to introduce her to someone important to me but I didn't give her any details and I'm pretty sure this isn't who she had in mind.

I open the door and find both girls waiting with Aaron right behind them. Shit. I'd completely forgotten he was coming too. I swallow hard and all three sets of eyes zero in on the little boy I'm holding.

"Hey, come on in," I say, ushering them inside.

Dressed in a knee-length hoodie dress and black K-swiss sneakers, Allie is beaming when she steps inside. "Is he yours?" she asks with open curiosity. I nod. "Oh, my God. He's adorable." She touches one tiny hand, her eyes shining with wonder as she gazes at my precious bundle. "How old is he?"

I swallow hard. "Nine months."

Her smile widens. "You did good, momma." She moves to the side, making way for the others, and I lead everyone through the kitchen and into the living room. "Told you," Monique whispers. I nudge her with my elbow playfully, grateful that things are off to a good start.

"My mom will be here in a little bit and she's going to hang out with him. He usually goes to bed around eight, but he didn't get a nap today, so he zonked out early," I say for everyone else.

Kasey moves closer and gives Luis a quick once over. She's dressed in ripped jeans and a flannel shirt over a black tank top. Her hair thrown in her usual messy bun style. "He's cute," she says in way of greeting. "Doesn't look anything like you."

"Kasey!" Aaron groans.

"What? It's not a bad thing. He'd still be cute if he looked like her too." She rolls her eyes and then turns her attention to Monique, a mischievous glint in her eyes. "I'm Kasey, by the way. You must be Dominique's sister?"

"In the flesh. I'm Monique, and I must say, I'm kind of obsessed with you. You have to tell me what it is that you do to my brother that gets him so worked up damn near every day. I need some pointers." Allie and I laugh, but Aaron has a pinched expression on his face I can't quit read, though he doesn't comment. I don't know Kasey or Dominique very well, but even an idiot can see there's something going on there. Whenever they're in the same room together it's like everyone else has to brace themselves for the oncoming explosion. I can't tell if it's hatred that fuels their responses or if they're secretly into each other. Either way, Dominique and Kasey in the same space for more than a few minutes is a recipe for disaster.

The girls head to the sofa just as my mom walks into the room, setting her purse and keys on a nearby hook.

"Sorry, I'm late. I had a few errands to run." She tells me, pulling Luis from my arms. She rubs his back and makes small shushing sounds when he squirms, and in no time he's back to being fast asleep. "We'll be upstairs, but you kids have fun." She waves to my new friends, exhaustion tugging on her features. She'd normally stop and chat for a few minutes, but I know she's been working late. Helping Miguel with some of his work at his office after she gets off from a full day of work herself.

"Thank you," I mouth and watch as she heads upstairs.

"Where's the baby going?" Allie whines, a mock pout on her lips. "I wanted to hold him."

"Why, with the way you and Roman fuck like rabbits every chance you get you'll probably have one of your own soon enough," Kasey remarks.

Allie smacks her arm, but there's a smile on her face that tells me she doesn't hate the idea.

"Sorry. Come over earlier next time and you can hold him. Promise." I tell her, secretly thrilled that not only do they seem completely fine with the fact I have a child, but genuinely interested in him too.

"Urgh, fine. But if he wakes up, I call dibs on baby snuggles. He's so freaking cute."

My heart warms and I hesitantly ask the one question that's been on my mind since we made plans to get together. "So ... you don't care that I have a kid?" I didn't make many friends in Richland. I wasn't there very long. But what friends I did make when we first moved didn't last long after having Luis. They always wanted me to leave him with my mom. They though it was inconvenient for him to be around even if all we were doing was homework or going to the mall. It was disheartening to say the least. And it's not like he caused problems. He was a newborn at the time. All he did was eat, sleep, and poop.

"Why would we?" Kasey asks. "He's cute. He's yours. I don't see what the big deal is."

"You seriously have no idea how relieved I am to hear that. I was so nervous to tell you guys."

Monique gives me an I told you so look just as Aaron steps forward and places a hand on my lower back. "He's a cute kid. And no one who matters is going to treat you any different for having him."

"Aww," Allie coos. "See. This is why we like having you around."

He snorts. "And here I thought it was for my good looks."

"Gross." Kasey retorts.

Aaron rolls his eyes. "Whatever, baby sis." He turns back to me with a shrug. "Having a baby isn't anything to be ashamed of, and friends don't turn their backs on one another for things they can't control." His jaw clenches at the last bit, his expression stony before he wipes it away and drops his hand, moving to sit beside Allie.

I give him a grateful smile. "Thanks, you guys. All of you. Really."

"Don't let that cute baby smile fool you, though," Monique says. "He can be a little devil when he wants to be." My heart shutters in my chest at her choice of words, but thankfully no one seems to notice. Or at least I don't think anyone does. But then Kasey asks, "So what is going on with you and Emilio?" And I freeze like a deer caught in headlights.

My eyes flick to Monique's, who's sporting a confused expression because I'm a terrible friend and still haven't told her who exactly Luis's father is or that I hooked up with him in a classroom after lunch.

"Yeah. Did you guys really have a thing before? I didn't realize you knew each other." Allie adds.

"Really well, too," Aaron interjects. "Pretty sure Emilio wasn't lying about that orgasm he gave you based on your face when he announced it to the entire class."

My cheeks heat and once again my gaze finds Monique's. Her eyes widen, sudden understanding dawning, and I implore her with my eyes not to say anything.

"Orgasm? You and—" she barely stops herself from blurting out you and Luis's father, but thankfully manages to catch her herself. "You and Emilio Chavez fucked?" she says instead, knowing exactly who he is with him being one of Dominique's best friends. "When? I'm your best friend. How did I not know about this? And eww... Emilio is one of Dominique's best friends. He's like an older brother to me." She visible shivers.

I bury my head in my hands. "Can we please not make this a thing, and we didn't have sex. There was no ..." I shake my head. "Just no. Let's pretend nothing ever happened. Okay? Okay. Glad we cleared that up."

Allie snorts. "You may not have boned but he gave you an O during school hours." She shrugs her shoulders. "I can't judge. Roman's caught me off guard a time or two too." A sly smile curls her lips. "But Emilio doesn't usually hook up on campus, and he's staying tight-lipped about the whole thing, which is unusual for him. It's driving me insane. So hard no. We are definitely not dropping it. I want all the details!"

Kasey snorts. "You mean because he usually brags about his conquests from the rooftops after spending the night at their place?"

My stomach drops, and Allie throws a sofa pillow at her. "He does not. He just..." She huffs and shakes her head. "Emilio is a great guy. A little bit of a man whore but a great guy."

Now it's Aaron who snorts though he raises both hands in surrender when Allie glares his way. "I wasn't disagreeing with the great guy part," he rushes to say. "Only the part about being a little bit of a man whore."

"Ignore him. The guys had a falling out and he's still a little salty. Emilio isn't that bad."

The face Kasey makes says she disagrees. "Right! He's so great that he fooled around with Bibiana and has been all over every senior and junior girl since."

I swallow hard, hating that she's right.

"Please tell me you're smart enough not to get involved with him as anything more than whatever it is you two are now? If you wanna fool around with him, have at it. Do the dirty. Just ... don't get attached," she warns.

"It's really not a thing. I made a stupid mistake. One I don't plan on repeating. Let's...talk about something else. Anything else."

"No way," Allie says. "There was mention that you guys hooked up before you moved. Is that true? Come on, please. Emilio is being so tight-lipped about it and getting anything out of Roman on the subject is like pulling teeth. I need the juicy details. I promise after you tell me everything, I won't bug you again."

"Way to sweeten the deal," Monique chimes in. "But I'm with Allie. Give us all the details." So not helping.

At the mention of our hookup, Aaron gives me a considering look. One that has me fidgeting in my seat.

"There isn't much to tell. We hooked up one time."

"Before you moved, right?"

"Yeah. I've lived in Sun Valley my whole life, so," I shrug. "We were bound to run into each other, but it was no big deal. Really. One hookup. That was it."

"Was it good?" Kasey asks. "I've always wondered why chicks throw themselves at him. I'm assuming he's at least decent in the sack. Is that why you fell for his act and fooled around at school with him?"

"Really?" Aaron admonishes his sister.

"What? It's a valid question."

I scrub my hands over my face. "It was fine. Good. But like I said, it was a one-time thing."

"So, the classroom was—"

"A mistake. And not sex. He just..." I look away and swallow.

"Aw, you like him!" Allie sing-songs and now it's me throwing a pillow at her.

"I'm getting food." I jump to my feet and rush off to grab some coxinha I made earlier. They're these little deep-fried balls of heaven filled with shredded chicken that my mom used to make for my dad. She doesn't make them anymore, but I still do from time to time, and hopefully with food in their mouths they'll drop the Emilio stuff, and we can get on with our night.

"Oh, what are these?" Kasey asks, popping one into her mouth when I return. She closes her eyes and moans. "Oh my god," she says around a mouthful because really, coxinha aren't small enough to be eaten in just one bite. "Soooo good."

I laugh as I grab one of my own. "Thanks. I figured since I dropped the baby bomb on you, I'd feed you. You know, in case having a kid was a deal breaker or something, I would bribe you with my culinary ways."

"You can drop as many bombs as you'd like," she says, eating another. "As long as you make these, I swear I will never care or hold anything against you."

"Deal."

We watch Five Feet Apart, which has all of us girls teary-eyed by the end and then take pity on Aaron and put on Enola Holmes. It's still probably not his cup of tea, but he doesn't complain, which I give him props for. I'm sure hanging out with four girls, one of which being your little sister, is probably not the highlight of his week, but he takes it all in stride and he seems pretty close with Allie so what do I know? Maybe this is how he likes to spend his Friday nights.

"I'm going to make some popcorn," I say hopping up from my seat and heading to the kitchen when it gets to the part when her brothers show up. I've watched this movie at least a dozen times and know the script almost by heart.

"I'll help you," Aaron says, getting up to follow.

"She totally needs help," Kasey mocks, and he throws a pillow at her, not bothering to respond.

"Did you want a drink or anything?" I ask once we're in the kitchen. I toss a bag of popcorn in the microwave and then grab two glasses from the cupboard, filling them both with water and handing one to Aaron as we wait for the popcorn to pop.

"Thanks." He accepts the glass and then leans against the kitchen island, a serious look on his face. "So, uh, I wanted to ask you something."

"Okay. What's up?"

He rubs the back of his neck in a nervous gesture. Is he gearing up to ask me out or something? No. That can't be right. Aaron hasn't shown even a hint of interest in me as anything more than a friend, and even that is still up for debate. Right now, he's tolerating me because of Allie, just like the rest of the Devils. So, I have no idea why he's acting so nervous all of a sudden.

"You said Luis is nine months old, right?"

I nod, not really sure where he's going with this.

"And you hooked up with Emilio two summers ago?"

My body goes on high alert. Shit. Shit. Shit.

I nod again. What else am I supposed to do?

"Kasey's right. He doesn't really look anything like you."

I frown. "Uh, okay."

"But he looks a hell of a lot like Emilio especially if you've seen his baby pictures like I have."

My mouth drops open. The microwave dings and I turn to retrieve the bag. "I don't know what you're—"

He doesn't give me the chance to finish. "I've known Emilio almost my entire life. I've seen the pictures of him that decorate his walls. The timeline adds up. You moved eighteen months ago. You hooked up with Emilio before you left. Tell me I'm wrong."

My back is still to him as I squeeze my eyes closed. This isn't how anyone was supposed to find out. What if he tells Emilio? What if—

"You need to tell him. He'd want to know. He'll want to be a part of that little boy's life."

I fist my shaking hands and force myself to turn around and face him, exposing myself in a way I haven't had to do before. "And what if he doesn't?" I ask, voicing my biggest fear. The thing that keeps me up at night when my mind refuses to go quiet. "What if he doesn't want the responsibility of a child? Aaron—" I force myself to slow down and take a deep breath.

"We had a one-night stand. It was never supposed to lead to anything more. He didn't sign up for this." I wave my hands around me.

"Neither did you," his words are softly spoken, not a hint of anger or judgement in them. "Bibiana, I can't imagine being a single mom in high school is easy."

I shake my head because no, it isn't.

"You didn't sign up for this either, but would you change it? Would you give him up?"

I vehemently shake my head. "Never. I love him. Luis is everything to me."

Aaron nods as though he understands, but his next words stab into my chest like a knife. "Don't you think Emilio deserves to love him too?"

Tears prick the corners of my eyes and I hastily wipe them away. "I was going to tell him. I am going to tell him." I suck in a breath. "There just is never a good time and whenever I try and get him alone or have an actual conversation with him—"

"He defaults into putting the moves on you?" Aaron says with a sad smile. I don't bother correcting him because no, Emilio isn't interested in me anymore. It's every other girl with a set of tits that he's chasing after. "I can see how that might be a problem but..." he hesitates then exhales a loud sigh, "you need to tell him. Soon. The longer you wait, the worse it'll be. You've already waited a year in a half."

Not on purpose. "I didn't know who he was." He must think I'm such a horrible person right now. "We didn't exchange information. Not even names. I had no way of letting him know I was pregnant after the fact," I rush to explain. I don't want him thinking I kept Emilio from his son intentionally. That was never the objective here.

"But you knew the first day you came to Sun Valley High?" he hedges.

I nod. "Yeah. I recognized him right away."

He considers me, tapping his forefinger against his chin. "It's been a week. I'll give you one more to find a way to tell him. It would be better if it came from you. But if you can't do it, I have to tell him. He deserves to know."

I swallow hard and open my mouth to ask for more time, but the front door opens and in walks Miguel, pulling both of our attentions his way.

"Hey, Bibi. Your mom upstairs?" Miguel asks as soon as he sees me. "Oh. I didn't realize you had a friend here." He scowls as he takes Aaron in. "Is Jae here too?" he adds, and there's an edge in his voice. I stop myself from rolling my eyes, because of course he would see Aaron and assume he's Jae's competition. It doesn't matter that I've told Jae and Miguel, and my mom for that matter, that I am not interested in dating anyone.

I just want to focus on graduating. Is that too much to ask?

"Who's Jae?" Aaron asks, taking Miguel's bait. Urgh.

"He's Bibi's—"

"Friend." I cut him off. "We're friends and no, he's not here. I haven't seen him since this morning." And only because he still insists on driving me to school every day. "And yes, Mom's upstairs with Luis. She went to bed early. She looked beat."

Miguel nods and grabs a beer from the fridge. "Yeah, she's been helping me with some of the accounting at work," he says as he cracks open the bottle and downs half its contents in one pull. Voices can be heard from the living room, and Miguel cocks his head, pointing his beer toward the hallway. "Who else is here?"

"A few friends. We're just hanging out. Watching movies."

"Sleepover?" he asks, a glint in his eyes that puts me on edge. He's been weird lately. I mean, he's always been a little weird but weirder than usual. Miguel's never been anything but nice to me. Sometimes overly nice and I usually just brush it aside. But right now, Miguel has a distinct creeper factor that is making me uncomfortable.

Just then all three girls come into the room. "Hey, what's taking so long?" Monique asks with a bounce to her step.

"Yeah, I was starting to wonder if you were making out with my brother," Kasey jokes, flicking her gaze between us before settling on Miguel. "But I can see that's not the case. Did you make the popcorn?"

"Here, let me help you out with that." Miguel says, taking the bag of popcorn from the counter and pouring it into a bowl. "What are you girls going to be up to tonight? Hopefully not getting into trouble," he says it with a smirk, and again the creep-o-meter jumps up.

No one answers him. Monique and Kasey are both giving him polite but wary smiles, meanwhile Allie's gone pale as a ghost.

"Are you okay?" I ask her but she doesn't look at me. Her eyes are trained on Miguel, her chest rising and falling at a rapid clip.

He turns his attention to her and recognition sparks. "Well, fuck me."

TEN

Emilio

"What's going on in that head of yours?" Dominique asks in the locker room. We just wrapped up practice and I'm sore as fuck. I drop my football helmet and pads beside my locker as I peel my sweat-soaked shirt over my head, rubbing my stomach in the process. I'm fucking starving.

"Nothing, man. I'm good."

"Liar," Roman says as he comes in the room and drops his gear beside mine.

"What's going on with you and Allie's new friend?" he asks. "Because whatever is eating at you, it has to do with her."

I shake my head. "I don't know what you're talking about. Nothing's eating at me. I'm good."

"Right." Dominique cuffs me on the shoulder. "So good you can't stop staring at the girl every time she walks into a room."

"Drop it," I snarl under my breath. "She's unimportant."

Dom snorts. "And you pissing all over the place to keep people away from her like she belongs to you totally supports that statement."

I clench my jaw and glower. "I'm not pissing on anything."

"*Mentiroso*," Roman says. *Liar.*

I ignore them and head for the showers, but of course the fuckers follow me. "Bro, you've claimed her. The whole fucking school knows it too. You beat the shit out of Carson Bailey during practice because he said she had a nice rack. Which she does, by the way," Dominique adds and my hands fist at my sides.

"See, that right there. That's my point." He indicates my tight fists and I force myself to relax, opening and closing them to bring back circulation. "I'm one of your best friends and you want to swing at me too. What the fuck, man?"

"Carson had it coming and you're being a dick." I stick my head under the running water and try and block out the voices of my friends as they do the same. Fucking Carson Bailey. He wanted her that night and the idiot made it known he was still interested. Sucks to be him though, because he's not getting anywhere near Bibiana if I have any say about it. And trust me, I have a say.

"E—" Roman snaps.

I wipe the water from my eyes and grab the soap, lathering it in my hands to take off today's layer of grime. "We hooked up. What's the big fucking deal?"

"You still hooking up with Sarah?" he asks and isn't that a loaded question. I tighten my jaw and rinse off the last of the suds before reaching for my towel and wrapping it around my waist.

"No." I offer the single-word answer, knowing the fucker is going to read more into it than he should. I'm not hooking up with anyone else and it's a fucking travesty because I should be. Sarah, Kathleen, Kaitlyn, I have a whole host of girls willing but none of them are her.

Neither Dom nor Roman say anything as we all dry off, getting dressed before heading for the exit. "What's the plan tonight?" I ask as we make our way to the school parking lot. It's Friday night and coach has us running two a day during playoffs since he's a sadistic bastard. I'm ready for the weekend and need the time to recharge and get my head on straight.

Antonio is home this weekend. Shocker. My older brother usually makes an effort to be anywhere but home, yet decided he'd watch over our little sister, Sofia, giving me a much-needed break. Sofia is old enough to be home alone but Raul —I refuse to call that waste of space "Dad"—has been hanging around more than usual, and none of us trust him where she's concerned.

I get that the man who contributed half of your DNA being home is probably normal for most families, but not for us. Not since Mom left. He spends most of his nights at the bar. Most of his days in some seedy motel with his flavor of the week. It's better this way. Safer for Sofia. For all of us. But he never stays gone for long. Not as long as he should, at least. He comes by the house on a near-weekly basis and when he does, he's usually drunk and angry. Never a good combination.

Lately, we've lucked out and Sofia's been at a friend's or kicking it at Roman's with his mom when Raul's stopped in. But I have a feeling our luck will run out eventually, which is why one of us is with Sofia at all times. And if we can't be, either because of practice for me or work for Antonio, then we make sure to coordinate a sleepover with a friend or she spends time with Maria. Roman's mom is the mom we never had and thank God she loves my sister as if she were her own.

Roberto should be here helping make sure she's safe, but he enlisted the day he turned eighteen. It was fucked up when he left, but I can't say I blame him.

"Dunno. Allie is kicking it at Bibiana's with the babies and Henderson."

"The babies?" I ask.

He smirks. "Yeah. Dom and Henderson's baby sisters. The babies."

Dominique scrubs a hand over his face. "Them meeting one another is going to come back and bite me in the ass."

"You're not wrong, man." I grip his shoulder and grin. "And I cannot wait to see your downfall."

He shrugs me off as we reach Roman's El Camino and Dom's Escalade. I rarely drive myself. Why bother when both of these two are control freaks and insist on driving. Nine times out of ten we're going to the same place. We don't need three rides to get there. "My place?" Roman asks and Dominique nods. I open the passenger door to Roman's ride when a cell phone rings. I check my pocket, but it isn't mine that's ringing. Dominique pulls his out and stares down at the screen, a scowl on his face. "What the hell is Kasey calling me for?" he bites out, letting it go to voicemail. As soon as he shoves it back in his pocket, it starts ringing again.

"Looks like things are about to bite you in the ass sooner than you thought."

He flips me the bird but answers the phone with a curt, "What?"

There's shouting on the other line and I freeze, straining to pick up what she's saying.

"Address?" Dom bites out. "Lock yourselves in a fucking bathroom if you have to, got it?"

He's shaking his head. "Dammit. Why can't you lis— Fuck. Put Aaron on the phone."

More shouting.

She must have given Aaron the phone because now Dom is listening, eyes dark as he runs his hands over his tightly braided hair, his fingers flexing as though he wish he could tear it out. "We're on our way." Dominique ends the calls and turns to Roman with rage in his eyes. "Follow me and call your pops on the way. I'll text Emilio the address so you can pass it along to him."

"What's going on?"

His jaw ticks. "Allie thinks she found her rapist, and Aaron is beating the shit out of him as we speak. We need to go."

That's all it takes to get Roman moving. We peel out of the school parking lot, taking the corner so fucking fast I have to grab the oh-shit handle, but I don't tell Roman to slow down. His girl is in trouble and there isn't a mountain on this planet he wouldn't try to move for her. He dials his dad's number, snapping out the situation, and I pass on the address Dominique texted me.

It's a fifteen-minute drive, but we make it in close to five, and before the car is even off Roman is jumping from the front seat and barreling straight for the front door, Dominique and I close behind. We're family. And none of us fight alone.

ELEVEN

Bibiana

Something is seriously wrong here and it has everything to do with Miguel. "Uhh... we're going to get back to our movie." I grab Allie's arm and half drag her toward the hallway, hoping everyone else will follow. Once we're alone I'll ask her what is going on. Her skin is so pale it's virtually translucent. I'm afraid she might pass out.

All of a sudden Allie digs in her heels and pulls her arm away from me, her spine straightening. "It's you," she says, but her voice is so quiet Miguel doesn't hear her. He's already gone back to his beer, and a part of me wonders if it isn't the first one he's had this evening. "It was you," she repeats, this time louder and he snaps his head toward her.

"I'm not sure I know what you're talking about," he tells her, but even I know it's a lie. He's not bothering to hide his smile or the heated look in his gaze as he eyes her up and down like a piece of meat. What is wrong with him? He has to know she's only seventeen.

"What's going on?" I ask, but Monique looks just as confused as I do.

"Allie?" Aaron questions, stepping closer to her and wrapping one arm protectively around her waist. "What's wrong?"

Tears are silently spilling down her face as she points at Miguel, her attention still wholly focused on him. "It was you. You were one of the men who..." She chokes on her words. "It was you." Aaron stiffens beside her and almost in slow motion turns to face Miguel. He tucks Allie behind his back and faces off with my mother's boyfriend, a furious expression washing over his face. "Kasey, call Roman."

"Wha—"

"Now. Tell him to call his dad and get here. Now, Kasey," he snaps.

Kasey pulls out her phone and starts calling, but it goes to voice mail so she tries again. And again.

"You sick sonovabitch," Aaron growls, taking a step forward.

Miguel doesn't even try to deny whatever it is they're accusing him of. He holds one arm out and waves his beer in the other. "Hey, man, you'd tap it too if you had a chance." My stomach rolls at his words. Is he...with Allie? No. No way. No freaking way.

Aaron launches himself at Miguel, and the two crash to the ground.

"Oh, my God," Monique gasps beside me.

I take a step forward but have no clue what to do. Do I intervene? Aaron is on top of Miguel, fists flying as he lands a right hook to his jaw before Miguel lands one of his own and manages to throw Aaron off him. I push the rest of the girls back as both men climb to their feet. Aaron's chest is heaving but he doesn't look to be in rough shape. Meanwhile, blood is running from Miguel's nose and the corner of his mouth. Yet he's smiling, eyes bloodshot and a manic expression on his face. He spits blood onto the floor and waves at Aaron as if to say come on. Aaron lunges forward again. The two begin rolling across the ground and it's all I can do to track their movements. One second Miguel is on top and the next, Aaron is. Limbs are flying everywhere, fists crashing into whatever body part they can find. A plant is knocked over spreading dirt across the tiles and it mixes with their blood, leaving smears of murk in horrific streaks or brown and red.

Aaron seems to have the advantage despite Miguel being the bigger of the two. He's younger and in better shape, and he makes good use of what advantage that affords him. The two manage to separate, but only for a few seconds before the front door crashes open and all eyes turn toward it. Allie visibly relaxes beside me when she catches sight of Roman—Dominque and Emilio right behind him.

A jolt of fear spears through me. Emilio is here. He can't be here. Not right now. Not like this.

Roman assesses the scene in a matter of seconds before he throws himself forward into the fight, fists flying as he tackles Miguel back to the ground.

Miguel has zero time to react before Roman is pummeling his face into the tile floor, a murderous look in his eyes.

A gasp on the stairs has me looking up to find my mom standing at the top of the staircase, Luis clutched in her arms as she watches the scene below. "What are you doing? Get off of him!" she shouts, and I rush to intercept her as she runs down the steps and heads right for Roman and Miguel. I pull Luis from her arms, my focus completely on my son's safety, just as Emilio steps up to my mother and says in a low voice, "He has this beating coming to him for what he did to our friend."

My mom tries to shove past him but Emilio sidesteps her, blocking her path. She pushes against his shoulders, but he refuses to move. "You can't do this. You have no right—"

"He raped a seventeen-year-old girl," Dominique adds, his expression stony. He hasn't moved since coming in, and despite his words being for my mother, his gaze is glued to the fight in front of us, almost like he's waiting for something.

"Miguel would never do that. Whatever you think you know is a lie. He—"

"Admitted it Mom," I say in a whisper, imploring her with my eyes. My vision blurs but I refuse to let a single tear fall.

She jerks back as if I struck her. "Watch your words, minha filha." My daughter. "You don't know the truth of it. Miguel would never do what they're accusing him of. I'm calling the police."

"They're already on their way," Dominique says, and as soon as the words leave his lips, we all hear the sirens in the distance.

"Time's running out," Emilio says, his words directed at Roman, but he doesn't hear him. Roman is straddling Miguel who's barely moving, his arms no longer able to defend against Roman's fists. "Roman!" Still no response.

His jaw clenches before he meets Aaron's gaze across the room. Silent communication passes through them before they both step forward and rip Roman off Miguel's body. Roman doesn't give up without a fight, and it takes both boys holding him back to keep him from throwing himself back at Miguel who's barely moving on the floor as it is. Roman looks crazed, his eyes ablaze and his lips pulled back in a snarl. "I'll fucking kill you," he shouts. "You're a dead man."

Allie rushes to Roman's side, her arms wrapping around his waist. His nostrils flare but he manages to pull himself together enough to wrap his hands around her and hold her tight against his chest.

My mother rushes to Miguel's side, pulling his head into her lap as she sobs over him, and I just stand there, holding my baby boy, my world falling apart all around me.

Two officers come through the door and one immediately begins barking orders.

"Roman, get Allie and get out of here. I'll get statements from both of you later." Roman nods and leads Allie through the open doorway and outside. The sound of a car starting and pulling out of the driveway can be heard from outside, letting us know they're gone. The officer takes one look at Miguel, who's still on the ground but has managed to push himself up into a sitting position, and says, "You're under arrest for the assault and rape of Allie Ramirez. Anything you say can and..."

I don't bother listening after that. I stumble backward until my back hits the wall and let my body slide down until my butt hits the floor, Luis clutched safely in my arms. Monique is beside me in an instant, but then so is Dominique. "Go wait in the car," he says.

She shakes her head. "I'm not leav—"

"Now, Monique. Don't make me call Mom."

Monique clenches her jaw and turns an apologetic look my way.

"It's fine. I'll talk to you tomorrow," I tell her. No way can she get mixed up in whatever all this is. Her family would never let her see the light of day if they found out what happened. They'd never let her hang out with me again if they knew what my mom's boyfriend was accused of doing. Dominique has the right to get her out of here before any more cops show up or the two who are already here decide to take statements from everyone and get names on the record.

"Call me later and let me know you're okay," she says, and I nod.

Dominique walks her out, but seconds later he's back and heading straight for Kasey. They argue but I can't make out what's said and the next thing I know he's throwing her over his shoulder and storming out of the room as she screeches at him to put her down. Aaron watches the entire thing with a resigned expression before following Dominique out the door, presumably to take his sister home.

The officers pull Miguel to his feet and begin to usher him out the door, my mom right behind them. "Mom—" I call after her and she turns to face me. "Where are you going?"

"I'm sorry, minha filha. But I love him." Tears fall down her cheeks, her expression torn.

My brows furrow. What is she saying right now? "Mom?"

She doesn't say anything else. She just shakes her head and follows the officers out. I'm still standing there, staring at the empty doorway she walked through when Emilio appears beside me. "You okay?"

I jump at his words, managing to startle and wake Luis in the process. How he managed to sleep through all the noise is beyond me, and I wish he would have stayed asleep a little longer because now Emilio is looking at him with open curiosity. "He yours?"

I swallow hard, but nod and push back to my feet.

He flicks his eyes between me and Luis. He opens his mouth. Closes it. Opens it again. I can the see the moment he puts two and two together. His mouth tightens, brows drawn, eyes glued to the boy in my arms.

"Come on," Dominique calls, ducking back inside. "Aaron's in his car with the girls. He'll drop them off and then head to Roman and Allie's so we can all figure our shit out. After Rome's dad drops Miguel off at the station he'll be heading there too. We need to get our stories straight."

Emilio doesn't move.

"E, come on." Dominique grabs his arm but Emilio jerks free and shoves him away. His chest is rising and falling at a rapid pace, his nostrils flaring.

"You have a son?" Pain slashes across his face and a muscle ticks in his jaw as he visibly fights to keep it together. When I don't answer, he takes a step back, and shouts, "I have a son?" It's as if the entire house shakes with the force of his voice.

I don't know what to do or what to say so I just stand there frozen in place. Dominique looks between us, seeing the baby boy in my arms, and his expression tightens. "Emilio, now isn't the—"

"Nah. No way, man. No fucking way." He shakes his head. "Do I even need to ask?" he says to me, and Luis starts to cry. I bounce him on my hip and make soothing noises in the face of Emilio's anger. He's fuming. If it were possible for steam to be coming out of his ears, it would be. His face is red and the veins on his neck stick out in sharp relief. All I can do in the face of his anger is swallow hard and hold Luis to me a little tighter.

Emilio catches the movement and his eyes narrow. "Are you fucking kidding me?" he barks. "You think I'd hurt him? My own kid?" His eyes narrow into slits, "Because that's what he is, right? Mine."

I hesitate.

"Answer me!" he roars.

Dominique steps forward and places a hand on Emilio's shoulder. "Hey, why don't we—"

"Fuck that. Tell me the truth. Is. He. Mine?" I nod, and Emilio shrugs Dominique off again, his movements sharp as he begins to pace. "She kept my kid from me. My son." He slaps a hand over his chest. "My son." His jaw clenches. "What the fuck, Bibiana? What did I ever do to you to warrant that? Huh? Am I not good enough?" His voice rises with each word until he's practically shouting at me, and all I can do is stand there knowing I deserve his anger. His rage.

Luis's crying increases at Emilio's harsh tone, and a silent tear slips past my defenses to trek down my cheek. This isn't how I wanted this to go. None of this is what I wanted.

"Emilio—" Dominique tries again. He flicks his gaze toward me. "Maybe you should—"

"No." He shakes his head, anger etched into every line of his body. "Give me my son." Emilio holds his arms out but I take an involuntary step back.

His eyes blaze. "Let me hold my son, Bibiana," he spits out my name with so much venom, I visibly shudder but manage to stand my ground and shake my head.

"You're angry."

"You would be too," he snaps.

I rock Luis in my arms, running my hand over the back of his head in a soothing gesture as I struggle to remain calm. "I know. I'm not saying you shouldn't be. But you're angry and right now, you're scary." Really fucking scary. I don't think Emilio would hurt me or Luis, but seeing him like this, it's unnerving to say the least. "I'm sorry. But I'm not handing him to you. Not like this."

I sway my body side to side and Luis's cries finally stop. He sniffles a few times before his head rests against my shoulder. Exhaustion finally taking hold. When his eyes close, I release a small sigh of relief and turn back to the angry boy before me. Emilio's entire body is taught like a bow string. I can tell he wants to argue but instead he gives me a stiff nod. He heads to the sofa and sits down, bowing his head and running his hands through his dark brown hair. His shoulders slump in defeat, and so many emotions run through me. Sorrow. Pain. Regret. I chance a look in Dominique's direction, but instead of finding anger or disgust like I expect, I find resignation. I'm not sure that is any better.

"This wasn't how I wanted you to find out," I say the words in little more than a whisper.

"I'm sure you had your reasons for not telling him." Dominique chimes in, not bothering to lower his voice, ensuring Emilio hears his words. "I can't imagine being a single mom is easy. You've had to make some tough decisions. Sometimes they're good ones. Other times maybe they're not."

I nod, worrying my lower lip. This obviously wasn't one of my better ones.

"But, I can see you love that little boy." He tilts his chin toward his friend. "Do right by him and give Emilio a chance to love him too."

It's all I've ever wanted to do. I didn't mean to keep Luis a secret. I wanted to tell him. It just never seemed like the right time. I'm so angry with myself for letting this happen. For letting it come out like this.

Dominique tosses his keys beside Emilio and heads to the door. "I'll catch a ride with Aaron. Call me if you need anything. We'll fill you in later when you have time." Emilio doesn't respond, not that Dominique waits for him to.

When the door closes behind him, I stand there for a few moments, almost afraid to move, before I muster up the courage to say, "I'm going to lay him down in his crib. If ..." I take a deep breath. "If you're still here when I come back and you want to talk, we can do that."

He doesn't answer, so I head upstairs and gently lay Luis down in his crib before slipping into the bathroom. My cheeks are red and blotchy, my eyeliner smudged beneath my eyes and the small wing at the corners long since rubbed away. I wash away the emotions of today and go back downstairs, almost surprised to find Emilio in the exact same spot I left him in.

A part of me was sure he would have left. I'm not sure if I should be relieved that he chose to stay.

When he hears me enter the room, he lifts his head and I freeze. Grief stands out in sharp relief across his face, and it twists me up inside to see him like this.

I sink down on the bottom step of the staircase, wrapping my arms around my knees. I don't know what to say, or if I should even say anything at all. So, I wait. Seconds tick by, turning into minutes as we stare at one another. I hope he can see how sorry I am. That my eyes can convey what my words have failed to give him.

When a full five minutes passes, he shakes his head and stands up, but he doesn't go anywhere. He just...stands there. The anger has drained out from his body, leaving behind a boy who looks lost and alone. Broken. And I'm responsible for that.

"I'm sorry I didn't tell you about him sooner," I say, my words whispered.

"Were you ever going to tell me?" he asks. "If I hadn't found out today, would you have ever said anything?" His words are equally quiet as though he's afraid of the answer.

I push to my feet and move closer to him. "I wanted to tell you the first day I saw you. I had every intention of letting you know right away but..." I bite my lip and Emilio tilts his head back staring at the ceiling. His Adams apple bobs as he swallows.

"But then you heard about my reputation." I exhales a harsh breath. "And then I finger-fucked you in a classroom. Fuck."

He reaches out and jerks me to him, wrapping his arms around my shoulders in a fierce embrace. "I'm so fucking mad at you for keeping him from me," he says into my hair and I tentatively wrap my arms around his waist. I have no idea why he's holding me like this, but I don't really care. I need this. Need the contact. I need to feel like things will be okay. That he isn't going to hate me forever.

"You should have told me. I don't give a fuck about everything else. You should have told me right away."

"It's only been—" He cuts me off, his body trembling beneath my hold.

"A week, Bibiana. It's been a week that you've been here. That's a week I can't get back. A week of not knowing I had a son and of him not knowing me."

"I'm sorry," I say, because he's right. If roles were reversed, I'd feel the same way.

"I want to hate you," he whispers almost too quiet for me to hear, but I do and my heart plummets to the soles of my feet. "And when my head stops spinning, I just might. I don't know if I'll ever be able to get over the fact that you kept him from me. I missed so fucking much." He releases me and takes two steps back.

I feel cold at the loss of contact and wrap my arms around myself.

"I—" I don't know what to say to that.

"I want to get to know him," he says, voice firm. "I want visitation and I want it in writing."

His last statement takes me by surprise, and I swallow hard as a trickle of fear worms its way through me before reason has me locking the emotion away. This is what I wanted. I want my son to have his father. I want him to feel wanted and Emilio demanding visitation is him showing that he wants to be in Luis's life. I take a deep breath and force out my next words.

"I'd like that too."

His eyes widen before he nods his head. "Okay. Good." He shoves his hands into his pockets. "When can I have him?"

I frown. "Um…"

"Can I pick him up tomorrow?"

"You want to pick him up?" I ask, licking my lips. "And take him where?"

"I don't know. The park. Maybe Roman's." He shrugs.

It's the middle of winter. What does he think they're going to do at the park? Luis isn't even walking on his own yet. "Have you ever looked after a baby?" I ask as gently as possible because I really don't want to fight with him about this. "Luis is only nine months old. He ...umm..." I can see that Emilio is about to argue so I rush out my next words. "What if you came here instead? You could take a few days to get to know him. Make sure he's comfortable with you and it'll give you a chance to learn umm ... how to look after an infant?" That sounds a lot more patronizing that I mean it to be.

He considers it and the silence stretches between us. "Fine."

I release a breath I hadn't realized I was holding. "Okay. Good."

We stare at each other for a beat. "His name is Luis?" he asks. His eyes keep flicking toward the staircase, and I know he wants to see him again.

"Yeah. Luis Afonso Sousa."

A muscle ticks in his jaw.

When he doesn't snap or yell at me, I move closer and tentatively reach out, tugging on his sleeve. "Come on," I say and lead him up the staircase to my room.

Outside the door, he hesitates for only a minute before following me inside. The lights are out, but there is a small night-light and sound machine beside Luis's crib that illuminates his sleeping form. Careful not to wake him, I wave toward my bed, indicating that Emilio have a seat. His eyes are glued to our son and a small smile curls the corners of his mouth as he takes a seat, leaning forward for a better view.

"He's perfect," he whispers, and I can't help but match his smile.

"He has your eyes and your mouth," I tell him, claiming the space beside him.

"He does?"

I nod.

We sit in silence, watching our little boy sleep, and despite today being a complete disaster of epic proportions, a small part of me is hopeful. Emilio wants to be in Luis's life, and that alone is more than I could have hoped for.

TWELVE

Emilio

I stay at Bibiana's until just past midnight watching my boy sleep, the steady rise and fall of his tiny body doing something to soothe the raging devil inside of me. I have a kid. A son. One she kept secret from me for all this time. Fuck. I scrub my hands over my face and look down at her. She drifted off to sleep close to an hour ago, her tiny body curled up beside me on top of her comforter. Exhaustion lines her face and a part of me is sorry for that, but the bigger part of me, the all-consuming asshole deep inside is furious with her. I'm having to try real hard not to explode.

What the actual fuck?

I shove to my feet and lean over the crib railing, giving Luis one last look. "I'll be back later, little man." I tell him, tracing a finger along his cheek. He's so small. Fragile. Looking at him brings home the fact that my entire world is about to flip upside down right now.

I head for the door, leaving Bibiana undisturbed on her bed. She said I could see him tomorrow. Well, technically today. But I need a few hours of sleep and a shower before I'll be in any sort of shape to meet my little boy.

I jog down the stairs, grabbing Dominique's keys along the way and head straight for my place. My mind is roiling and my stomach is twisted into knots. I want to call Roman, but I know he's got his hands full with Allie's shit right now, and she needs him more than I do. And isn't that a fucking plot twist. Bibiana's what? Stepdad, or whatever he is to her, is one of the sons of bitches who raped Allie.

My blood boils as an entirely different sort of anger thrums through my veins. I need to do something. Hit something or someone. I slam my palm against the steering wheel and scream out my frustrations. What the hell am I going to do?

Bibiana seems onboard with me being in his life, but that could be the adrenaline of the night's events talking. A lot has happened. What if she wakes up in the morning and changes her mind? What if she decides I'm not good enough? Or fuck, worse, what if she takes off again? She might. She's done it before and with her mom taking that asshole's side. What if—

Shit. I still don't have the girl's fucking number.

I'm about to turn around and go back when my phone pings with the sound of an incoming text message.

Allie: Are you okay?

I pull over to the side of the road and stare down at the illuminated screen.

Me: I should be asking you that. You good, vanilla?

I take a deep breath through my nose and exhale loudly through my mouth as I wait for her response. I can't even imagine what she's going through right now, and the fact that she's still worried about me... I hang my head. She's too much. Too good. This is why we all liked her when she transferred in. She's not like other women. She isn't selfish. She's there when you need her. The girl is the strongest person I know.

Allie: I'm ok. Dom told me what happened. I didn't know.

Even if she did, I could never be mad at her. Allie is...I don't know. She's my friend. But she's more. Like a sister but not. I don't know how to describe it. What I do know is that she never gives up. She puts everyone else's needs before her own. But this time, she needs to put herself first. She doesn't need my shit. I love her for it. But I'm gonna figure this out. I don't want her worrying about me when she has her own mess to handle.

Me: Not your fault. Get some sleep. We can talk about it later. You have enough on your plate.

Allie: It's going to be okay. Love you, E.

Me: You too, vanilla.

I pull back on the road and go straight home, pausing in the driveway at the sight of Raul's beat up Civic. Shit. I do not have time for this right now. I climb out of the car and head for the door, only then spotting that it's standing slightly ajar. Fuck me.

I take a deep breath and push it open. A broken bottle sits discarded in the entryway. I listen, but don't hear anything. No voices. No footsteps. I creep through the house, careful to keep my steps quiet. Where the hell is my Antonio? Where's Sofia?

One of my questions is answered when I find my brother passed out on the living room floor, dried blood beneath his nose and mouth. Fuck. I drop down to my knees and check for a pulse. It's steady. He's just knocked out. I shake his shoulders and he stirs with a start.

"What the—"

"Where's Sofia?" My heart races as I scan the room for our little sister.

He groans and I know his head has got to be killing him. I help him into a sitting position. "The bastard took me by surprise."

I clench my jaw because that's what he always does. You never know when or if he's going to swing. There's no way to read Raul. One second, he's fine and the next he's in a manic rage trying to kill his own fucking children.

"Sofia," I prompt when my brother doesn't say anything else.

"Shit." He pushes to his feet. "What time is it?"

"Maybe twelve-thirty. Where is she, Antonio?"

His shoulders relax and he heads for the hallway that leads to our rooms. There's more broken glass here and a few drops of blood splattered across the floor. I'm assuming those belong to Raul because they all lead toward his room at the very end of the hallway.

Antonio raises his finger to his lips in the universal sign to be quiet as he slowly opens the door that leads to my bedroom. We step inside and he goes straight for my closet. Sofia is asleep inside, her tiny body curled into the fetal position. We both stare down at her, relief sweeping through me once I can see for myself that she's okay.

I lean down to lift her out, careful not to wake her as I lay her on my bed and tuck the blankets around her. When she's settled, I follow Antonio back into the hall, locking the door behind me. It only locks from the inside, so she can let herself out when she wakes up. I won't be able to get back in until then, at least not without waking her. But it's better this way. I need to talk to my brother and find out what the hell happened, and I can't do that and worry about the bastard down the hall getting to my baby sister.

"What the hell happened?" I asked, my voice pitched low as soon as we're a safe distance away.

He rolls his neck and scrubs a palm down his face, wincing in pain when he brushes over his bruised cheek. "What always happens. He showed up maybe an hour ago." Antonio shakes his head. "I heard his car roll up and hid Sofia before he stepped through the front door. Made her promise not to come out and to keep quiet."

I nod my head. That's what we usually do when Raul comes around. She's looking more and more like our mom as she gets older, and the sight of her alone has been enough to set him off the few times he's dropped by recently.

"You okay?"

Antonio nods. "Yeah. I'm good. I don't remember much after the second punch, but I didn't fight back so he must have gotten bored."

"You should go to the—"

"I said I'm good," he snaps. Antonio hangs his head, palms clenched into fists at his sides. "I fucking hate this." He moves further down the hall to the kitchen and pulls out a bag of frozen corn before taking a seat at the table. He holds it against his face and mutters out a few choice words.

I grab two beers from the fridge, open both, and hand one to him across the table before taking a seat. "What's the plan?" I ask, hoping he's come up with something. Raul is getting worse, and we all have shit going on. We do our best to protect Sofia, but one of these days he's bound to come up on her alone, and none of us knows what will happen when that day comes.

"I don't know, man." He's fighting exhaustion. Shit. We both are. Too much has happened today. Too many things to process. To try and figure out.

"What are you doing home so late? I figured you'd have been here earlier, or later if you crashed at Romans."

I debate telling him about Luis, but before I can make up my mind, my brother proves just how well he knows me with his next words. "What happened?"

"It can wait."

Antonio shakes his head. "No. Don't do that. I know you've got your boys, but you got me too. Come on, Emilio. What happened?"

I grind my teeth down as frustration radiates through every cell in my body. I want to tell him. I want his support, but Antonio doesn't do well when his plate is full. He's like Roberto. He bails rather than dealing with it. He might be doing better than our oldest brother—when shit got too real, he enlisted in the military and never looked back. Antonio, at least, stuck around after his eighteenth birthday—but he still takes off sometimes for a week or more at a time.

"E?"

"Don't you dare bail, you got me?"

His eyes widen, but he nods. "I won't bail."

"I'm serious, Antonio. I can't deal with Raul and my own shit right now. Not by myself."

He nods his head, his face twisted into a solemn expression. "I won't leave."

"Okay." I hesitate and have to swallow past the lump in my throat. "I have a kid."

His eyes widen to the size of saucers. "You knocked a girl up?"

"Yeah," I rub the back of my neck. "A year and a half ago. I just found out tonight."

He curses and drops his head into his hands. "Shit. Are you sure it's yours?"

I nod. "I'm sure. The timing lines up and he looks just like me. Damn near identical to my baby pictures at that age.

"You should get a paternity test," he suggests.

"I don't need it. He's mine. I haze zero doubts. You'll feel the same when you meet him."

He doesn't like my answer, but thankfully doesn't argue either. "We need to call Roberto."

"What?" I shove away from the table. "Why the hell would we call him? He left!" I hiss, but Antonio just shakes his head.

"Can you think of a better option? Raul is a problem. A big one. And now you have a kid. What are you going to do if you have him here and Raul shows up? Huh? Have you even thought that far?"

My blood turns to ice as I digest his words because no, I hadn't thought that far. I'm still dealing with the fact that I'm a dad. That Luis is mine. I hadn't even considered just how vulnerable he is. How dangerous having him with me could be for him. Shit. If Bibiana found out what I was dealing with, no way would she let me be in his life. Fuck. Fuck. Fuck.

"He doesn't have leave coming up. There's nothing he can do—"

"He'll get leave."

"But—"

"Let me handle it, okay? Shit. Boy or Girl?"

Huh. It takes me a second to understand his questions. "Oh. Boy."

"What's his name?"

"Luis," I tell him.

Antonio nods to himself for a second before a wide grin splits his face. "So, I'm an uncle."

I muffle my laugh with my fist. "Yeah, fucker. You're an uncle."

Silence stretches between us, both of us thinking of all the things that have gone wrong and all the possible things that can still happen. It's times like this when I can't breathe. When the pressure builds too much, and I need to find a release. I'm tempted to call some random. It'd be easier if I called Sarah, worked out some of my frustration while Antonio was here but that's not a tree I want to be barking up right now. Fucking her holds zero appeal for me. I don't know what is wrong with me but obviously something is. Maybe it's just her. Our last fuck was awful. But...whatever. I can't leave Antonio and Sofia to deal with Raul on their own whenever he wakes up anyway.

My family might be fucked up, but we do what we can for as long as we can. Let's hope we all have enough fight left in us to deal with whatever comes next.

THIRTEEN

Bibiana

I wake to Luis's garbled baby jabbers and roll over to find the space beside me empty. A glance at the beside clock. It shows that it's just past nine. Emilio must have left sometime after I fell asleep. I pick up my Luis almost as though I'm on autopilot and go through our usual morning routine.

Nurse. Fresh diaper. New clothes. When he's all set, I put him down on the floor with some of his toys and get myself ready, taking a five-minute shower with the door open to try and wash away some of the strain of last night.

Clean and feeling more awake, I straighten up the small mess Luis made before we head downstairs. I pass my mom's room on the way, her door open and the bed empty. I wonder if she ever came home last night. I need to talk to her but I'm not sure what to say.

The entryway and kitchen are a disaster. A lamp is laying on its side, shards of glass scattered in the general area. There are blood smears across the floor. Chairs toppled over and dirt from a potted plan strewn about.

I sigh, already knowing I can't leave it like this. I deposit Luis on the floor in the living room with a few of his favorite toys and turn on some cartoons. "Mommy will be right back."

I grab a garbage bag and the broom, cleaning up all of the dirt and glass and throwing away anything not salvageable. Luis wanders into the kitchen a few times, so the clean-up process takes a little longer having to go back and forth and pause long enough to play with him for a few minutes before he's distracted enough for me to slip away and finish my task.

The blood has stained the off-white tiles leaving them tinged with pink, but I've been scrubbing at them for close to half an hour so it's as good as it's going to get. I'm just about to go dump out the blood-tinged water when there's a knock at the door.

I dry my hands on my pants and head over to it to answer, surprised when I find Jae standing on my doorstep. "Hey," I say opening the door wider for him to come in.

His hair is disheveled. Instead of being neatly pulled back into his usual bun, it hangs over one side of his head, and a sprinkling of scruff covers his jawline. "Hey. Sorry. I would have come sooner, but I didn't want to wake you."

"Is everything okay?"

Luis chooses that moment to crawl into the kitchen. His eyes light up when he sees Jae and he stretches his little arms up in the air. His way of demanding to be picked up. Jae complies, bouncing Luis in his arms for a second. "Hey, little man," he coos, and I don't bother fighting my smile. Jae has always been great with Luis. It's why I always felt like a jerk for never giving the guy a chance.

"So, what brings you by?"

He turns to face me, and his expression grows stony. "I was at the precinct all night. I know Miguel was arrested."

"Oh. That." I'm not sure what else to say. He works for Miguel. They were kind of friends despite the age difference between them. I know Jae looked up to him almost like a mentor. "Did you see my mom?"

He shakes his head. "No. She was at the hospital with Miguel. She called me for help but then I found out what he was being charged with ..." He hangs his head. "Did he... "

"No. It wasn't me. He didn't." I shake my head. "Not me."

He exhales a relieved breath. "Your mom seems to think—"

"He did it. He all but admitted it in front of me. He isn't innocent."

He jaw clenches. "I kinda figured."

"You did?" I ask, surprised. He and Miguel always seemed close, almost like he looked up to him.

"Yeah. Miguel is in some shady shit. The way he talks sometimes when it's just the guys," a shrug. "I brush it off as just talk but now ..."

I place a hand on his arm. "Not your fault. You couldn't have known. None of us knew he was capable of something like this."

"I know. But, I'm... I'm sorry, Bibi. I told your mom I couldn't help. Wouldn't. If he's guilty, I'm not going to use the firm's connections to get him off. They'll have to figure things out on their own."

"Good." Miguel can rot for all I care.

"It's just..." he hesitates. "It looks like your mom is going to stand by him on this one. He's in the hospital. He'll be taken to the precinct once his injuries allow it but..." he trails off.

Moisture pools in the corners of my eyes and I blink it away. I shouldn't be surprised. She'd said as much yesterday.

"So..." I trail off, unsure what it is that I'm asking exactly.

Jae holds one arm out while his other supports Luis's weight. I step into his embrace, relishing the security and comfort of just being held. "I'm here for you. I'm worried about you," he says, conviction in his voice.

I slowly pull away and stare up into his eyes, a fierce determination on his face. "We're not your problem," I tell him, and his jaw tightens.

"You're my friend. That's reason enough to give a damn about your well-being."

Fair enough. "I'm not sure there's really anything you can—"

"Move in with me," he says, his words taking me back.

"What?"

He hands Luis back to me and shoves his hands into his pocket, squaring his shoulders. "Move in with me."

I can't be hearing him right.

"Miguel has an entire team of lawyers working for him. Even if he doesn't get off, he will get out on bail. They're already drawing up the paperwork for his release. You're not safe here. Neither is Luis. I think you should move in with me."

Before he finishes, I'm shaking my head. "I—I can't move in with you." I say, though what choice do I have if what he says is true? If Miguel gets out, this is his house. His home. I can't stay here if he's here. And Mom... I don't even know what she's going to do. We haven't talked since she ran out to follow him. I need to call her. Figure out what she's planning. Convince her that he isn't someone worth defending.

"Bibi—"

I raise a hand to stop him. "I'll think about it," I tell him, and I will. "But he's not here yet. He's still in the hospital and it's the weekend. At best, he'll get out Monday." With any luck it'll be later than that. "Let's just hold off a bit and see what happens."

He doesn't look happen but nods. "Okay. But if you need anything,"

"I know. And thank you. You have no idea how much I appreciate that." I've made friends at school but they're new. Fragile. It's not like I can call Allie or Kasey and ask to move in with them and while Monique would want to help, no way would her family approve. I'm grateful I have Jae at least.

He looks around the room, spotting the garbage bag and bucket of bloody water. "I know he was arrested and is accused of raping a student at Sun Valley High. Wanna fill me in on the rest?"

For whatever reason, I completely unload all of last night's events on Jae. From the second everyone arrived to Emilio finding out he's Luis's father. It's takes twenty minutes to give him all the details and when I finally finish, he's wide-eyed with a stunned expression on his face.

"Shit. That's a lot to process."

"No kidding."

"Do you know what you're going to do next? What he—"

A knock at the door halts his next words. "Let me get it," he says, moving to answer the door. Emilio is on the other side, freshly showered, his hair still wet. His eyes are narrowed at Jae, but they soften when he spots Luis in my arms behind him.

"Hey, can I come in?" He barely acknowledges Jae's existence.

I nod and have to tug on the back of Jae's shirt when he doesn't step aside to let Emilio in.

"Yeah. Follow me. We can go in the living room."

I lead him through the house where Luis's cartoons are still playing. Jae takes a seat on the sofa, a wary look on his face as he sizes Emilio up. I'm not sure what he's looking for, but whatever it is, he doesn't find it because his expression only seems to darken as the seconds go by.

"This is my friend, Jae. Jae, this is Emilio. Luis's—"

"Bio-dad. Got it," he bites out.

I scowl at him, not sure where his hostility is coming from, but also not having the energy to deal with it right now. "Do you think we can get together later?" I ask. "Emilio and I..." I pause. What do we need to do exactly? Talk, I suppose. I'm sure he wants to meet Luis. Play with him maybe.

"I can stay if you'd like," Jae suggests, but I don't miss the narrowing of Emilio's eyes. "It might be good to—"

"That's okay." I cut him off. "This is probably something I should do alone."

His jaw tightens, but he nods and climbs to his feet. "Okay." He kisses the top of my head before doing the same to Luis. "Catch you later, little man. And Bibi," I wait. "Think about what I said. Okay?"

"I'll consider it," I tell him, watching as he leaves. I wait for the sound of the front door closing behind him before I turn and face Emilio.

"Something I should know about?" he asks.

I shake my head. A part of me knows he would have a problem with me living with Jae and it's not something I want to argue about right now. Not when we should be focusing on Luis. "No. It's nothing."

I take a seat on the floor, Luis in my lap and hand him a few blocks to play with. "He takes a few minutes to warm up to strangers," I tell him, immediately regretting my choice of word. "But if you give him some time to adjust, he'll make his way over to you on his own and hand you blocks or cars to play with him with."

Shoulders stiff, Emilio nods and lowers himself to the ground across from me. He shrugs out of his coat, laying it on the sofa behind him. His shirt stretches across his broad shoulders, the fabric hugging his muscular form. I wet my lips and wring my hands in my lap.

Luis captures his entire attention, his gaze never straying from our boy. I watch emotions play over Emilio's face. Curiosity, wonder, joy. He's enamored with him already and a fist squeezes my heart inside my chest seeing the open affection he already has for him.

We both watch our son toddle around the room, one second crawling and the next walking as he collects his toys into one pile before throwing them as far as he can—which isn't that far—across the room one by one, laughing as they hit the hardwood floor.

"He's kind of a terror, isn't he? Emilio asks, affection clear in his voice.

I smile. "Yeah. He likes the sound the blocks make when they hit the floor. It's his favorite pastime these days." One block lands particularly close to Emilio, and Luis crawls toward him to retrieve it. Emilio freezes when Luis sits up on his knees, brown eyes curious, as he holds the block out in his hand for Emilio to take.

"That for me?" he asks. His face is the softest I've ever seen it as he looks down at our son, carefully taking the toy from his tiny fingers. "Thanks." Luis stares at him a moment longer before crawling right into Emilio's lap and turning himself to the side to get comfortable. He reaches for the block in Emilio's hand and he gives it to him, both arms winding around Luis's small body and a wonder-struck expression on his face.

Luis doesn't allow Emilio to hold him long before squirming in his arms to get back on the ground to play and Emilio reluctantly releases him.

"So..." I begin, because there are a lot of things we should probably talk about. "We should talk about, um, what it is you want." God, even to my own ears that sounded lame.

His dark brown gaze finds mine and anger flashes for a split second before he nods once, rubbing the back of his neck. "Yeah. Well, I figured it's pretty obvious." He looks to Luis and his jaw clenches. "I want to be in his life. I want to be his dad."

Okay. That sounds good and all, but...

"And I want regular visitation."

I swallow hard and force my breathing to slow despite the rapid beating of my heart. What he's asking for isn't unreasonable.

"And I want it in writing, Bibiana. I want to be added to his birth certificate. I want our visitation schedule in writing and signed or notarized or whatever it needs to be for it to be official. I need to know you're not going to disappear again and take him from me."

My breath hitches and a trickle of apprehension slips beneath my skin. "I never meant—"

"It doesn't matter. You did. I'm not risking that again, so those are my terms. I'll pay child support or whatever. We'll figure it out and I'll do my part, but I want everything in writing so there is zero question that he is mine and I have rights."

I lick my lips. "And if I don't want to put everything in writing?" I ask because there is a needle of fear that tells me if I give him what he's asking for, it will make it all the easier for him to one day take Luis away from me. I'm not saying he would, just...it's a possibility. I don't know Emilio. Not really. What if we get into an argument? What if he wants to take Luis out of town or to visit a distant relative and then never comes back. I know they're what ifs, but that little boy is my entire world. The thought of losing him—

"Then we'll get the courts involved. I don't want to do that, Bibiana. I don't want things to get any uglier than they already are but..." He trails off and shakes his head, turning his focus to Luis. "I won't risk losing him."

The mention of that word—court—makes my mouth run dry. He could take me to court, make demands, ask for even more than he's asking for now and there is a good chance he would get it. I know people assume that the judge always favors the mother, but will that still hold true if they learn I kept his son from him? That he missed out on the first nine months of his life because of me? No. I don't think it would. If he takes me to court, I could lose everything.

I drop my head and close my eyes, pulling in a lungful of air. "Okay," I whisper, my heart aching in my chest and I raise my gaze up to his. "We'll put it in writing."

He nods once.

"But—"

He frowns.

"The rest we do my way. I'm his mom. He doesn't know you yet, and you're a seventeen-year-old guy with no clue how to look after a baby. I'm not going to just send him off with you after one introduction."

His jaw clenches, his nostrils flaring. "I won't let you keep him from me, Bibiana."

"I don't want to. I just..." I exhale a loud breath. "He's only nine months old. He's still breastfeeding."

His eyes drop to my chest, and a dark look passes over his face before he blinks it away.

"I think you should come here for visits, at least to start," I say and when it looks like he's about to argue I rush to add, "Let him get to know you. Let...let me get to know you so I don't freak out when you walk out the door with the most important person in my universe. Please."

The muscle in his jaw ticks. "Fine," he manages to bite out, and I release the breath I'd been holding.

"Thank you."

FOURTEEN

Emilio

T his moment is surreal, seeing my kid play with his toys and bring them to me like he knows me. As if we've been doing this his whole life.

My kid.

Fuck. I still can't wrap my head around the fact I'm a dad.

Luis stumbles across the floor, his tiny legs unsteady, and with each step he takes, I tense, waiting for the moment when he loses his balance and I need to catch him. Somehow, he manages to stay on his feet, his arms held out and a drooly grin on his face.

We watch him play for half an hour when all of a sudden he gets angry with one of his cars, yelling at the thing like it somehow offended him before crawling to Bibiana and shoving his little hand down the front of her shirt.

"Sorry." Her cheeks turn pink. "I think he's hungry." She gets up from the floor, about to leave the room and I realize I don't want her to. It would be one more thing I don't get to be involved in.

"Feed him here." It comes out like an order. She scowls and is about to argue when I add, "Please."

She nods once, and her cheeks turn an even brighter shade of pink.

I try not to stare as she lifts him up and positions herself on the sofa, my boy in her arms. She grabs a blanket from the back of the sofa and attempts to cover herself up as she pulls her shirt up just enough for Luis to reach her breast, but he isn't having it. If anything, her attempts at modesty make it worse because instead of burying his face in her boobs— something that, I won't lie, sounds appealing because she's got great tits—he's fighting with her, yelling and flailing his tiny hands in the air to get the covering off.

I'm sure she'd like a few minutes of privacy, but I can't bring myself to give them to her.

Bibiana huffs, finally giving up, and lets the blanket drop to the side, her full breast exposed save for the back of Luis's head blocking my view of her nipple.

She visibly swallows and won't meet my gaze. It's fucking adorable. Not that the thought should be running through my head. I've cooled off some since last night but I still can't shake the feeling that she did this on purpose. That she didn't think I was good enough for our son. I hate that.

"You good?" I ask. Not that I should care, but seeing her feed our son, take care of him, it awakens something primal inside of me. Fire burns in my throat as she turns her head and meets my stare head on, and want flickers in the recesses of my mind. What the hell is wrong with me?

"Yeah. Just ... didn't want to make you uncomfortable." She shrugs.

A smile curls my lips. "You can pop those out anytime you'd like. Trust me, I'm far from uncomfortable."

Her cheeks go from pink to scarlet. I like it. Like making her uncomfortable. Uncertain.

What she's doing isn't sexual. Far from it, in fact. But ... I exhale a harsh breath. Without letting myself think about what I'm doing, I get up from the floor and move to sit beside her. She gazes up at me, a furrow between her brows, but I've already turned my attention to Luis. His little fists are balled up against her breast, his eyes closed and a relaxed expression on his face.

Emotion threatens to overwhelm me and I almost don't recognize the sound of my voice as I utter my next words. "Marry me," I say, surprising myself, but I don't try and take back the words. Actually, now that they're out in the open, it makes sense. Getting married, I mean. It would resolve all our problems. We wouldn't need to work out custody or visitation. There wouldn't be any worries or unknowns. We'd be a family, for Luis.

Her head snaps up. "What? Are you serious?"

"Deadly."

"No."

I grit my teeth and try not to be offended by her response, even as my chest squeezes all the air from my lungs. "Why not?" It comes out angrier than I intended and her eyes narrow. I was right, a voice in the back of my mind tells me. I'm not good enough.

"Because I don't know you. And you don't know me. We can't go off and get married just because we have a child together."

"Yes, we can," I bite out. It would make things easier, too. We'd be a family. That's what Luis deserves. Why wouldn't she want that? "Luis deserves both parents—"

"And he'll have them. But I'm not going to marry someone I don't even know—who doesn't even like me—just because we have a child together."

My jaw tightens. I like parts of her just fine. Her ass. Her tits. Her tight pussy. There are plenty of things I like about Bibiana, but I don't bother voicing them aloud, already aware that isn't what she means.

I glower at her as though my stare alone can change her mind, but she doesn't cower. If anything, her chin lifts higher in the air.

Okay, so no marriage. For now. We'll shelf that conversation for another day because I sure as shit am not giving up on it. My son deserves everything I never had and more. "Fine."

She releases a breath.

"We'll date first." I can be reasonable. Compromising is important in a relationship. See, very reasonable.

Her blue eyes widen and she shakes her head in a definitive no.

I try not to let my annoyance show. But, why is she being so difficult? I know she's attracted to me. We have chemistry off the charts. This is a win-win situation.

"Let me guess, you have reasons for not wanting to date me too? We've already fucked. Is dating really such a big leap here?"

Her lips press together and she turns her attention back to Luis who's fallen asleep in her arms, his mouth open and her glistening nipple on full display. She covers herself up, careful not to disturb Luis before she rises to her feet. My dick twitches in my jeans and I glower down at my crotch. Now is not the fucking time.

"I'm going to lay him down in his crib. I'll be right back."

I suck on my teeth as I watch her all but run from the room without answering my questions.

She returns a few minutes later and I decide I'm not going to give her the easy out she clearly wants. "Date me," I say again, ignoring my semi. I swear my dick gets excited just by her walking into a room.

She claims a seat on the sofa across from me instead of sitting beside me like before. "No."

A muscle ticks in my jaw.

"Emilio—" Her voice is soft and I can feel the careful let down she's about to deliver and I don't fucking want it. "I don't know you."

"Then get to know me." That's what dating is for, right? I've never done the whole exclusive thing before but I know how it works. You date before you decide to marry. I'm not missing a step here. At least I don't think I am.

"Aren't you seeing someone? Sarah or Kaitlyn or," she rolls her eyes on a forced laugh, "I don't know, half the senior class? All the girls at least."

Is that what this is about? My reputation? I sleep around, sure. But that doesn't mean I have to. I haven't been with anyone since she came back. I sure as shit don't belong to anyone else. I've never been exclusive with a girl. Bibiana would be the first. The only.

"No," I deadpan. "I'm not seeing anyone. I'd like to see you. The mother of my goddamn child." Why is this such a difficult concept for her to wrap her mind around? I know our cultures are different but we're both Hispanic or Latino or whatever the fuck you want to call it. I'm Honduran. She's Brazilian. Our upbringings couldn't have been so different that she wouldn't at least see the appeal in raising our son together. I'm trying to do the right thing here. Why is she making that so difficult?

"I don't know you," she repeats. Again.

"You know me well enough to let me finger-fuck you in a classroom."

Her eyes narrow to slits.

I run my hands through my hair and try to tamp down my frustration. "Will you get to know me, then? I think our son deserves at least that much from us."

"For Luis?"

Fuck, yes. Fine. "For Luis," I agree.

She nods. "Okay. I'll get to know you."

That's still not an agreement to date.

God dammit.

We spend the next three days getting to know one another. All day Saturday and Sunday, and then I show up right after football practice Monday evening. We agreed my next visit would be on Wednesday but Bibiana wasn't at school today and she didn't answer any of my texts. There's an irrational fear inside me that says she's bolted with my boy, but when I show up unannounced on her front porch, she lets me in without question and for the first time, Luis reaches for me.

There are dark circles under her eyes and her hair is haphazardly thrown up into a bun thing on top of her head.

"You look," I pause choosing my words carefully, "tired. Everything alright?"

She sighs. "Yeah. Luis is teething so we didn't get much sleep last night."

Oh. "Is that why you weren't at school today?" It makes sense. I pluck Luis from her arms and follow her inside.

Despite her oversized shirt, I can tell her spine is stiff as she hastily picks up Luis's toys from the ground. "Umm... no. My mom usually watches Luis while I'm in school but she's dealing with Miguel stuff today so..." she trails off and then hastily adds, "I have it sorted with my teachers. It's not a big deal."

My brows furrow. Something in her voice contradicts her words, but I decide to leave it alone, knowing it isn't my place. "Cool. Is it alright if I hang for a bit with Luis?"

She nods. "Yeah that would be great actually. Do you care if I take a shower and catch up on some homework? You can have some one-on-one time with him?"

My smile widens and I turn to Luis. "What do you think, little man. Wanna kick it with Dad?"

He gurgles and waves a fist in the air which I take to mean hell yeah, so I turn back to Bibiana with a grin. "Sounds good. Shower away." I try not to think about her naked and wet in said shower but my mind wants to go places it shouldn't. It's been nice these past few days, which is better than I could have expected.

At first it was terrifying. There is so much I don't know and when Luis is tired or hungry, it's not like he can tell me. I don't know his cues, but I learned real fast that my boy has a temper. If I take too long trying to figure out what he wants, my man loses it. Who knew something so tiny could be so explosive? And the diaper changes, my god. Nothing this cute should smell that bad.

The uncertainty has mostly faded now. I still don't know everything there is to know, but I'm learning, and Bibiana's been good about filling me in if she thinks he's trying to tell me something. She doesn't have to make this easy on me. She isn't required to help me figure out how to be a dad. But she has been. Helpful, I mean. And while it's the least she can do after keeping him from me, I guess, I don't know, I appreciate it. Hell, I'm grateful, really. Not that I'll tell her that.

We haven't talked about the whole dating thing again but I think I'm winning her over. It's slow moving, but I can be patient.

She heads upstairs and I move with Luis to the living room, finding the basket of blocks and cars she keeps close by for him. We play on the floor for a bit before grabbing a snack from the kitchen, one of those food pouch things he seems to like.

When he finishes with that he yawns and I know he's ready for a nap, but I haven't quite figured out his routine for that yet. From what I've seen so far, he usually just falls asleep after nursing and well, I don't have tits for my little man to get what he needs. But, I don't want to call Bibiana for that either.

"How's everything going?" she asks, poking her head into the room, as if me thinking of her somehow conjured her here. Her wet hair hangs in loose curls around her make-up-less face. I'm stunned for a moment at the sight of her. She's fucking beautiful.

Wearing an army green tank top that hugs her chest and waist like a second skin, she shows off every inch of her delectable curves. Fuck me. I haven't seen her in anything form fitting since the night we met. She looks good enough to eat. My mouth waters and I wonder what she tastes like.

"We're good," I say, hoping my voice doesn't betray me.

"Do you need me to—"

I shake my head. "Nah. I got it." I give her a wink. "Go. You have homework, right?"

Her eyes are conflicted but she nods and leaves the room with a muttered, "Call me if you need me." But, I'll figure it out. He ate. He played. I check his diaper and we're good on that front too.

I rock Luis in my arms, adjusting his position a few times until we find one that's comfortable for him. He fusses a little but I manage to keep him quiet for the most part. I don't want Bibiana thinking I can't handle this. I want to take him to meet my sister which means she needs to trust me enough to let me take Luis on my own. We agreed we'd do this her way, and I don't want to push, but my baby sister was bouncing off the walls as soon as I told her she's an aunt. I know Antonio wants to meet him too. Hell, Allie was even me asking today at school when I'd be bringing him over despite all the shit she's dealing with right now.

And none of that can happen if the mother of my child barely trusts me alone with him when she's right there in the next room.

"We've got this, don't we, little man?" I whisper and rub circles on his back until his head rests against my shoulder. Holding him in my arms reminds me of how fragile he is. How easy it would be for him to get hurt, and I have to fight back the urge to squeeze him tighter to me. Miguel is Bibiana's mom's boyfriend and he hurt Allie. He beat her and then the fucker raped her. I haven't brought it up with her yet because I don't want to start an argument but I'm nervous about what will happen if the bastard is released. I don't want him anywhere near my kid.

Roman's dad can't make a case for the rape. There isn't sufficient evidence and Allie didn't report it when it happened, but he's doing his damnedest to keep the asshole locked up for something else. They're digging into all of his financials and looking for any skeletons he might be hiding in his closet. Allie was attacked because of something her father did. Some business deal gone wrong that Miguel was involved in.

If the people you work with are shady enough to rape your daughter because you pissed them off, chances are that shit isn't above board, and with any luck, Chief Valdez will find something to pin the fucker with. Then I won't have to bring the subject up with Bibiana at all.

Luis falls asleep and I take a chance, slowly dropping onto the sofa and centering him on my chest. When he doesn't stir, I sigh in relief and look down at the mop of dark brown hair on his head, pressing my lips to his temple.

I prop my feet on the coffee table and settle back in my seat, letting my eyes close as I listen to the steady inhale and exhale of his breaths.

I'm completely content to sit here until he wakes up. There isn't anywhere else I'd rather be.

FIFTEEN

Bibiana

The shower is heaven. I haven't been able to take one that wasn't rushed in longer than I can remember. I almost feel guilty for taking my time and going through the motions of shaving my legs and deep conditioning my hair, something it desperately needed.

When Emilio showed up on my porch, I realized I like having him here. In a way, it helps. Sure, I've always had my mom but she never really stepped in for the parenting parts. If Luis was hungry, I fed him. If he needed a nap, I was the one to put him down. If he was having a rough day and insisted he be held twenty-four-seven, I was the one who held him. Mom helps me out if I can't be there because of school, but if I'm home, the responsibility of caring for Luis falls directly on my shoulders. As it should. I'm not complaining.

But with Emilio around, there's someone to help carry that load, even if all he does is play with him on the floor while I shower or make a something to eat. I never noticed how much easier it is to accomplish simple tasks without carrying a baby around with me while I did them.

I towel my hair dry and after checking in to make sure Emilio is doing okay with Luis, I turn on my laptop and check to see if any of my teachers emailed me back. I let them all know last night after I got off the phone with Mom that I wouldn't be there. I came up with an excuse that Luis was sick and thankfully it doesn't seem like any of them are disgruntled about it. They're probably all married with kids of their own and while Luis isn't actually sick, I couldn't very well say, "My mom's boyfriend is in custody and she's refusing to leave his side so I don't have childcare." Well, I guess I could. But I don't really want to air out all of our dirty laundry if I don't have to.

Miguel's in the hospital after the beating he took. He's still under arrest. Handcuffed to his hospital bed according to Mom. But since he's not actually in prison where she can't see him, she's adamant that he needs her and that she has to stay with him while he recovers. I'm not sure what she's hoping for. He raped a teenage girl. Someone who happens to be the same age as her daughter. That she's even speaking to the man is beyond me, but I can't very well tell her all that over the phone.

This might be one of those things she needs to work out for herself, and with any luck, once Miguel is carted off to jail, she will. I don't think the reality of the situation has hit her yet. She's still trying to process everything and still clinging to the hope that this is all some horrible misunderstanding.

It isn't. I've spoken to Allie on the phone a few times since Friday night and she's confident he's the one who attacked her. And after seeing his reaction to her with my own eyes, I believe her.

I download the assignments my teachers sent and get to work on playing catch up. Mom said she'd come home at least long enough for me to go to school tomorrow so with any luck I won't fall too far behind only, I don't know what will come next and I hate being unable to plan.

I spend the next hour catching up on my reading and assignments. There's an exam in my economics class on Friday and I want to make sure I do well. With that finished, I head back downstairs and freeze at the sight of Luis fast asleep on Emilio's chest.

Wow. I'd like to blame what I'm feeling right now on my hormones, but I have a feeling the sight of this arrogant playboy asleep with our son in his arms is something I'll never get used to.

He must not have been too deeply asleep because the next second Emilio is cracking one eyelid open and smiling my way.

"Hey, momma." His voice is rough with sleep. Why do those words make my toes curl? Visions of Rio from Good Girls comes to mind and I have to force myself to walk further into the room instead of standing there dumbstruck. Does Emilio have to be so hot? This would be so much easier if, I don't know, he was average and said all the wrong things instead of unraveling me with his words and voice alone.

"How was your nap?"

His smile grows impossibly wider. "Fan-fucking-tastic. Isn't that right, little man," he whispers, and kisses the top of Luis's head. I swear my ovaries are on overload right now.

"How long has he been out?"

He cranes his neck toward the wall clock, his Adam's apple bobbing before saying, "Maybe twenty minutes."

"His evening nap is usually an hour or two. Do you want me to go put him down in his crib so you can move?"

He shakes his head and beams at me. "Nah. We're good."

The sight of his smile tugs at my heartstrings. Emilio is more than I expected. "You're pretty good at this dad stuff, huh?"

"Learning from the master," he tells me and pats the space beside him.

I take the seat, leaning in to brush a lock of hair from Luis's forehead.

"We made a great kid," he whispers, and if it weren't for the fact I'm sitting down right now, I would melt into a puddle of goo right here on the floor. "You did good, momma."

A lump forms in my throat. "Thanks."

Almost reverently, he rubs Luis back with one arm, his other thrown across the back of the sofa, and his fingers absently stroking my bare shoulder. I'm not sure if he even realizes he's touching me, but I don't bother to point it out.

"Can I come back tomorrow?" Emilio asks, his voice hesitant. "I know we said Wednesday and I know I wasn't supposed to be here today but ... I've missed so much already, and I swear the kid changes every day. I don't want to miss out on even a second of his life that I don't have to."

"I—" A trickle of worry worms its way into me before I push it aside. This is great. Emilio wanting more time with Luis is a good thing. I need to get over the irrational fear that him spending more time with Luis somehow means I'll have less. This isn't a competition, and right now, more time is not only good for Emilio, but it's good for Luis and that's what is more important. "That would be great."

"Really?" His arm drops down from the back of the sofa and he squeezes me to him in a side embrace.

"Yeah. Really."

He kisses my temple, taking me by surprise. "Thank you."

I laugh off his words and his touch with a roll of my eyes. "Don't thank me yet. One of these days Luis is going to clock you in the face with a car and we'll see then how you really feel."

"I'm looking forward to it."

I ignore the fact that his arm is still around me, that I'm still pressed against his side, and decide to just be. I rest my head on his shoulder and place the other on our son, content to share this moment with the man I created this tiny human being with.

"How goes fatherhood?" Dominique asks when I take my seat beside him in fourth.

"Amazing," I tell him and pull out my phone to show him the pictures I snapped of Luis earlier in the week. It's Thursday and I've been at Bibiana's every day as soon as football practice let out. Antonio is keeping to his word. He's been watching Sofia, getting her to and from school and making sure she isn't alone while I focus on Luis.

Raul hasn't been back since last week, and I'm hoping our luck holds out a little bit longer.

"There's a lot of Bibiana in this reel," he tells me, quirking a brow.

"She's his mom and she's there. Don't read too much into it." I haven't told any of them that I asked her to marry me. And I sure as shit am not going to mention that she turned me down.

"Don't read too much into what?" Allie asks as she takes her seat, Roman following suit beside her.

"The fact that most of the pictures Emilio has of Luis on his phone are also shots of Bibiana."

"Oooo, let me see," Allie says and without bothering to wait for me to hand it to her, she snatches my phone and begins scrolling. "Oh, my god, he is so freaking cute." She shows Roman a few of the pictures and he gives me his nod of approval. Asshole. Though despite myself I have to try and not puff up at his response. Roman is the head of our little trio, err, foursome. Is that what we are now that Allie is around?

Hold up. Do Kasey and Aaron count? And if they count, what about Bibiana? She's the mother of my child so she better fucking be included, right?

I rub the back of my neck. I'm not even going to try and figure all of that out right now, but whatever we are size-wise, Roman is our fearless, asshole-ish leader, so yeah, him being happy for me gives me those warm and fuzzy feelings I won't admit to out loud. I'm a dad. A teenage dad, which I'm sure comes with the same stigma as being a teen mom, but none of my friends have batted an eye at that. No one is giving me shit. I'm grateful. Roman and Dominique, they're my family. Just as much as Roberto, Antonio, and Sofia are. I want them to be a part of Luis's life, and that they're so clearly interested in my boy is a relief.

"My mom wants you to bring him by. She said she's only going to wait so long to meet her first grandchild before she comes and hunts you down," Roman adds gruffly.

I grin at that. "Aww, you bitter I gave Mama Valdez a baby first?"

He snorts. "No. I'm hoping since you gave her a baby she'll back off with her questions about when Allie and I are getting married and when will we pop out some grand-babies for her."

"Good luck with that."

Allie laughs. "We have time. Right now it's just, when are you going to get married and stop living in sin?"

Roman snorts. "Don't delude yourself. That woman wants babies. I vote we pimp out Emilio's."

I roll my eyes but I'm cut off from responding when our teacher starts his lesson. I don't pay attention for most of it. All of this feels like refresher coming off winter break and my grades are better than most, so I let my mind wander to my future now that Luis is in it.

I have a full ride to Suncrest U after graduation just like Roman and Dom do, but unlike them, football isn't all I've been considering.

For Roman, it's always been football. His pops wants him going to the academy. Having a police chief for a dad puts on some added pressure, but Roman has never once even considered it. He wants to go pro.

Dominique wants to go pro too, and with an arm like his, the fucker is good enough if you ask me, but he also comes from money. He could go to any college in the country and his parents would pave the way for him. Hell, they'd probably prefer he go somewhere else. Suncrest U is a state college, but it's a division one school with the top-ranking football team in the nation which is why we're all going there.

But Dom's parents are loaded and they've got plans for him to take over the family empire at some point. Only time will tell if he makes it playing ball before they drag his ass off the field.

I play cornerback for the Sun Valley Devils. And I'm good. Really good. But, I got offers for educational scholarships too. It helps when you get a 1340 on the SATs and carry a 3.9 GPA, not that I advertise that shit. I could rock the 4.0 if I wanted to, but I cut one too many classes and let's be honest, no one likes an overachiever.

Football has always been the plan for me. Getting a degree in engineering is just a backup plan. But with Luis, where does being a dad fit into things? Next year, I'll have classes, training, my free time will be thin. If I took an educational scholarship instead, gave up on playing ball, I'd have more time in the day.

A rock forms in the pit of my stomach. No. I'll figure something out. I don't need to do the college scene. That was never the plan anyway. Fuck the parties and the booze. I'm going to college with one goal in mind, so I'll have plenty of time if I keep my eye on the prize. Luis, football, school. That's it. I can plan my schedule so it's tight. Back-to-back classes with a break between them and practice so I can see my boy.

I don't need to get a killer GPA in college. I just need to pass well enough to keep my scholarship. No one cares about your grades as long as you walk away with your degree. And fuck, if I get drafted, then my grades really won't mean shit.

I can make this work.

I have to.

The bell rings, snapping me out of my thoughts. I look up to see Allie's gaze locked on mine. "Everything okay?" she asks.

"Yeah, Vanilla. Everything is good."

Roman scowls but I roll my eyes. He isn't the only one allowed to call her that. He pulls out his phone and reads an incoming text. "Practice is cancelled," he tells us.

"Friday funday, fuckers."

"For you, maybe," Allie complains. "I have a shift at the diner."

"You two coming over?" Roman asks Dominique and I as we all make our way out of the classroom. "I'm dropping Allie off at work and then I'll be at my place. We can go over plays. Watch a few recordings."

I shake my head. "Can't. I'm heading to Bibiana's."

"Has she mentioned when she'll be back?" Allie asks, and I hear the worry in her voice.

I suck on my teeth. "No, actually. It hasn't come up. But she said she has it handled with her teachers." I shrug.

Allie doesn't look happy about my response. "I'm worried about her. She can't afford to miss this much school. She was already struggling to meet graduation requirements."

My brows pull together. "What are you talking about?" She hasn't mentioned any of this to me.

Allie sighs. "It's not really my pla—"

"Come on, Vanilla. Help a man out. Please."

Her eyes soften. "Fine." She runs a hand through her hair as we all navigate our way through the parking lot to our cars and I force myself to slow down my steps so she doesn't have to increase her pace to keep up. She's almost as small as Bibiana but not quit. "Her mom isn't coming home until her loser boyfriend is either released or in jail, so she has no childcare."

I stop. "What?"

"That should be any day now. Roman's dad has enough to bring charges and his injuries are mostly healed since Aaron and Roman beat the crap out of him." Roman smirks at that and not gonna lie, Aaron's part in all this definitely makes it harder to keep hating on him.

Speak of the devil. "Hey," Aaron calls out and we all turn to find him a few car lengths away with Kasey beside him. "I'm heading to the diner, want a lift?" His words are meant for Allie but it's Roman who answers him.

"No. I can take her."

Aaron comes closer as Kasey rolls her eyes and climbs inside his Subaru WXR. "Don't be a dick, Roman. I'm working with her. I can take her to work and you can pick her up before shift ends."

"Sounds like a plan," Allie says, not letting Roman argue as she gives him a kiss on the cheek and turns to leave.

"Hold up. What all am I missing about Bibiana?"

She pauses beside Aaron. "Her mom isn't watching Luis for her until things with her boyfriend are sorted." Her lip curls in disgust. "I don't know what is wrong with her. She's acting like her boyfriend isn't a rapist asshole when he is. When he could do to Bibi what he did to me." She shudders. "It's not my problem but I feel bad for Bibi and what she's going through. It's hard knowing that your mom is standing by someone like that."

My jaw tightens. Shit. I didn't know.

"Roman's dad said they'll bring charges against him today. Once they do, he can request bail so they're going to time it with the weekend and hold him as long as possible. Bibiana should be back next week if everything works out. With that creep in jail her mom should be around but," she shakes her head, "I don't know. She can't afford to miss much more school. Even if she manages to keep up on assignments, there are attendance requirements she won't meet. We talked yesterday. I don't know the specifics but I know she's barely treading water."

"Fuck." I run my hands through my hair. "She didn't tell me that. She said she had it figured out."

The look on Aaron's face says it all. I'm an idiot.

"I didn't think—"

"About what it was like to be a single mom, raising a kid on your own when you still have school and shit to worry about?" Aaron finishes for me. Allie smacks him in the chest, but he's not wrong.

"No. I didn't." Dammit. "I gotta go. I'll catch you guys later." I need to talk to Bibiana. Figure this out because she needs to graduate. Luis is my kid, too. She doesn't have to do this on her own anymore. What happened to being a team? Co-parenting? That means I do my part, but I can't if she doesn't keep me in the fucking loop.

SEVENTEEN

Emilio

S he opens the door like she has every other day this week, only this time, Luis is nowhere in sight. "Hey," she says, stepping aside to let me in. "You're here early."

"Yeah. Practice was cancelled today," I tell her.

She nods and I debate how to go about this. Bibiana is proud. She won't want me inserting myself into her life. Not on her account. I've noticed this week she's fine when I offer to do something for Luis, but anytime I try to help her, she brushes me aside.

"That's probably nice," she says. "Gives you a chance to rest up before next week's game." I'm surprised she knows our schedule. She hasn't been to any of our games, not that I've made a point of inviting her or anything. I'm not sure she'd want to go even if I did. We're not together, and watching me play feels like a girlfriend thing to do.

"Yeah. I'm always down for a break." Coach has been running us hard. We made it through playoffs and earned our regional championship titles. You would think that'd grant us a reprieve, but, if anything, it's only made things more grueling. Coach isn't going to let up until we take state next week, and then we can all breathe a little easier.

Sun Valley High has won state the last three years in a row. If we win this year, it will be our fourth. I think Coach is worried it'll also be his last with all three of us Devils graduating this year. He's been pushing the underclassmen on the team to step up, asking us to spend more one-on-one time with them than typical so that he has something decent to work with next year. We don't. Well, Roman and I don't, at least. Mingling with the new recruits isn't exactly something we do, but Dom is the school's quarterback so he's been handling business, giving the rest of the team pointers and getting their asses in line.

"Where's my little man?"

She brushes a few stray pieces of hair out of her face. "He actually just went down for a nap. I'm sorry."

I shrug. "No worries. Mind if I hang out until he wakes up?"

"Umm... sure. I guess. I mean, yeah. That's fine." She's nervous but she has no reason to be. Bibiana leads me through the house and into the kitchen, pausing behind one of the barstools at the kitchen island where it looks like she's been doing her schoolwork.

"Keeping up?" I ask, nodding to her open textbooks.

She sighs. "Yeah. I've got it handled."

I step closer to her and tilt her chin toward me. "It's okay to ask for help sometimes," I tell her.

She tugs her chin away. "It's not your job to help me. I've got it covered. Besides, Mom should be back next week."

I clench my jaw. "You said that before and it's been a week already. Can you afford to keep missing school?"

Her expression tightens. "I'm not your problem, Emilio."

I swear this girl is going to be the death of me.

EIGHTEEN

Bibiana

"I'm not your problem," I tell him.

"What if I want you to be?" he asks. Brown eyes search my own, trying to understand what's going through my head. But if I'm honest, I have no idea. This week has been ... different. Not bad different, though I'm not sure if it's good different either. It's just, different. I feel like I'm playing some elaborate game where we each have a role and a character we're expected to be and I'm terrified to get my part wrong.

I'm already coming to rely on him and it's only been a week. He plays with Luis in the evenings while I get caught up. He helps with bedtime and he makes being a single mom so much easier than it ever was before.

I'm getting attached when I shouldn't be. I don't want to mess everything up. Emilio's only concern should be Luis. I'm not his responsibility. We need rules. Boundaries.

But ... his words from earlier this week come to me.

Date me.

Would that be such a bad thing?

Emilio's eyes darken when I still don't answer, and his thumb drags along my jawline. "Mariposa?"

He hasn't called me that since...

"Why did you call me that?" I ask and yeah, I'm avoiding his question. I'm woman enough to admit it. Doesn't mean I'm going to feel bad about it.

The corners of his mouth quirk up. "Because the night we met, you decided to spread your wings and fly. You transformed from the shy prep-school girl into a sexy-as-sin vixen. *Mi mariposa.*" My butterfly.

My breath hitches. "A moth," I correct for no real reason. I know mariposa translates to butterfly in Spanish, but I need to dispel this moment.

Emilio dips his head toward me, his warm breath skating across my cheek.

"Fine. You can be the most beautiful moth if you'd prefer."

I swallow hard. How does he manage to make that sexy?

"Do you remember that night? How good we were together?"

I gasp when he leans even closer, his stubble scraping along my skin. Heat rushes between my legs and my thighs clench as memories assail me. That night was so much more than I'd expected.

A strong arm wraps around my waist and pulls me flush against his chest, and his free hand cups my jaw, right before his lips press against mine. My heart pounds in my chest as his mouth teases my own. Sucking in a breath, I pull back before the kiss can go much further.

"Emilio—?"

His eyes are hooded and glazed with desire. "Don't. Don't overthink this. I want you. And I'm pretty sure you want me too."

I exhale in a rush as Emilio's hands find their way to the back of my head, tangling in my hair. He tugs me toward him again, his lips an open invitation I'm not strong enough to deny. I didn't realize how badly I craved him. How much deeper my need for him has grown these past few days.

I sag against him, allowing the kiss to deepen, and the next thing I know, he's lifting me onto the kitchen counter and wedging himself between my thighs, the height just enough to line our bodies up perfectly. He devours me as though starved, his kisses deep and hungry. His tongue slips past my defenses, the taste of sweet oranges and chili an addictive flavor I can't seem to get enough of.

For a second, I consider pushing him away, but then he groans into my mouth, his hard length pressing against my center, and any thoughts of putting an end to this escape me.

"Emilio," I breathe. "God, you feel so good." Oh my god, did I just say that out loud?

"Fuck," he moans. "I can't get enough of you." His fingers slip under the hem of my sweatshirt and the next thing I know he has it tugged up and over my head. I gasp as cool air hits my overheated skin and my arms instantly wrap around my middle to cover myself.

He pulls back, a furrow between his brows as I tear my gaze away from him, hunching my shoulders in a vain attempt to hide my body. This was a mistake.

"Hey."

I turn, my eyes scanning the room for my sweater, but he's thrown it on the floor behind him and out of reach.

"Bibiana?"

"I need my sweater," I tell him, hoping he'll grab it and give it back to me. He doesn't. Instead, he takes two steps back, folds his arms across his chest and stares at me. My nursing bra isn't sexy. It's simple. A black full coverage bra that hooks in the back and has snaps above each cup for easy access should Luis get hungry. It's not what I would have chosen if I knew anyone else was going to see it, but it's not the worst bra I could be wearing either. At least this one has shape and isn't one of those uni-boob sports bra types that I happen to have buried in my drawers.

What I'm more worried about is that I didn't have a shirt on underneath my sweater, so not only is my bra on full display, but so is the rest of my body and it isn't pretty. It isn't...what he's used to. The body he's seen before.

My cheeks heat in the worst possible way and I blink back my complete and utter humiliation, refusing to cry over something like this. Stupid hormones. Come on, Bibi. Pull yourself together.

"What happened just now?"

"Nothing, I just want my sweater back. Can you hand it to me? Please." I hold my hand out but he doesn't move.

My vision blurs. Dammit. I shouldn't care. It's not like I want to impress him. What he thinks of my body shouldn't matter. But it does. I don't let people see me like this. I cover up. I wear baggier clothes. I hide the changes having a baby has made to my body. I don't want his scrutiny. His disgust.

"Hey—" His voice softens. "Talk to me. What just happened? We were good and then it's like a switch went off as soon as I..." His brows pull together. "You want your sweater?" he asks, as if that isn't exactly what I've been asking for this entire time.

"Yes. Now, please."

He picks it up from the ground but doesn't hand it to me. I huff out an exasperated breath. "Emilio. Give it to me." I'm still covering my stomach or I'd reach for it myself.

"Why?"

"Because I want it back." I snap. I shouldn't have to explain this to him.

His eyes roam over my body.

I clench my teeth, bracing myself for the look of revulsion I'm sure will come once he realizes what I'm hiding.

He steps closer and I all but lunge for my sweater, but he shifts to the side, keeping it just out of reach. "I want to see you."

The first tear falls. "No. And we shouldn't be—"

He doesn't give me the chance to finish. His lips crash into mine and my mouth opens on a moan. His tongue flicks out, sending tendrils of desire straight to my core. His hands loosen the hold I have on myself as he guides my arms around his neck, pressing our bodies impossibly close so my stomach is flush against his.

He abandons my lips to trail kisses along my neck, sucking and nipping at my skin gently. Shockwaves ripple through me when his hand cups my center, his palm pressing firmly against my clit through the fabric of my jeans.

"You're so goddamn beautiful," he tells me. I wish I could believe him but—

His tongue drags back up my jaw and to my mouth before he pulls back just enough to look me in the eye. "You are beautiful. This body is perfection. Do you understand me?"

I swallow past the lump in my throat. "But—"

He shakes his head. "No buts. You're perfect. Don't ever hide from me." He kisses me again. "I want to see all of you. Every inch so I can worship your body the way I've been dreaming about."

His words undo me and I force myself to relax. If he's repulsed by my body, I'll find out soon enough.

My stomach is soft. My stretch marks visible. That won't ever go away. And if it's going to be a deal breaker, I may as well find out now before putting my heart on the line.

His palm slides down my side, over my hip and to the button on my jeans. He pops them open as I pull at the material of his shirt, tugging it off and exposing his broad chest and muscular abs. My eyes catch on the tattoo that spreads across his chest. A gothic woman's portrait, her hair flying all around her as ravens tug on the strands.

I trace the intricate ink. It wasn't there when we first met. It's amazing. "Is this new?" I ask and there's a note of wonder in my voice. It looks so lifelike, the woman almost familiar.

"Got it on my eighteenth birthday earlier this year," he tells me.

"She's—"

"You."

I jerk my hand away from the tattoo. "What?"

He smirks. "I knew what I wanted, and I needed a description for the girl, so when I got the ink, I described you."

My eyes widen. "Why would you do that?"

A shrug. "Because you were the most beautiful girl I'd ever seen—you still are," he adds with a savage smile. "Being with you that night was a memory I didn't want to forget. Even if you ghosted me after the fact."

My chest squeezes. "Emilio, I—"

He places a finger against my lips to stop me. "We have history. We have a kid. I want to see where this goes. Where we can go. Don't you?"

God, yes. But ... so many things could go wrong. What if this blows up in our faces?

He mistakes my hesitation as acceptance and kisses me, and I'm too far gone to stop him. His fingers hook into the waistband of my pants, and I decide to hell with it. I'm going to be the girl I was when we first met. Reckless and free. I'll spread my wings and soar with Emilio right beside me.

Our breathing is heavy as he drags my jeans and underwear down over my hips and I lift myself up a few inches for him to get them past my butt and down my legs. I hiss when my bare ass hits the counter and he chuckles. "Cold, baby?"

I bite his bottom lip.

He grunts. "Why don't you let me warm you up." His fingertips leave a fiery trail of heat across my skin as he inches closer to my center. I squirm on the counter, one of my legs hooked over his hip. I tug at his jeans, wanting him just as naked and exposed as I am. I haven't been with anyone else. There isn't a lot of time to explore your sexuality when you're pregnant, and there is even less when you have a newborn. I'm desperate to feel his skin against my own.

Unbuckling his belt, I push his jeans and boxers to the floor and his impressive cock springs forward. I swallow hard. I remember him being big, but...did it grow?

"Everything okay?" he asks just as he sinks one finger inside my wet heat.

My back arches toward him and I whimper, needing more.

"Fuck, you're tight." He thrusts in and out of me before inserting another finger and I cry out, tightening my legs around him. He cups my nape and devours my mouth as skilled fingers bring me close to the edge of orgasm. My fingers bite into his biceps, the muscles flexing beneath my touch.

"I have dreamed about fucking you ever since you left. Replayed your moans in my mind every night since you came back."

"I didn't leave, I—"

"You left," he growls. "I'm not letting you go again." He adds a third finger and uses his thumb to stroke my clit and I explode, my body tightening around him as shock waves wrack my system.

I'm shaking as he withdraws his fingers, and the satisfied smile on his face is absolutely savage. He grabs a condom from his jeans pocket and rolls it on his hard length before lining himself up with my center and meeting my gaze. His eyes are hard but his voice is tender when he asks, "You ready for me, baby?"

My chest rises and falls as I struggle to catch my breath. "Mmm hmm." I'm beyond words at this point.

He circles his cock around my opening, teasing every sensitive nerve ending I have before plunging himself inside me in a single hard thrust. I gasp his name as he pulls out only to dive back in, harder than before.

I buck my hips up and he increases his pace. Triumph is stamped across his face as he buries himself inside me, his thrusts coming faster and more urgent. My body responds, arching toward him and leaving me breathless. It feels so good. I can't help but watch him as he towers over me. His muscles bunch. His jaw gets tighter. Sharper. He's beautiful like this—consumed with need.

He drags the cup of the bra I'm wearing down, exposing one breast as he fucks me, and before I can tell him to stop, he's squeezed my breast in his palm before pinching my nipple and drawing a moan from my throat. Sensations surge through me and moisture coats my breast but he doesn't seem to care. He spreads my milk across my chest before exposing my other breast and giving it a similar treatment. Kneading and squeezing the tender flesh.

"Fuck," he swears before leaning forward and raking his teeth against my sensitive nipple. A second orgasm slams into me and I can tell his is close behind. He slams into me, his entire body trembling. His control starts to slip. His movements grow erratic as he thrusts deep into me three more times before his dick is pulsing inside of me. He hisses out a sharp, "Fuck," when he finds his own release and slumps against me, his sweat-slick skin hot against my own.

I wrap my arms around his shoulders, clinging to him as the gravity of what we did settles over me. Milk leaks from my breasts onto his chest and I pull away, looking for something to clean myself up with before he stops me.

"There you go hiding from me again," he whispers. One finger trails down my stomach and I realize he's tracing a particularly dark and thick stretch mark.

I push his hand away. "I'm leaking," I confess, completely mortified.

His mouth smiles against my own as his hand cups my breast and his thumb flicks over my still sensitive and leaking nipple. "Is that supposed to bother me?"

I bite my bottom lip. I mean...shouldn't it?

"Because it doesn't. Like I said, everything about you is perfect."

Luis's cry shatters the moment and as though we're both on fire, we lunge away from one another and for our clothes then rush up the stairs. I manage to grab Emilio's shirt and throw it over my head just as I reach the door and throw it wide.

Luis stands in his crib, eyes red and angry, but he hiccups to a stop when he sees me.

"Hey, benzinho," I coo. My baby. "Come here." Emilio is right behind me. He's managed to slip on his jeans and stands barefoot, his naked chest pressed against my back.

"Hey, little man."

Luis turns toward Emilio and a smile spreads across his face. He gurgles and babbles and whatever he was upset about is history now that he sees his dad. "You wanna come see me?" Emilio asks, putting his hands out, and Luis reaches for him.

"Why don't you get cleaned up and little man and I will wait for you in the living room?" He presses a kiss to my temple and bounces Luis in his arms. "Don't worry, momma. I've got this."

NINETEEN

Bibiana

The weekend passes and I somehow manage not to throw myself at Emilio every time he comes over, despite the heavy tension between us. My mind is a jumbled mess. I don't know what the two of us sleeping together means, and it's driving me insane.

We haven't talked about what this is. I'm not even sure what I want it to mean.

We've kissed. Touched. But we haven't had sex again. My body wants him. Craves him. But my mind tells me I need to slow down. There is too much on the line to rush into whatever this is turning into. I want to believe we can be one big happy family. What girl doesn't want her Cinderella story? But it all seems too good to be true.

Emilio doesn't do commitment. I've heard enough stories. Rumors. The thought that he'll tire of playing family is a feeling I can't shake.

On top of that, I've given up on my mom being available for Luis. I need to take matters into my own hands. This, at least, is something I feel confident in working out.

I walk into my first period class with Luis on my hip. The bell will ring in just a few minutes, so I'll need to make this quick. The rape charges against Miguel were dropped, and he's since been charged with securities fraud and money laundering in addition to extortion. I have no idea what all they found, but the combined charges can lead up to a combined twenty years behind bars and over five hundred thousand dollars in penalties and fines.

He's in jail now, but his bail hearing is set for Wednesday afternoon, and Mom is frantically trying to figure out a way to pull the money together for his release. We don't have it. Miguel doesn't have it stashed away somewhere that I know of either. Which is a relief.

It's insane how ignorant she's behaving. But the fact that the rape charges were dropped just confirms in her mind that he didn't do it. He has her convinced the rest is false. Misunderstandings or mistakes made by his associates. She is completely blind to the fact that he's a criminal and a rapist.

Don't get me wrong, I'd love for Miguel to be innocent. My mom loves him. Truly and completely loves him, but she didn't see the look on his face when confronted with Allie in the kitchen. She didn't hear his admission of guilt. And that's what that was. An admission. He knows what he did, and the fact that he won't be charged for his crime is wrong.

I've never had a great relationship with Miguel, but I never had issues with him either. He was just always ... there. It creeps me way the heck out to know that all this time, I've been living with a rapist. Would he have done to me what he did to Allie if given enough time and opportunity? What if he tried to hurt Luis? He's just a baby, unable to tell me if anyone tries to hurt him.

I shiver just thinking about. It keeps me up at night. Knowing he was there. I'm glad I never left Luis alone with him. Never trusted him enough to watch my boy.

Heading toward Mr. Albert's desk, I consider what I'm going to say just as his head lifts from a stack of assignments he's been grading, judging by the red pen in his hand.

"Ms. Sousa." He gives Luis a curious once-over. "Can I help you with something?"

I shift Luis's weight to my other side and nod. "Yeah. Sorry. I won't be in class today. Actually, I probably won't make it all week. Again." I exhale a sigh. "I was hoping you'd let me make up this week's assignments somehow, and any quizzes we might have coming up since I missed Friday's exam?"

His lips purse and he looks a little closer at the baby boy in my arms. "He yours?"

I nod and offer him a small smile. "Yeah, he's mine."

He nods to himself. "Okay. When you first enrolled we were informed you had a child. I didn't realize he was so young. We'll make it work."

"Thank you so much. I really appreciate it. You have no idea. I promise to stay on top of things. I can even drop my assignments off daily after school gets out. Whatever you—"

"Ms. Sousa, I believe you misunderstand me."

My stomach drops. What? I thought...

"I didn't mean I would send you home with independent study assignments. I meant you could continue coming to class and bring your son with you."

"To class?" No way am I hearing him right. What high school teacher is okay with a nine-month-old in their classroom?

"Yes. And before you leave I'll have you write down the names of your other teachers and get things sorted out with them. If they don't want you in the classroom you can use the teacher's lounge to do your assignments away from other students, or perhaps the library if you'd be more comfortable there."

Emotion clogs my throat and my vision blurs. "Why?" The single word passes my lips in a whisper, and I suck in a shaking breath as I struggle to maintain my composure. "Why are you jumping to help me like this?" Because that's exactly what he's doing. He doesn't have to go out of his way for me. Emailing me assignments and letting me retake tests is already going above and beyond but this ... letting me complete my senior year as a student. This is so much more.

Mr. Albert stands from his chair and moves around his desk. He reaches a tentative hand out and Luis latches onto his finger waving his arm and jabbering away with a drooly grin on his face.

"Ms. Sousa, you are one of the brightest students I have ever had the pleasure of teaching. You are diligent. Studious. You think outside of the box and your creativity in thought knows no bounds. You can make something of yourself should you decide to. Having a child does not mean you have to sacrifice your opportunities. If anything, it means you must get a little ... creative in how you achieve your goals."

I sniff and blink away my tears. "I really appreciate this. You have no idea. But, I'm not so sure the school will let me—"

"You let me take care of that, okay?"

I nod just as the bell rings, signaling that first period is about to start.

"Do you need to miss today or do you have your materials and everything you need for your son with you?"

"I just have to run to my locker. But I have all my things." It's part of why I decided to come in person originally. To pick up some of my books I'd left behind the last time I was at school.

"Good. Do that and hurry back. We're covering the devastating effects of European diseases on native populations. Wouldn't want you to miss any of it."

I smile and rush to grab my books, ignoring the startled looks of my peers as I hurry through the hallway and to my locker. I shove Luis's diaper bag inside, grabbing his favorite toy and a bottle out and shoving that into my backpack before grabbing my history textbook and heading back to class.

I'm almost there when I spot Dominique hovering outside the door to the classroom beside mine. "Everything okay?" The bell rings just as the hallway empties. "I thought I saw you and this little guy but wanted to be sure." He runs a hand over his tightly braided hair.

"Yeah, Mr. Albert is working it out so I can still attend classes with Luis."

He nods his head like this all makes perfect sense to him. "What do you have second?"

"English."

"I have a non-schedule. I can take him and chill in the library if you're cool with that?"

My brows pull together and I worry my bottom lip. "You want to babysit for me?" I ask, making sure I'm hearing him right, because Dominique doesn't seem the type to want to hang out with a baby.

He shrugs. "Why not? He's Emilio's which makes him mine. Don't be surprised when Roman asks you for some time with him too. This little man has a lot of people who love him."

I fight back a wave of unexpected emotion. "Oh. I mean, yeah. That'd be cool."

He nods and steps backward toward his class. "Alright. I'll meet you out here after class." And then he slips inside, leaving me to do the same.

Class is uneventful. I get a few interested looks when I first walk in, but eventually people ignore that I'm sitting there, bouncing Luis on my knee as I take notes. Toward the end Luis gets a little fussy, but before I can even try and soothe him, Mr. Albert comes and plucks him from my arms and goes back to teaching the class while swaying my boy in his arms. I'm not sure I've ever felt this grateful in my entire life.

As promised, Dominique is waiting for me outside the door when class lets out.

"Do you have everything I'll need?" he asks, and I fall into step beside him.

"We'll grab his diaper bag from my locker and then you'll be set."

Emilio is waiting beside my locker, a wide grin on his face as soon as he sees us. I texted him earlier that I'd be here, but he didn't respond, so I'm assuming he got my message.

"Hey, momma." He tugs me close and kisses me, uncaring of who sees. When he pulls away I'm a little breathless and Luis is jabbering away, vying for his daddy's attention.

"There's my boy," Emilio says, lifting him from my arms and carefully tossing him up in the air before catching him and hugging him close to his chest. There are a few interested looks directed our way, and I do my best to ignore them. I don't know how Emilio feels about everyone knowing he's a dad. We never discussed if we were going to keep his involvement secret or—

"Ah! You brought him," Allie's voice calls out, and all heads turn her way. "Bibi, your and Emilio's little boy is the freaking cutest." And that answers that question. By the end of the day everyone will know Luis is ours, and a part of me is surprisingly happy about that, though I don't miss the intense glares from some of the girls who pass us.

"What can I say, I make cute kids," Emilio jokes. "Where are we heading, momma?" he asks, and I can't help but smile up at him.

"To class. Dominique was nice enough to offer to babysit during his non-schedule."

Emilio lifts a single brow. "Uncle Dom, already making moves to become the favorite?"

Dominique takes the diaper bag off my shoulder and pulls Luis from Emilio's arms just as Roman stalks up behind Allie and wraps his arms around her waist.

"I won't have to try very hard. Between me and this fucker, I've got favorite uncle in the bag."

Emilio snorts. "Tell that to Antonio. He'll fight you for the title."

Everyone laughs. "Who's Antonio?" I ask, not recognizing the name.

"My older brother," he tells me. "I have two. A baby sister as well. You'll meet them soon." He tugs me into his side and leads me toward my second period class. "Little man has a whole host of people who are going to compete for his attention."

The thought makes warmth spread through my chest. This is what I wanted. Family. People who will love Luis as much as I do.

"Are you sure you'll be okay with him?" I ask Dominique one last time.

He nods and grins down at my little boy. "Yeah, I've got it. We'll see you guys at lunch."

TWENTY

Bibiana

Second period is nerve-wracking knowing Dominique has Luis. It isn't that I don't trust him. I know he wouldn't hurt Luis. But he's also a teenage boy. What if Luis gets hungry or tired? What if he throws a fit and Dominique doesn't know how to calm him down? Will he come get me? Get Emilio? This wasn't my best idea. I appreciate the help but I should have said no.

I twist my hands in my lap, watching each second tick past on the clock above the door. "So, is it true?" a voice whispers behind me.

I turn around in my seat.

"Is what true?" I ask the girl, who so far has never bothered to talk to me before. She usually just sits in the back of class and files her nails or texts on her phone.

"Is it true you and Emilio Chavez are together? That your kid is his kid?" Her brows are raised high in open curiosity. News certainly travels fast, though I'm not sure what I expected. Emilio is a Devil. I doubt he could sneeze without someone knowing about it.

"Yeah." I shrug. "We have a son together." I whisper the words over my shoulder and turn back toward the front of the class. I might not be paying attention, but I don't want to get in trouble either. Mrs. Jennings isn't known for being tolerant of disruptions in her classroom.

"No wonder you're always in baggy clothes."

I scowl and turn back around. "Excuse me?"

She smirks and flicks her platinum blond hair over her shoulder. "I mean, the kid probably destroyed you, right? I get it. I'd want to hide that too." The corners of her mouth dip in a mock display of sympathy before she adds, "My sister had a baby two years ago. Absolutely wrecked her. The stretch marks, the loose skin." She shivers. "I am never having children. No, thank you."

I grit my teeth together to keep from snapping at her. My body isn't wrecked. It's different, sure. But it's not...urgh.

No, Bibi. Do not go down that road. Don't let her get to you. She isn't worth your time.

I turn back around again. This class cannot end soon enough. I'm grateful to be here, but I have enough on my plate. I don't need pettiness added to it.

"So, you and Emilio?" she whisper-shouts behind me, and Mrs. Jennings jerks her head in our direction, her ever-present frown on her face.

"Ms. Crisp?"

"Yes?" the girl chirps.

"Is there a reason you're talking instead of paying attention in class?"

I don't need to see the look on her face to know she doesn't care one lick about the reprimand. "Nope."

Mrs. Jennings' scowl deepens. "Refrain yourself then, please. Or you can stay behind after class to catch up on everything you're intentionally missing."

Our teacher returns to the board and I slink down in my seat, but Kaitlyn Crisp, the girl sitting behind me, still doesn't shut up.

"Are you going to answer or not?" she hisses in my ear. My nostrils flair and my lips press into a thin line.

"Shut up," I tell her. "You're going to get me in trouble."

"I'll take that as a no, then," she says with satisfaction.

I ignore it. I don't want to confirm or deny anything when I, myself, don't know what the situation is. Emilio asked me to marry him. God. What was he thinking? And then to suggest we date, as if the proposal is no big deal. It's a huge freaking deal. How can he be so flippant about marriage? But now, I don't know what this is.

Are we dating? Are we simply friends with benefits? I have no clue. Do I need to say yes? To the dating part, I mean. Or is it assumed that we're a thing because he technically asked me, even if I didn't say yes at first.

This is all such a mess.

He kissed me in the hallway though. He isn't treating me like a dirty little secret. Then again, he's never kept any of his relationships secret, if you can even call them that.

We're in this weird going-with-the-flow stage and I'm not sure how to feel about that.

The bell rings and I rush to shove my books in my bag and haul ass toward the cafeteria. We need to talk. I don't like the uncertainty of what is happening, and I'm cognizant enough to know that by not talking I'm setting myself up for heartache. I'm already developing feelings for Emilio, and I don't want to get hurt.

I run into Dominique halfway there and am relieved to see a smiling Luis in his arms.

"How was he?" I ask, reaching for my boy.

He grunts, but there is affection in his voice. "A terror."

"What did he do?"

The corners of his mouth curl into a smile. "Crawled down almost every row in the library and yanked every book he could reach onto the floor." He pats Luis on the head. "Our librarian might not be his biggest fan but we cleaned up the mess and it kept him entertained."

"Did he eat anything?" I ask, hoping he drank the bottle I pumped for him earlier. I don't remember if I gave Dominique specific instructions on that.

He nods. "Downed the entire thing and I changed his diaper. You're welcome."

"Thank you!" I tell him and I mean it. We fall into step beside one another, heading toward the cafeteria, when Emilio comes into view, a pretty blond standing close beside him. I give her a closer look and realize it's Kaitlyn, the girl who sits behind me in second period.

My steps falter. They're right beside the cafeteria doors so I'll have to pass them if I want to go inside. I hesitate, assuming he'll dismiss her after a moment, only he doesn't. He laughs at something she says, and she twirls a piece of her hair, a come-hither expression on her face.

Dominque see's what I'm looking at and his brows pull forward. "I thought he was—" He shakes his head. "Whatever. Come on."

My heart plummets to the bottom of my stomach. Is she... are they... no. I'm getting ahead of myself. For all I know, she's just asking for his notes or something from class. It's harmless flirting. Right?

I force myself to move forward and follow Dominque when I see her press her hand against his chest and lean up on tip toe to plant a chaste kiss on his cheek. He shakes his head and says something to her I can't hear before turning around and going through the open double doors, leaving her behind, but still not noticing me.

I swallow hard.

It's nothing, I tell myself.

When I get to the table, everyone is already there. Roman, Allie, Aaron, Kasey, and Dominique.

"Hey, momma," Emilio says, a wide smile on his face as he shifts to the side and makes more room for me. I accept the seat and he plucks Luis from my arms, handing him a french fry off his tray. "How was your time with Uncle Dom?" Emilio asks him, to which Luis gurgles and grins. "That good?" He turns to Roman. "Looks like you've got your work cut out for you," he tells him.

Roman rolls his eyes, but it's Aaron who surprises us when he holds his arms out and Luis immediately reaches for him. "Hey, what's this?" Emilio says in mock offense. Luis grips Aaron's cheeks and gives him an open-mouthed kiss as he all but tries to eat his nose.

"Who were you saying was his favorite?" Aaron asks and all three of us girls laugh at the boys stunned expressions.

"He was over for girls' night," I remind everyone and then wince. "Sorry."

"Don't be," Allie says, nudging my foot with her own under the table. "Girls' night was good. Besides, I needed the closure, you know?"

I nod, still unconvinced, but I don't want to dig into the topic either.

My phone buzzes in my pocket and I pull it out to see a text flash across the screen.

Jae: He made bail. They're releasing him today.

I gasp. What? It's too soon.

"What is it?" Emilio asks. I turn wide eyes toward him, not wanting to say anything, but everyone's eyes are on me, waiting.

I lick my lips and chance a furtive glance at Allie. "Miguel made bail."

She visibly swallows and nods. Roman tucks her into his side, his jaw tight and his hand fisted on the table.

"I'll call my dad. We'll figure out—"

I block out the rest of his words as my fingers fly over the keyboard.

Me: When?

Jae: This afternoon. Bibi...

I wait.

Jae: Let me come get you. Help you pack. You can't stay there.

Emilio nudges my shoulder and tilts his chin to my phone. "What's going on, momma?"

I hesitate for only a second before forcing a smile. "Nothing. Just Jae filling me in on what's going on."

"Jae?" Emilio scrapes his teeth over his bottom lip. A muscle ticks in his jaw but whatever is bugging him, he decides to keep to himself.

Me: Give me until the end of the day to think about it?

Jae: Can I at least go to your house and grab some of your things? In case he's there when you get out of school.

Me: Yeah. That would be great. Thank you.

I shove my phone back in my pocket and try to enjoy the rest of lunch, but the mood at the table has drastically shifted. This isn't just bad news for me. It's upsetting for all of us, and I'm not sure how any of us are going to handle what happens next.

TWENTY-ONE

Emilio

The rumor mill is running rampant. I can see it eating at Bibiana. She's not used to all of the attention. Personally, fuck what people here think. Let them look and whisper. I'm proud to be a dad. I know she is too — of being a mom. The way she is with Luis, there's just something about it that makes my heart beat faster, my chest squeeze tighter.

I don't want to mess this up.

Everyone is acting like this is some big thing. It's not. Luis is mine. End of discussion. I don't need to explain myself. They all want to know why they never heard of him before. Why we kept him a secret for so long. But that isn't my problem.

It's not my job to keep these fuckers informed, and I sure as shit am not going to throw my girl under the bus and tell everyone I didn't know about him.

My girl. I like the sound of that.

I might be new to this relationship shit, but I know that's not the way to get off on the right foot.

People here should know by now the Devils don't explain themselves. A few words in the halls shut most of the guys down, and the team knows better than to question any of us. But the girls — fuck, they're the worst.

My phone is on silent and I swear it vibrates in my back pocket every other minute. I read the first three this morning before deciding to ignore it the rest of the day. I don't have time for that shit. I thought if I ignored them, they'd eventually stop, but the ones who are bold like Kaitlyn Crisp have taken it upon themselves to just ask me about it in person.

She thought she was subtle, asking how things are going. If I like being a dad. Telling me how cute my boy is and then hinting that being a single dad must be so hard. Puh-leez. She's angling to find out if Bibiana and I are a thing. Single dad. I roll my eyes.

I need to take a page out of Dom's playbook and be the broody, unapproachable asshole so I don't have to deal with people and their bullshit. The bell rings and we all dump our trays in the trash. Aaron reluctantly passes Luis back to Bibiana and I walk her to her next class.

"See? This all worked out," I tell her, placing my hand on the small of her back. She offers me a hesitate smile, shifting Luis's weight to her other side.

"For now. What happens when Luis is sick or has a meltdown?"

I press my lips to her temple. "We deal with it. If he's sick, I'll stay home with him. We'll watch cartoons and chill in my room. And if he has a meltdown," I shrug. "Kids do that. We'll cross that bridge when we get there."

She doesn't look convinced, but she nods. "Okay."

"Do you want me to take him for third?"

She shakes her head. "No. I can manage."

I tuck a strand of hair behind her ear and face her once we reach her classroom door. "I know you can manage, but we're a team, remember? Luis is my responsibility too. Fifty-fifty. If you need a break, tell me."

She nods. "I will."

I scrutinize her looking for the lie, but she seems genuine, so I leave it at that. "I'll see you in fourth." I run my hand over the top of Luis's head. "See you soon, little man."

TWENTY-TWO

Bibiana

"Need a lift?" Emilio asks when the final bell rings and we all head outside, the school day officially over. It was stressful at first, but by the end of the day having Luis with me felt ... normal. I can totally do this. Especially with everyone else helping out.

Dominique has volunteered to take Luis every day during second since he has a non-schedule. I found out today that Aaron TA's third and he's offered to take him then. We're all together during fourth so there are plenty of hands on deck should I need them. This is completely do-able, and there is this giddiness inside of me at the knowledge that not only is everyone willing to help, they want to. They want that one-on-one time with Luis. I know people say it takes a village, but I never realized the true meaning of those words until now.

I catch sight of Jae's Acura TLX as soon as we get outside. He offered to pick me up today, but I didn't realize just how much he'd stand out. He's parked front and center, leaning against the hood with his arms braced behind him. Several girls stop and give him appreciative looks, a few are brave enough to introduce themselves, but he barely glances their way, his eyes focused on me and a genuine smile on his face.

"What is he doing here?" Emilio asks, dark shadows crossing over his face.

"He's my ride," I offer with a shrug. For whatever reason, these two decided to immediately dislike one another. Too bad they're going to need to work past all that, especially if I move in with Jae which is sounding more and more likely. Okay, it's pretty much a done deal. I've thought about his offer all day today and to be honest, it's not like I have any other option. I don't know what this is between Emilio and I, but I do know it's too new for us to shack up together. I texted Monique during class when my teachers were distracted to get an outside opinion and she seems to agree. If I want things to work with Emilio, we need to move slow.

Besides, Jae is my friend. He's always been there for me and I appreciate him being there for me now. If he wasn't, I'm not sure what I would to. I'd probably have to drop out. I'd need a job to support myself and Luis, and I'd still be in a bind when it came to childcare.

Emilio's arm wraps around my waist, his hold possessive and his voice filled with irritation when he says, "Why? Allie or Aaron can take you home on their way to work. Your place is on the way to the Sun Valley Station. Hell, I'll let coach know right now I'll be a few minutes late to practice and I can take you. It's not a big deal." His fingers clench on my hip and I wince.

If it's not a big deal, why is he trying to turn it into one? "Jae is my friend. He offered. I accepted. He's literally been driving me to school all quarter already, so this isn't new. Don't make a big deal out of nothing," I plead.

If anything, his face only darkens. "I don't know him," he bites out.

"And he doesn't know you. Why don't you two make nice and be friends?" It sure as hell would make my life easier.

He snorts. "Not happening."

I rub my temples and remind myself that now isn't the time to get in a fight. Especially over something as stupid as who drives me home. I can already tell that moving in with Jae is going to be a problem. One Emilio is just going to have to deal with.

"I'm going to go home. Go to practice before you're late."

Emilio's nostrils flare, and the next thing I know he jerks me up against him. Luis is still in my arms, but that doesn't stop him as his mouth presses down on my own. One of his hands tangles in my hair, holding me in place while the other cradles our boy so neither of us drops him. The kiss is angry. His teeth bite at my lower lip until I open for him and then he devours my mouth like I'm his last meal.

It ends almost as quickly as it began, and I'm left standing on shaking legs when he steps away.

"Just a ride?" he questions, as though I'm somehow the untrustworthy one. I force my irritation down and give him nod.

"Yeah, man. I'm just giving her a ride," Jae says, having moved closer. His words are innocent enough, but there's the hint of suggestion in his tone and Emilio doesn't miss it. "You all set?" Jae asks, ignoring the tension that's building between them. He places his hand on my shoulder and Emilio's eyes laser in on the touch, his hands now fisted at his sides in a white-knuckled grip. Dominique and Roman both take steps forward, flanking their best friend in an aggressive show of support.

You have got to be kidding me. They can't possibly think it's okay to act like this.

"Really? You guys are going to go all machismo now? Don't you dare even think about starting something. Jae is my friend. What are you thinking?" Roman and Dominique say nothing. Stupid Devils.

Allie tugs Roman's arm and he reluctantly allows her to pull him away, but not before shooting a warning look at Jae that screams, *I can and will hurt you.* I roll my eyes before giving Aaron a pleading look and tilting my head in Dominique's direction just as Kasey joins our group. He gives me a shake of his head. So much for being one of the girls. All right then. No help from him. I try Kasey next and I can tell she's considering it. Her eyes flick between Dominique and Emilio, her lips pursed together. I catch a spark of mischief in her gaze, but also hesitation.

"Please," I mouth.

Jae plucks Luis from my arms and habit has me letting him. Immediately, I know it's a mistake. It's only confirmed when I hear Emilio bites out, "I don't want him around my kid," as he takes a step closer. I shift to intercept him.

"Excuse me?" Where is this possessive asshole crap coming from?

"One of us will get you to and from school. You don't need him to do that, and I don't want him around Luis. I don't know him and I sure as shit don't trust him with my son."

I rub my temples with my fingers, a headache already blooming. Jae says nothing for which I'm grateful. His eyes narrow into slits but he does the right thing and keeps his mouth shut, letting me deal with Emilio's sudden hostility. Luis grabs for his cheeks, smooshing his face and attempting to blow raspberries against his skin. It'd adorable, but only serves to piss off Emilio more.

"Can you buckle him in his car seat?" I ask Jae and he nods, turning to put Luis in the car. Before Emilio can argue I grab his hand and tug him closer to the building away from the growing crowd that is all too interested in what one of the school's Devils is getting himself into. Sometimes I really hate high school.

"You don't get to dictate who I spend my time with," I remind him as soon as we're a safe distance away. "And you do not get to dictate who I have in Luis's life."

"I'm his dad—"

"And I'm his mom. Jae giving me a ride and being in Luis's life doesn't change that any more than Dominique or Roman being in his life."

The muscles of his jaw flex. "You know he has a thing for you."

I don't answer because yeah, I do. And admitting that right now isn't going to do me any favors.

"Jae has been there for me. As a friend," I rush to add when Emilio opens his mouth. "I'm not going to all of a sudden cut him out of our lives because you say so."

Emilio's stare burns through me as he takes a step forward until we're little more than an inch away from one another. His hand comes up to wrap around the column of my throat, his hold possessive. He runs his thumb over my jaw and slowly over my bottom lip. I stay still the entire time, waiting to see what this beautiful boy will do when his anger rides him like this.

"You and Luis are mine."

I quirk a brow.

Fire licks his gaze as his teeth scrape over his bottom lip. "Say it."

"Say what?"

His grip tightens just enough to be a warning. "You're mine."

"What happened to getting to know one another?" I ask. "Taking things slow."

He backs me up against the wall and presses his body against mine. I can feel his cock dig into my stomach, already hard. "You said you wanted to take things slow. I never agreed." He captures my lips in a drugging kiss. How does he undo me like this? His hand moves from my throat down to my chest where he squeezes one breast before trailing down my body to rest his hold on my hips.

"People are watching," I gasp, tearing my mouth from his.

"You think I care?"

I push at his chest because while he might not, I certainly do. His mouth trails kisses down my neck and he presses his pelvis against me, letting me feel every glorious inch of him. My pussy clenches and I force myself to keep from melting into his touch.

"Emilio—"

"Bibiana—" There's a warning in Emilio's voice and he bites at the juncture between my neck and shoulder. I hiss and before I can do more than that, he steps back. I rub at the slight sting and turn an accusing glare his way.

"Was that really necessary?" I ask.

He shrugs. "Just marking what's mine."

"You don't own me," I remind him.

"Keep telling yourself whatever you need to hear."

I shake my head and brush past him, Jae already seated in the driver seat of his car.

I check on Luis to make sure he's properly buckled and that his chest clip is resting where it's supposed to before climbing in the passenger seat. I meet Emilio's stare through the windshield, his face still tight and eyes glaring.

Jae squeezes my knee in reassurance. "Everything good?"

I nod. "Yeah. Let's go."

He puts the Acura in drive and Emilio steps out behind the car, watching us leave. I sigh. I have a feeling he isn't going to take the news of me moving in with Jae very well. Which is why I'm not going to tell him. At least, not anytime soon if I can help it. Now, I just need to figure out a way to keep him from finding out. Easier said than done.

TWENTY-THREE

Emilio

I'm supposed to be defending my receiver, but I'm taking every chance I get to slam into my teammates during scrimmages. Fuck the plays. I'm going on the offensive. There's a fucking monster simmering beneath the surface of my skin and I need a release. Bashing helmets isn't going to cut it.

What was that guy even doing here? Jae. Pfft. And why the hell would she call him? Today is her first day back. I told her I'd be there. That I'd help. Pull my weight. I thought we went over all of this at her place. I told her she was my responsibility too. I want to take care of her and Luis, but she doesn't even give me the chance.

Dominique throws the ball long, aiming for Roman who is rushing toward the end zone, his cleats flying across the field as the ball spirals right for him. We're playing blue, the other half of our team wearing red. I see one of the guys in red coming my way and I bend my knees, angling my shoulder to take him right in the gut. My smile is savage when our bodies connect, and I hear the air rush out of him as he takes the full brunt of my aggression. My feet slide back across the wet grass, but I manage to stay upward as he stumbles back, crashing flat on his back.

"Fuck!" he shouts, his chest rising and falling as his fists hit the ground beside him. He doesn't get up and I hear Coach's whistle putting an end to the play. I walk over to my teammate, seeing his number and knowing right away it's Carson-fucking-Bailey. "Did you have to lay me out like that?" he growls, trying and failing to push himself up with his hands. He slumps back, his helmet bouncing on the ground and I shrug.

"Yeah. I did."

Coach comes up beside me and slaps my shoulder, but I barely feel it. "Hold onto that fire for this weekend's game. We need it," he tells me as he reaches down to pull Carson up. "But lay off your teammates." He pauses. "At least my starters."

I chuckle. "Sure thing, Coach."

Carson tears off his helmet and flips me off as soon as Coach turns away. "Fuck you, Chavez. I thought we were cool?"

I take my helmet off and brush past him, making sure to shoulder check him along the way. "Not sure what gave you that idea."

He curses. "I didn't even talk to her, man."

I don't bother turning around. He doesn't deserve my anger, but it fucking sucks for him because he's going to get it. "Line up!" Dominique shouts and everyone hustles back into line.

"I'll be in on the next play," I tell him and nod toward one of the juniors on the bench. "You're up."

He startles to attention and then runs for the field, Dominique already shouting for him to hurry his ass up. I stalk toward the locker room and drop my helmet on the bench. I need to get my head on straight, but I can't get the image of her sitting with him out of my head, my kid in the back seat. They looked like the perfect fucking family. Is that why she said no to marrying me? Fuck. To dating me. Because she's already got her eyes set on someone else?

I drag my hand over my face and kick the locker. I need answers. Spinning in the combination to my lock I tear my locker open and dig through my bag for my cell phone, but before I even have a chance to unlock the screen, a call comes in.

Antonio's name flashes across the screen and my stomach drops to my feet. Shit. My fingers fumble as I rush to answer, bringing the phone to my ear, my heart lodged in my throat. Is our little sister okay? Did Raul do something?

"What's up?" I ask as sooner as the call goes through.

"Where are you?" His voice is tight, and my panic increases tenfold.

"School. Football practice," I tell him.

"Can you get away? Somewhere quiet where you can be alone?"

My brows furrow. He doesn't sound upset, just... tense.

"Already am. I'm in the locker room. I needed a breather. What's going on?"

"Sit down."

"Bro— " I cover my apprehension with a laugh. "Get to the point. Who died?" I joke, because if anything had happened to Sofia, he would have told me by now.

"Raul."

What? I stumble back onto the bench and clench the phone to my hear, hunching over as I stare at the ground. There's a ringing in my ears. Antonio is still talking but I can't make out his words. I catch pieces of what he's saying but none of it is making any sense. "Missing. Found at ... drunk. Choked on his own..."

I shake my head to clear it. "He's dead. You're not fucking with me right now?"

There's a beat of silence. "Dad is dead."

I haven't heard him call Raul "Dad" since Mom left, and for some godforsaken reason, hearing it makes my insides twist into knots. It hurts. A physical pain I can't describe, and all because a fucker who needed to die finally did.

"Don't call him that. We haven't had a dad in years. If Raul died, as far as I'm concerned, good riddance."

"Fine. We'll skip over the tears and heartfelt trip down memory lane. But we have a problem?"

I snort. "No. We just got a solution to our problem. A big fucking one at that." There's movement on the other line already, like he's stepping into another room.

"We have Sofia," he reminds me.

"What about her? She's safe now. We don't need to worry about that fucker hurting her anymore." I rub at my chest, trying to alleviate some of the ache. Maybe I took a hit on the field and didn't realize the pain at the time. I can't think of another reason for feeling this way all of a sudden.

"No. Now we have to worry about social services taking her."

Hold on a minute. "You can't be serious." She's our sister. Our blood. We're family. You don't take family away. Social services didn't give a shit about us when Raul was leaving bruises behind. Why the hell would they get involved now?

"I've already gotten a phone call. When the police were called after a maid at the hotel found his body, they ran his records. They know he has kids, and they know Sofia is a minor."

"She has us. It's not like she's alone. You and I are both over eighteen. We've got this."

He exhales a harsh breath. "You're an eighteen-year-old high school senior," he reminds me, and I can hear the thread of panic in his voice. He's serious. Sofia can be taken from us all because our deadbeat father kicked the bucket. Will this man never stop ruining our lives? He even has to do it from the goddamn grave?

"You're not. You have a job. You can be her legal guardian." I still don't understand what the problem is.

"I have a record, E."

All the blood drains from my face. "That was three years ago. They can't—"

"They can. It was assault with—"

"You were defending yourself!" I roar, slamming my fist against the locker. "You were defending us." Antonio did what he had to do to keep us safe, but our asshole of a father pressed charges even though he was the one who swung first.

"I know. Doesn't matter though. That's not how they see it."

"Fuck." I start to pace. "What are we going to do? How do we fix this?" There has to be a way. Letting social services take Sofia is not an option, I'll run with her if I have to. I know Antonio will too. My mind strays to Bibiana and Luis. Shit. I can't take my sister and run. I have my own kid to think about too. Goddammit. What a mess.

Would Bibiana leave with us? I could convince her if I had to, right?

"Roberto is on his way. I called him before calling you. He put in for leave when I told him about Luis. It was approved."

"But for how long? We can't count on him to—"

"We'll figure it out, okay? We have to."

I grind my teeth together and nod, not that he can see it. I don't have a lot of faith in our eldest brother, but if he can stick around long enough for us to figure this shit out, that'll be enough. Then he can crawl back to whatever desert they have him stationed at and go back to pretending his family doesn't exist.

"So, what do we do in the meantime?"

"You get your ass home. We need to show the case worker that we're a stable, loving, family. That we can provide the type of environment Sofia needs to thrive in. They'll be here tomorrow to interview us. I need—"

"I'll be there."

He lets out a relieved breath. "Thank you."

I snort. "You don't have to thank me. She's my baby sister too."

"I know." He sighs. "But you've got your own kid now and—"

"And nothing. I'll let Bibiana know I'll be busy for a little while. She's bringing Luis to school now, so I'll still get to see him every day. We'll figure it out."

"You still need to bring him home sometime. I want to meet my nephew."

"I know I will—"

"Only maybe after we get all of this figured out."

Sounds good to me. I don't want my kid anywhere near where social services is sniffing.

The sound of voices approaching lets me know the guys must have finished up with practice. "I gotta go, but I'll be home in half an hour. An hour max. Okay?"

"Okay. See you soon."

I hang up and shove my phone back into my bag before peeling off my pads. I need a quick shower before the rest of the team uses all the hot water, and then I need to haul ass home. I consider calling Bibiana to let her know what happened, but I never told her about Raul in the first place. Better to leave well enough alone. I'll just tell her I can't come by this week because of practice. She'll understand. She knows we have the state championship this weekend, so it won't be a big deal.

Right?

TWENTY-FOUR

Bibiana

When Jae said he'd grab some of my things from my mom's, I didn't realize he'd meant all of my things. My room wasn't very large to begin with back home, so I didn't have a ton of stuff, but all of my clothes are hanging in the guest room closet and six large boxes lay against one wall filled with Luis's clothes and toys. He even packed my books and knickknacks.

There is a playpen set up beside the bed, and it looks like my makeup and toothbrush are sitting on the nightstand. I can't believe he thought to grab them from my bathroom.

"Did you leave anything behind?" I ask jokingly, though also somewhat serious, because this makes the move feel permanent and that can't be what he has in mind. Right? I mean, no. Of course, this is temporary. A few weeks. Maybe a couple of months at most.

He rubs the back of his neck, his expression sheepish. "I mean, I didn't bring the bed. Or the crib. But we can go back for it if you'd like."

"No. This is fine. Great actually." The play pen is new. I definitely didn't have that before, though Luis is fine to sleep beside me if need be. Half the time he winds up in my bed anyway.

I set Luis down and place a hand on Jae's forearm. "You didn't need to go through all this trouble. I'll figure something out soon. I promise." Maybe I'll get lucky and can wait out Miguel's trial, though from the sounds of it, that could take months, and I don't have months.

"Don't." He sighs. "I mean, you don't need to, and it wasn't any trouble. Living by yourself is overrated. I have this whole place to myself. It could use some life in it, don't you think?"

"Are you sure? Because if you're not—"

"I want you here. You and Luis." His eyes implore me to stay, and without an alternative, I relent.

"Okay. Thank you. I promise we won't get in your way."

He chuckles. "I want you two in my way. That's the entire point of moving you in here so get comfortable. Leave Luis's toys all over the house and help yourself to whatever you need."

I can't help my smile. "You know you're a pretty great guy, right?"

The corner of his mouth lifts into a smile. "Yeah?"

"Yeah. You're going to make some girl insanely happy one day."

His smile dips and he licks his lips, a nervous gesture. "That isn't you though, is it?"

I open my mouth. Close it. Swallow and take a deep breath. "I think Emilio and I are..." I trail off. I'm not sure what we are, but it's something, and I don't want Jae getting the wrong idea. Because even if Emilio weren't in the picture, I just don't feel those sparks with him. It isn't in the cards for Jae and I.

He forces a laugh. "No worries. I get it." He swoops Luis into his arms and rubs his nose against his, giving him an Eskimo kiss. "I hope he knows how lucky he is. And I hope you know if he screws up, I'm available." He winks.

I can't help the laugh that bubbles out of my chest. "Stop. You are not going to be anyone's second choice."

He steps closer and places a chaste kiss along my temple. "I'd be your second choice in a heartbeat if you'd have me."

My breath hitches.

"But I won't push. I value our friendship too much and I want you comfortable while you're here. Why don't you unpack while Luis and I grab a snack?"

"I really do appreciate—"

He shakes his head. "Enough with all that. You and me, we're good. I don't mind being friend-zoned as long as that friendship weathers any storms that might come up. Okay? I know you and Luis's dad are together."

I scowl.

"Or maybe not together?" he corrects.

"I have no clue, to be honest."

"Yeah, guys are stupid at his age." He shrugs. "But you're something, or you're working out what you are to each other at least, and I respect that. Just don't let him shove me out of your life, okay? I remember being eighteen and an idiot too."

"You're not that much older," I remind him.

He smirks. "Old enough to grow out of my idiot phase."

I roll my eyes.

"He's going to be jealous. Possessive too. Can't say I blame him but"—he hesitates, and I can see that this is really important to him—"hang on to the people you want in your life."

"I will. Promise."

"I'll hold you to that."

I spend the next hour unpacking and making sure I have everything I need. I try calling Mom, but she doesn't answer so I shoot her a text hoping she'll see it eventually and respond.

Me: Staying with Jae for a bit. Call me if anything changes with Miguel.

I'm not used to radio silence from her. We've always been close. Especially after Dad died. She talked to me. Told me things most mothers probably wouldn't tell their daughters, but it was okay. I liked the shift in our relationship. I liked knowing she needed me but now—I need her.

I try to push back the emotion bubbling up inside of me. An empty crater opens in my chest and I rub at the ache, hating the hollow feeling inside of me.

"You're not some little kid anymore," I remind myself. I close my eyes and take a deep breath. Everyone has to leave the nest at some time. Now just happens to be mine.

I set my phone on the bedside table before picking it back up. I debate calling Emilio next.

Every day this week he's come over to the house after football practice. But he's clearly upset with me today. It's stupid and beyond immature. I get the feeling he won't stop by today but if he does, I should be the one to tell him. It'll only make him angrier if he shows up at my house and my mom is the one to tell him I moved in with Jae. I don't know how he'll take it. But I imagine it'll be worse than if I tell him myself.

Indecision swirls through me. I don't want to tell him. I want to just pretend like this isn't a thing. Because it shouldn't be. Where I live should play no part in our relationship, whatever it may be. And that kiss. I press my fingers to my lips, remembering his touch. His taste. He's always sweet with a hint of spice, much like the *palerindas*—a tamarind-flavored sucker—I see him eating sometimes.

But I know this is going to be a thing between us. It'll cause a rift and Mom being the one to tell him will only make it so much worse. She knows Emilio is Luis's father. We had that fun, awkward conversation and it went about as well as can be expected.

She thinks he's too young. That I should be careful. That I shouldn't give even an inch when it comes to Luis because he'll take a mile. It's like she expects him to try and take Luis from me or something.

It doesn't help that she's always been a fan of the idea of Jae and I getting together. Luis being around puts a damper on her plans and knowing Emilio was there when Miguel was arrested, doesn't give him any points in her book. I don't need this to boil over into a bigger deal than it needs to be. I love my mom but, she's not thinking clear right now.

Resigned with the knowledge that I do actually have to tell him, I pull up Emilio's number and hit dial, listening as it rings. Once. Twice. Five times. I hit his voicemail. Relief sweeps through me as his voice says, "This is Emilio. You know what to do." The line beeps and I hang up. Voicemail isn't the best way to tell him I've moved out, right? I'll try again later. Probably. But at least I can say I did try.

I check the time. Practice should be out already but be could be running late, or maybe he decided to take a shower or something. Should I send him a text? Maybe just to ask him to call me when he has a moment. Before I can decide, my phone vibrates in my hand and I jump.

Emilio's name flashes across the screen and my fingers fumble to open the incoming message, nerves already slamming into me.

Emilio: Had some family shit come up. I'll be busy the next few days.

Oh. My shoulders slump. He'll be busy? What is that supposed to mean? Like, is he too busy for Luis and me? I chew on my bottom lip. Is he really that mad at me that he'd make up some story about family drama?

I shake my head. No. I'll give him the benefit of the doubt. Besides, I wanted to put off telling him I moved out anyway. This at least buys me some time. I sit on the edge of the bed and stare down at my phone.

This is good. Helpful, even.

I exhale a harsh breath. So why does it feel like my stomach is trying to escape through my feet right now?

If he wants to avoid me, there isn't anything I can do about it. It just royally sucks to know that he does.

Me: Okay. See you at school.

I hit the send button, refusing to let on how much this bothers me. Doubt creeps in and I wonder if this is going to be a recurring thing? Get mad at Bibi and suddenly become unavailable?

Three little dots appear on the screen and I wait for him to respond, but after a few seconds, the dots that signal he's typing fade and no new messages arrive. I sigh. Whatever. Boys are dumb anyway.

TWENTY-FIVE

Emilio

I t's been three days since I found out Raul died, and life
has been an absolute shitstorm. I didn't even make it to
practice the last two days, and I barely see Luis. I
mean, I see him at school since Bibiana brings him but getting
my kid for all of thirty minutes during lunch and then sharing
him during fourth period isn't enough. This isn't going to
work for me.

I remind myself that it's temporary. As soon as we figure shit
out and make sure Sofia doesn't go into the system, I can
spend more time with Luis. With my girl. Bibiana has been
acting strange. Reserved even. It's like she's folding herself
back into a shell and I'm not sure what to think about it. I
want to let her know what's going on, but what if she freaks
out? I won't risk her keeping Luis from me. I'd like to think
we're past that. That she'd never keep him from me, but I
can't shake the feeling that she might. I mean, what mother

wouldn't be worried with social services sniffing around, right?

"Thank you, boys. I believe that's everything I need for now." The social worker—a Miss Patricia Morgen—says, getting to her feet. She holds a legal pad in one hand, the first few pages littered in notes. About what, who the fuck knows. She's been here twice now in three days, and I won't be surprised if I see her again.

It's clear she has decided she doesn't like our situation. She keeps making statements about how important it is to for a young girl to grow up with a mother. And yeah, I'm sure it is. But we don't have one around, and it's more important for Sofia to stay with her family than to be carted off to live with a bunch of strangers. Mother or not, she needs us too.

The possibility of that happening is getting to my baby sister and it shows. Not in a good way either. She's pale and acting skittish. She inches back every time this Morgen lady asks her a question, as if she is trying to sink into the furniture, and she flicks her eyes toward me and Antonio before she answers. It makes her look guilty as hell. If I were Patricia Morgen, I would be concerned too. But she doesn't know us. Dropping in on people and putting the fear of God in them in your first meeting isn't a great way to make someone comfortable.

Antonio jumps to his feet to walk her out and I stay on the couch, pulling Sofia into a hug. God knows she needs it. Her tiny body shudders against mine and I tuck her head beneath my chin. "She's going to take me away, isn't she?" she whispers, tears lodged in her throat.

"Nope. This is all just protocol, baby sis. No one is taking you anywhere." My voice is firm, but inside I'm reeling. They could take her from us and there isn't a damn thing we could do about it.

A few hours pass and the mood in the house is decidedly grim. Sofia's retreated to her room to read her *Meet Josefina* book—they really need to come up with a Honduran girl for that shit—and Antonio are I are sitting in the garage. He's drinking a Modelo while we both stare out across the street, lost in our separate trains of thought.

A car I don't recognize rolls up and I lean forward in my seat. The passenger door opens, and a man steps out. Dressed in combat greens, my brother turns to face us, a military duffle slung over one shoulder. The driver takes off as Roberto stands there, waiting to see his reception.

Antonio is the first to stand up. He meets our brother halfway across the drive and the two embrace. Roberto has filled out since I last saw him. He's both taller and broader, damn near engulfing Antonio in his arms.

They separate and walk together to the garage, Roberto stopping a few paces in front of me, a quirk in his brow. "Long time, *hermanito*." Little brother.

I nod and push to my feet. "Four years," I remind him. Four years with damn near zero contact, I might add. But I don't bother saying that out loud. He already knows how long he's been away.

Roberto ducks his head and releases a harsh breath. "I'm back now."

Obviously. He's standing in front of me. But the question is, for how long?

He flicks his gaze to the side, his jaw stiff before returning his hard hazel stare back to mine.

"Cut him some slack," Antonio asks.

Before I can respond Roberto adds, "I'm out now."

"What's that supposed to mean?" I ask.

He's standing stiff, shoulders squared, and feet almost perfectly spaced. "It means I was eligible to re-enlist when Antonio called. He told me about your kid." A smile splits his face, one of the few genuine smiles I've ever seen on my brother's face. "I decided not to. Even before I knew about Raul." He hesitates, his voice dropping low. "I know I left you. Left like mom. I don't blame you for being pissed off with me. I should have called. Or written." He huffs out a breath. "Look. I'm sorry. But—I'm here now. I want to be here. For Sofia. For you. I want to put our family back together the way it should be."

I work my jaw and give him a stiff nod. "Okay."

"Okay?" he questions, as if he doesn't believe me. I hold my hand out and he clasps it.

"Yeah, man. Okay." I gave up my grudge years ago. He did what he needed to, and I can't say I wouldn't have made the same decision in his place. Okay. Lie. I know I wouldn't have, but still. This, I can let go. For family. For blood.

TWENTY-SIX

Bibiana

"We're going to a party this weekend," Kasey says as soon as I sit down for lunch.

"Uh, you do know I have a kid, right?"

She nods, blond hair bobbing around her face. "Yup. I already took care of it." I look at Allie and she shrugs.

"And how exactly did you take care of my child?" I ask just as Emilio and the rest of the boys join us.

"What's this about our child?" Emilio asks, plucking Luis from my arms. He gives me a quick kiss on the cheek and then turns his attention to our son, making faces and blowing raspberries on his neck.

"I got you a sitter," Kasey adds, and I frown. I'm not going to leave Luis with just anyone. "Relax, it's Monique."

Oh. My shoulders relax. "I didn't know you two talked."

Dominique grunts and a wicked smile spreads across Kasey's face. "All the time," she says with a pointed look toward Dominique. "I'm learning so much. That girl is a wealth of information."

I snort, but quickly smother my laugh. I can only imagine what these two are getting up to. "Okay. I'll bite, since I trust Monique, why are we going to a party this weekend?"

At the mention of party, four scowls greet me. Emilio, Aaron, Dominique, and Roman.

Kasey ignores all of them. "The guys have the state championship game this weekend."

"Exactly," Roman says. "So why the fuck would any of us go to a party?"

"You're not invited," she tells him with a flick of her hair.

"If the guys have a game, why wouldn't we go to that?"

Emilio shifts beside me. "You wanna see me play?"

I shrug. "Why not?"

His back straightens and the corners of his mouth curl into a smile. "You guys should come to the game."

Kasey just shakes her head. "We don't do school games, remember?" She gives a pointed look in Allie's direction and everyone at the table is suddenly nodding.

"What am I missing?"

Kasey hesitates, so it's Allie who answers. "When I was... uh... assaulted," she swallows hard, "it was at a football game. They're still kinda a sore spot for me."

Oh. "I'm so—"

She shakes her head. "Don't be. But I'm with Kasey. Let's get out. Go to a party. I haven't been to one since we all got together at Shadle Creek. I could use a fun night with everything going on right now."

Roman places his arm around her and she leans into him. I've been such a crappy friend. I've barely checked in to see how she's holding up with all of the Miguel stuff going on right now. That last I heard from Jae, since he's been keeping tabs on everything for me, is that Miguel was offered a plea deal to give up the other man who assaulted Allie with him.

It's looking like the recent charges are going to stick, and Jae said Miguel is considering it. They offered him a lesser sentence. Ten to fifteen years with a shot at parole for good behavior, so he could be out in as little as seven if he turns on his buddy. We'll see what happens.

"Are you holding up okay?"

She shrugs. "As good as can be expected. I just want it all to be over, ya know? I want to finally put all of this behind me and move on with my life."

I reach across the table and squeeze her hand. "So, girls' night out?"

She nods. "Girls' night out."

I smile wide. I haven't been to a party since... well, since I got pregnant with Luis.

"I don't like the idea of you three going out alone," Emilio says, setting Luis on the table where he promptly twists in an attempt to crawl across the surface.

"Give me," Allie says reaching for him. "I need the baby snuggles."

"We're not going to be alone. We'll be with each other." I shrug.

"Bad idea," Dominique adds. Roman and Emilio both nod in agreement. "Shit could happen. Someone could spike your drink. You guys could get hurt."

Kasey snorts. "It's at Sarah's. I live literally right next door. We don't have to worry about rides or designated drivers and none of us are heavy drinkers. Stop being spoilsports. We'll call Aaron if we get in a bind."

Aaron shakes his head. "I've got plans. You three are on your own."

Kasey whirls on him. "Plans? What plans?"

"Personal ones that my nosey baby sister doesn't need to know about."

Her eyes narrow but surprising us all, she drops it. "Whatever. It doesn't matter. We don't need—"

"No," Roman deadpans like his word is law and all three of us girls raise a brow.

"No?" Allie says, a tilt of her head and a gleam in her eyes. Oh, this is going to be good.

"Vanilla, you know this is a bad idea."

"What I know is that I'm having a much-needed girls' night. And I know you have a football game. State championships in fact, that I also know you can't miss. That's what I know."

Kasey and I both snicker.

Roman opens his mouth to argue and then thinks better of it before he curses under his breath and then steals Luis from her. "I thought you both hated Sarah."

"We do," Kasey chimes in. "But that doesn't mean I'll turn down free booze and a night out."

His lips mash together and Allie smirks in triumph as Roman starts making baby noises and faces at Luis. It's weird how fast his mood shifts.

"Can I keep him next period?" she asks. "I want some nephew time." I love that she considers him family already. That they all do.

"Sure. But don't you have class?"

She nods, holding a finger out to Luis, who tries to bite it. He's teething and everything appears edible, or at least chewable these days.

"Just gym so we'll roll a ball around or something. No one will care."

"Why not?"

The bell rings and we all push up from our seats. "See you in fourth," she calls, claiming my diaper bag as she and Roman head toward the exit.

I'm about to follow when Emilio reaches out and captures my arm. "A party?" he asks, his voice low. "Is that a good idea?"

"Why wouldn't it be?"

He tugs me into falling into step beside him and we spill into the crowded hallway. "Because the last time you went to a party you—"

"Had a one-night stand? Got pregnant?" I grin. "Worried it'll happen again?"

He drags me into an empty classroom and closes the door behind us before spinning around and pressing me up against the wall. My breath hitches as he trails his nose along my jaw line and takes a deep breath. "It better not happen again, unless I'm the one who puts another baby in this oven." He presses a hand against my stomach. My eyes meet his hooded gaze in question.

"Already planning on knocking me up, again?" I joke, but he doesn't smile.

"What if I was?"

My brows furrow. "You're kidding right?"

Silence.

"Emilio..."

"I wasn't there the first time. I missed all of that. Maybe I want to see what it's like." He shrugs like it's no big deal, but there's an emotion in his eyes I don't recognize.

"We're not even—"

"Yeah. We are." He presses himself against me, his lips hovering a hairsbreadth over mine. "We're a thing. You can tell yourself whatever you need to but this, you and me, it's not nothing. This is a thing. And it's exclusive."

I shiver in response. "Emilio Chavez is capable of monogamy? Who could have known?" I only half joke, because despite his words, I have my doubts. Especially with the way he's been acting these past few days.

"You know now," he says, kissing me, his lips ghosting across my own in a way that has me chasing to follow. "And you're the only one who matters." He cups the side of my face and tilts toward me until his lips are pressed against mine. This time, the kiss lingers for a moment and my cheeks heat when I feel the hard press of him against me.

The bell rings, jerking me out of the moment and we break away from one another, but just barely. "We should get to class," I mumble, but make no move to leave.

"We should," he agrees, but Emilio doesn't move either.

My chest rises and falls as my heart pounds in my chest. There's a savage glint in his eyes and a wicked curl to his lips. "Or..."

"Or?" My voice is breathless.

"We could stay."

I swallow hard and lick my lips. His eyes track the movement and the next thing I know he's lifted me into his arms. My legs wrap around his waist and he grinds into me, his hard length pressed tight against my center. "I need to be inside you," he murmurs against my mouth.

"We..." I gasp. "Can't do that... here." I can't catch my breath. His kisses are drugging, stealing the air inside my lungs. He nips at my chin, my jawline, my neck.

"I'll come over after practice. Things are settling down with my brother in town."

I arch against him as his words make their way through a haze of desire. Come over? Today? Brother? Shit.

I pull away and drop my feet back to the ground. Emilio scowls and reluctantly sets me down. "Your brother is in town?" I wrack my brain for any earlier mention of him. I know he has two. And a little sister. I haven't met them yet, but I assumed they all lived here.

"Yeah. My oldest just got out of the army. He's back for good now that..." he trails off.

"Now that what?"

He takes a deep breath and steels himself. "My dad died."

"Oh, my god." My hand flies up to cover my mouth before I rush to hug him. "I'm so sorry," I murmur against his chest.

Emilio pulls away and looks down at me, a strange look on his face. "He was an alcoholic who liked to hit his kids. Don't be sorry he's gone. I'm not."

Oh. I had no idea. "Are you..."

He rubs the back of his neck. "I'm good. Really. I don't want to talk about him though. What I want is," he kisses me again, "to fuck you, preferably in a bed but I'll settle for a desk."

I groan against his mouth. "We are not having sex at school. Someone could come in."

"Fine. Your place tonight."

When I don't answer, Emilio leans back, holding me at arm's length. "Unless you don't want me to come?"

I shake my head. "It's not that..." How do I explain?

"Then what is it?" There's a bite in his tone.

I take a deep breath and decide to rip off the band aid. "I moved out." There, I said it.

"When?"

"Earlier this week. Miguel made bail so..." I shrug.

He steps back and folds his arms over his chest. "And you weren't going to tell me?"

"It's not that I wasn't. I mean, I knew I had to tell you eventually, just..."

He taps his foot.

"I moved in with Jae?" It comes out like a question even though it isn't. As expected, his face reddens and steam practically comes out of his ears.

"Jae? The guy who would fuck you in a heartbeat, Jae?"

"We're just friends."

He shakes his head and backs away from me. "Are you fucking kidding me right now?"

I rush toward him. "Keep it down. It's not a big deal. I needed a place to crash and he offered. Nothing is happening. I swear."

He tugs at the strands of his hair, but instead of yelling at me some more he surprises me and backs me into one of the desks. "Nothing is happening between you two?" he bites out.

I shake my head. "Nothing."

"But I can't come over and fuck my girl at his place. Is that what you're telling me?"

When he says it like that it sounds bad, but still, "It would be weird. Don't you think?"

He quirks a brow and one hand comes up to grip my chin. "You're mine, Bibiana Sousa. Only mine."

I press my lips together to hold in my retort.

"Say the words. You. Are. Mine."

I hesitate and he bites my bottom lip. Hard. Ow. Fuck.

His hand grips my ass and tugs me tight against him. "I'm going to fuck you until I own every part of your mind, body, and soul," he growls.

My pussy clenches in anticipation.

"I won't be gentle," he warns. "You kept something from me. I thought we agreed, no secrets?" There's a savage glint in his eyes, but he waits, almost like he's silently asking for my permission. I swallow hard but manage a nod. "Okay," I tell him, knowing that despite the anger riding him, he needs to hear that I'm alright with this.

He wants to... punish me. I think. For not telling him about Jae. Probably still for the other day when he picked me up from school. I should balk at this, but I don't. I've accepted that Emilio isn't like other boys, and I'll happily take my punishment if it means I can have him.

At his core, Emilio is a good guy. He doesn't want to hurt me. He just needs...

"Turn around," he commands, his voice thick with lust.

I hesitate for only a second before doing as he instructs. I turn around and press my hands down on the desk in front of me, my chest heaving and my heart racing. Emilio presses his cock against me as he drags the waistband of my leggings down. Cool air brushes over my skin, the thin scrap of satin that covers my rear hardly enough to keep the chill away. "What if someone—"

"No one is going to come in. The door is locked. You'll just need to stay... quiet." There's a smirk in his voice.

His fingers trail along my inner thighs, digging into my flesh before sliding up to hook into my panties. Practiced fingers tug them down, but they're left to tangle with my leggings at my feet. My fingers tighten on the edge of the desk. This is really happening. I'm going to let him screw me in a classroom.

My pussy pulses with need and he steps back. I turn to look at him over my shoulder. His eyes burn with want. "So pretty," he coos darkly, but he isn't looking at my face. His eyes are locked on my bare flesh as he licks his lips like the savage devil he is, intent on devouring me. He lowers himself between my thighs, pressing his face against my ass. His hands roam up and down the inside of my legs, forcing them wider for him.

Anticipation hums through me as he parts the folds of my pussy with his thumbs and he licks me front to back like I'm his favorite treat. I cry out at the explosive sensations, but he's just getting started.

"Stay quiet," he warns. My eyes close, but I force them back open and bite my lip to keep my moans locked up inside. He presses a wet, hot kiss to my core and his tongue goes to work as he circles my clit and works me into a frenzy before plunging inside me with his tongue. My back arches and I push back, chasing his sinful mouth.

"So fucking sweet," he says. "Come for me Bibi. I want you to unravel."

"Oh God," I gasp, a little embarrassed at how breathless I sound. How exposed I am.

"Hold still, baby. I've only just begun."

I cry out when he adds his fingers, plunging one deep inside me before adding in a second. I clench around him, my body so starved for contact that I can feel my release hovering close. "Emilio," I gasp as the pressure builds. He thrusts into me with his fingers, curling them inside me as his mouth works my clit and my orgasm tears through me. I buck against his mouth, my body writhing as wave after wave of sensation rockets through me.

He continues sucking on my clit, prolonging my orgasm until my legs feel like jelly my body sated and my limbs boneless. But he isn't finished. He rises to his feet behind me like an avenging angel.

Devil would be more accurate.

I hear him loosen his belt and undo his zipper. I turn back to watch him, kicking off my leggings and panties with my other foot so they're not in my way. His impressive cock juts out and he meets my stare, grinning like the devil himself as he rolls a condom on his impressive dick. "You taste like sin, Bibiana Sousa." He steps back to me and covers my body with his as he cups my jaw, forcing me to twist right before he slams his mouth against mine. I taste myself on him and something about that turns me on. "It's a good thing I'm a Devil." Before I can respond, he releases me and tugs my hips back against his cock.

"Now, I'm going to fuck you like one."

He thrusts inside of me, stretching me as I'm forced to accommodate his size.

"Fuck," Emilio grunts, digging his fingers into my hips in a way I know will leave marks. "You're so fucking tight." He spreads my ass cheeks, exposing me in a completely different way as he pounds into me harder, faster. Taking zero time to let me adjust to his size.

I clutch the desk like my life depends on his, his thrusts so forceful that with nearly each one, we slide forward, forcing him to follow to hold the connection. "You like that, don't you?" He growls and my body coils tight, chasing my release.

I press my face to the desk, hoping it will muffle my moans, but I know it isn't enough. There's a knock at the door and I gasp, but Emilio doesn't stop. If anything, his thrusts become harder, more frantic. Again and again until the knock at the door is all but forgotten. My orgasm tears through me and stars explode behind my vision. But Emilio doesn't relent. He shifts his hips, finding a new angle and milking my orgasm for all that it's worth. His thrusts quicken with mounting urgency and I moan his name.

His grip tightens, his hands on my hips hurting as he pumps into me with wild abandon. His cock nudges my cervix and I see stars. Oh. My. God. He's so deep inside me I can feel him in my throat. And another orgasm threatens to wash over me. "I can't—" I gasp. Unable to get the words out.

It's too much. Too deep. Too everything. But I don't want him to stop.

Just when I think he's about to come, he surprises me and pulls out, spinning me around and pressing me down until my face is level with his shaft. He tears the condom off, weaves his fingers through my hair and thrusts his cock between my parted lips.

I groan around him as he thrusts into my mouth, his cock nudging the back of my throat and inducing my gag reflex, but he doesn't stop. He fucks my mouth mercilessly, sweat glistening on his brow as his eyes bore into mine. "That's it, baby. Suck my cock," he grunts the words, his entire body tense. "Good girl."

God. Why does hearing him say that turn me on? If anything, I should be offended right now, but I'm not. I like this. Hell, I love it.

My pussy clenches just as his cock pulses in my mouth and it's the only warning I get before his hot salty cum coats my tongue and shoots down my throat.

I take all of it, every drop he has to offer and swallow it down greedily. Pulling out, he yanks me up to him and slams his mouth down on mine again, the taste of both our pleasure a heady combination.

"You are mine," he growls the words against my mouth. My heart thumps loud behind my rib cage as I fight to recalibrate my brain and slow down my breathing. "Say the words, Bibiana. I need to hear them. You. Are. Mine."

We stare at one another in the silence, electricity crackling in the air between us. His savage grin is firmly back in place and I wish I knew what to say to him. But clearly, I was supposed to say something because when the silence continues to stretch, he reaches out and grips my jaw. "Mine," he enunciates the word. "Do we have an understanding?"

"Are you mine?" I bite out with a flare of irritation. Now that I've had a few seconds to recover, my brain is kicking back into gear, reminding me again of all of my doubts. The girls I see who flock to him. The flirting. But he does the unexpected and instead of telling me no, he nods his head in agreement. "I'm yours as much as you are mine. Which is to say completely and unequivocally. If you let another man touch you, Bibi, make sure you hate him because he won't be walking once I'm through with him."

My mind instantly snags on Jae and I know this is no idle threat. He grips the back of my head, slams his mouth on mine again and then releases me, all in the span of a few short seconds.

"Don't forget that," he warns before tucking himself back into his jeans. "I have zero intention of sharing you or my son with another man." He reaches for my leggings and panties, picking them up off the floor and handing them to me. Some of the tension has left him as he trails a hand down my neck, my shoulder, and then drags his fingers along my arm.

The knock at the door again startles me and I jump, but Emilio only laughs. He waits a few seconds as I rush to put my clothes back on and he takes care of throwing away his condom. I finger comb my hair and when he opens the door it's to reveal Allie with Luis fast asleep in her arms.

"Skipping school again?" She tsks and my cheeks heat, but Emilio only shrugs.

"From what I hear, you and Roman have made some good use out of an empty classroom a time or two."

Her eyes widen before she masks her horror with a groan. "Of course, you would know about that."

Emilio carefully reaches for Luis, tucking him into his arms and rocking him so as not to wake him.

"Everything okay?" I ask, peering down at my boy in Emilio's arms.

She nods. "Yeah. We ran out of his bottle and he was getting fussy, so I came to find you. Only you were," she smirks, "busy. So I walked around the halls with him until he fell asleep."

"Thank you."

She smiles and the bell rings, doors thrown open and students spill into the hall.

"That would be our cue," she says, tugging me beside her. "Best to slip out now before everyone else knows what you two were up to."

TWENTY-SEVEN

Emilio
_____

I'm pissed as fuck that she moved in with Jae and didn't tell me. That my kid is living with the guy. He's already comfortable with him, but now, living there...

I lean back in my seat in fourth period, Luis fast asleep on my chest. I don't like the idea of another guy being around him. I don't want it confusing him. What if he wants Jae more than me? He's my kid, but he's still getting to know me. How is that supposed to happen now?

I try to push my worries away. There isn't anything I can do about. I understand why she moved out. Hell, I'm glad she did. I just—fuck, I wish it wasn't there.

Class moves at a snail's pace and I'm so done with all this shit. I'm ready to graduate. Move on with my life. We have five months left before we can blow this taco stand, and I'm counting down the weeks. Only shit is different and it's getting more and more complicated as time goes by.

I shift Luis in my arms, slumping lower in my chair to make him more comfortable. I hate not seeing him every day. I hate that I'm not a part of his day-to-day life. We agreed to a visitation agreement, had it submitted to the courthouse and all that shit, but it isn't enough. Bibiana isn't keeping him from me, but I want more time. I want every day.

Living with Jae needs to be a temporary situation, which means I need to figure my shit out so we can get a place. I know she wants to take things slow, but slow with that girl just isn't in my vocabulary. Roman and Allie moved in together, so I don't see why we can't. We were all going to stay in the dorms together when we went off to college, but that plan has changed with Roman and Allie being together, so it was going to be just Dominique and me. With Bibiana though— we could do what Roman and Allie are doing. Get our own apartment. Somewhere not too far away.

I consider what I'd need to do to make that work. Income is going to be our biggest obstacle. Allie has a job. And she got a trust fund from her bio dad the day she turned eighteen, so rent has never been an issue. I don't have that. I'll need to get a job to support my family, but where will I find the time between classes and football? I can work nights maybe, but juggling a job, school and practice and game days will make spending time with them that much more difficult.

Shit. No matter how I look at this, it's a fucking mess. My scholarship covers room and board in the dorms, but they're not co-ed and no way will the university let me waltz my girl and kid in. I suck on my teeth. I need to come up with something. I don't have any other choice.

Game day rituals are a must. We all have our things and I stick to mine like a religion, only today I'm off and I know exactly why. Bibiana. Coach goes on about what we're here to do but I tune most of it out. Since the Devils are the reigning state champs, the game is taking place on our field. This should be a big deal. I promised myself this year would be all about football. But all I can think about is the fact that Bibiana is going out to a party. With Kasey, of all people, which means those girls are going to get into trouble. Even with Allie around no way are they going to be on good behavior. And the last time Bibiana went to a party—that dress...

Dominque slams the locker door beside me jerking me from my thoughts. "Get your head in the game, man."

I suck on my palerindas and flip my friend off before turning to Rome.

"How are you dealing with this?" I ask him.

He doesn't bother pretending like he doesn't know exactly what I'm talking about. "I know my girl isn't interested in anyone else's dick. Not much to worry about." He shrugs. "Besides, I'd be more worried if she were here."

I nod because yeah, Allie and football games don't mix. "Any news?" I ask. I've been out of the loop and haven't wanted to bring the matter up with Bibiana.

He nods. "Fucker's days are numbered. He made bail but he is also accepting the deal. He has until next Friday to surrender himself."

"How long?" The longer the better, as far as I'm concerned.

Roman pushes to his feet, keeping his voice down so Coach doesn't lose focus. He's on the whole this-game-can-change-your-lives, so-don't-fuck-up roll. It's his shit way of motivating us and scaring the underclassmen.

"He'll do six years minimum even if he gets parole." His jaw clenches.

"You're obviously not happy about that."

"Would you be?"

I shake my head. "Hell, no. I wouldn't be happy until the fucker was six feet in the ground if he did that to my girl."

"Agreed. But he gave up the other guy. He's looking at three years, so at least Allie will get some time to... fuck. I don't know. Breathe."

"Three? That's it?"

Roman nods. "Crimes of sexual assault come with the least severe punishment. It's a bullshit system if you ask me, but my pops says it's the best we're gonna get unless Allie wants to go to trial."

"Fuck that," Dominique barks and Coach turns to look at us. We draw back further into the locker room.

"I know. I'm not putting her through that."

"I thought the rape charges couldn't stick. How is this guy getting three years—"

"Because he confessed. They won't stick to Miguel because we have no proof, but when they dragged in the other guy, some William Chaiton or some shit, they told him Miguel flipped on him and he told them everything." He exhales a harsh breath. "He told them every goddamn twisted detail and we can't use any of it to nail Miguel because the deal's already been signed.

I push my sucker to my cheek. "Fuck, man. That's rough."

None of us say anything after that. The situation is a dumpster fire. Our system is broken and the fact that two asshole rapists are getting off so easy makes me sick to my stomach. I'm glad they got Miguel for something, even if it wasn't for the rape, but it's still bullshit.

Coach blows his whistle, and we all grab our gear, heading for the doors. Dominique slaps my shoulder, his voice grim as he says, "Focus on getting through the game, kicking their asses, and then we'll go collect what's ours from the party."

I lift a brow in silent question. Ours. Really? We making confessions now?

Dom's jaw locks tight and he gives me a stiff nod, refusing to say anything else as we spill onto the field. Well, isn't that interesting.

TWENTY-EIGHT

Bibiana

A llie picked me up and we dropped Luis off at Monique's before going to Kasey's to get ready.

I eye the dress Kasey has picked out for me, having flashbacks to the night I first met Emilio. "No." I shake my head and throw the dress back at her.

"Why not?"

Allie plops down on the bed and settles in for the show, already dressed and ready in a red body con dress with long sleeves and a short hemline.

"Because my body is not like your body and I am not going to put every dimple and bulge on display."

Kasey rolls her eyes. "You're right. Your body isn't like mine," she says and my shoulders slump. Ouch. I mean, it's true but still. "It's better. Because you have curves I would kill for but am still a few years away from developing. And you have a rack most girls would die for. So, put on the damn dress."

My brows pull together. "Uh, thanks. But still no."

"Come on, Bibi. Just try it on," Allie pleads.

"I'm serious when I say it's going to look awful. And it's backless. I can't go braless. I will literally leak everywhere."

Kasey's face scrunches up. "Okay. You might have me there." She returns to her closet and flips through the hangers before pulling out a black lace dress with skin colored lining. "Try this one." She tosses me the dress and Allie steps up beside me, fingering the lace.

"This is hella pretty," she says, and I can't help but agree.

"Okay. Give me a minute."

I use Kasey's attached bathroom to slip into the dress. The zipper is on the side, making it easy to get into on my own. I rub my hands down the front, smoothing out any wrinkles as I look at myself in the mirror.

"Woah."

The door opens behind me and Kasey and Allie both step inside.

"Damn," Allie says.

"Told you." The corner of Kasey's mouth lifts into a smirk. "Curves in all the right places."

"Too bad Emilio can't see you like this."

Kasey whips out her phone, her fingers flying over the keyboard. "Oh, he will," she says, right before snapping a picture and sending it to him.

I groan. "I'm pretty sure knowing that this," I wave at myself, "is how I'm going out tonight isn't going to make him happy."

She grins. "I know. Which is exactly why I'm sending it. The guys were already planning on coming over after the game so this will give Emilio a little added encouragement to hurry his ass up."

Allie and I both laugh. "God. The guys aren't wrong. You really do like to stir the pot."

She smirks. "Duh. Hi, I'm Kasey. Have we met?"

There are too many people here. It's loud and the strobe light in the corner of the room is giving me a headache. I might have thought I missed out on the whole party scene since having Luis, but now that I'm here, I'm beginning to think I wasn't really missing out on much of anything.

I check my phone for the hundredth time, knowing Luis is fine. Monique has been sending me updates. It's just that this is his first overnight and it's making me anxious. I've had to run back to Kasey's to pump and dump once already which makes me feel horrible as I pour my liquid gold down the drain. Normally I'd save it, but we're drinking. Or at least Kasey and I am. She suckered me into taking a shot with her before we left, and after being reminded of whose house we're going to, I figured it was necessary. Now that we're here, I know I was right.

Kasey walks through the house like she owns it, making a beeline for the bar covered with booze. "What do you like?" she asks me, and I consider this. I don't drink. I've had the shot at her house—which was disgusting by the way—and I've had a mimosa. Beyond that, my knowledge of alcohol is nil.

"I'm not much of a drinker," I tell her with a shrug.

She rolls her eyes. "Well, you are tonight. I want to have some fun!" she shouts over the music. I glance toward Allie who gives me an expectant look.

"No one is going to make you drink if you don't want to, but how many opportunities do you get to let loose a little?"

I purse my lips. "Okay. One drink." Kasey jumps up and down before turning to the teenage boy manning the bar. He's familiar. From our school, but not someone I've talked to before. She tells him what she wants, and he makes quick work of lining up three red cups and filling them with various liquors before pushing all three toward her. She takes them and hands one to each of us before retrieving her own.

"What is it?" I ask, looking down at the vibrant blue concoction.

"Blue Hawaiian. You'll love it."

I take a tentative sip. Oh. Yum. "That's really good." I take another drink and decide maybe this whole alcohol thing isn't so bad after all. Shots though, I don't need to try those again.

We follow the sound of music to a makeshift dance floor in the middle of the living room and, cups in hand, start dancing to some early two-thousands reggaetón. My hips sway to the beat and I relax a bit.

"So, what's going on with you and Emilio? Are you guys official now?" Kasey asks and Allie smacks her arm.

I take another drink and consider her words. "I mean, I'm not sure. He does this whole caveman thing saying I'm his, but I don't think we have labels or anything. He's never called me his girlfriend or anything like that."

"Do you want to be?" Allie asks, waving a boy off who tries to dance with her.

I shrug and drink a little more. "I don't want to rush into anything. I don't want to mess things up. You know?"

She nods. "Yeah. You have Luis to think about."

Exactly.

"You do realize you're past the whole girlfriend bit, right?" Kasey says. I stare at her and she huffs out a breath. "You have a kid. You can't really date like normal teenagers, so you've basically skipped that part, but you're not *not* a thing. And you're definitely past the whole, this is my boyfriend-girlfriend bit."

"You think so?" I ask, genuinely curious because if I can't figure out what we are exactly, maybe Kasey can shed some light on things for me.

"Absolutely."

The three of us are quick to finish off our drinks and after a second trip to the bar for another blue drink, I'm feeling great. The lights aren't giving me a headache anymore and my body tingles, my cheeks slightly numb.

"You're buzzed," Kasey says, dragging Allie and I back to the dance floor, and I don't deny it. I've never been intoxicated before, but I definitely understand the appeal now. This is pretty fantastic.

TWENTY-NINE

Emilio

"She's trying to get a rise out of you," Dominique says as I stare down at my phone, my jaw tight.

"She's succeeding," I tell him with a shake of my head. Why does Kasey always have to pull this shit? And fuck, why does Bibiana have to look so damn good? I love that dress on her, but I'd love it even more if no one else but me saw her in it. And I'd really like it if it were on the floor and she were naked beside me right now.

I save the picture to my albums because ima need that later, and then I shove my shit in my locker. "Let's roll out," I tell him and he's quick to nod.

"I'm ready." Dominique shoves his gear in the locker and pulls on a clean shirt.

"Shower?" Roman questions with a quirk of his brow.

I send Kasey a text. It's been maybe an hour since she sent the first picture, but knowing Kasey, she'll have her phone on her and respond right away.

Me: Send Roman Allie.

She replies almost instantly with a winking emoji.

Seconds later Roman's phone buzzes and he looks down at the screen. A switch flips and he goes from tired and worn out from our game—which we won, by the way—to tense and ready to throw the fuck down. "What the hell were they thinking?" he bites out and I smirk. He's not too keen on that shower now is he?

"Really? You thought they were what, going to go out to a party in sweats? *Estúpido*." Stupid. I shake my head. "Don't act surprised. But hey, if you wanna take the time to shower..." I trail off as his nostrils flare. "I mean, we could wait. Right, Dom?"

"Fuck that. Let's go get our girls," Rome bites out.

Like I thought.

We roll out in Dominique's Escalade. Roman rides shotgun while I sprawl out in the back seat. Kasey gives me a fucking play by play of their evening with a series of photos, now that she knows she's got our attention, and it's easy to see Bibiana is having a good time. Her smile is bright when Kasey catches her unaware as she dances beside Allie, red Solo cup in hand. Shit. She's drinking. Does she do that? Hell if I know. What if she can't handle her liquor? What if some asshole tries to take advantage of her?

"Should we call Aaron to get his sister?" I ask with feigned innocence, curious to see what Dominique thinks about the idea.

He grunts but doesn't say anything. That's cool, the fucker doesn't have to. I don't miss his hands tightening on the steering wheel, and I swear if it weren't for the fact he's black, he'd have a white-knuckled grip. He isn't fooling anyone. I don't know why he's pretending he doesn't want to fuck Baby Henderson. He's already admitted it before so there's no reason to act disinterested now. Hell, if anything, he should hurry his ass up before he turns eighteen because then shit can get complicated.

Just to piss him off, I dial Aaron's number, putting him on speakerphone so Dominique and Roman can hear.

"What?" he says as soon as the call connects.

"Nice to talk to you too," I deadpan. *Cabrón.* Like he isn't happy to talk to me. We all know I'm the lovable one out of the bunch.

He huffs out a breath. "Kinda busy," he says, and I hear movement in the background.

"Who is it?" a feminine voice asks.

Ooh. Damn. Someone really is busy.

"No one. Go back to the bedroom," he murmurs.

"Yo. Henderson's getting some action, boys."

"OH! Ow. Ow!" Dominique and Roman howl from the front and for a second, it's like old times, before the rift between us all developed. Where we mess with each other and give Aaron shit just for the hell of it. There was a time when I considered him as much family as I do the two fuckers sitting in front of me. I rub at my chest and remind myself we're not cool like that anymore but maybe... maybe Roman has the right of it. Maybe it is time to let that shit go.

Aaron groans, but there's a laugh mixed in there as well. "What do you fuckers want?" I can hear the smile in his voice and don't bother fighting my smirk.

"We're about to go crash a party, but I can see you're indisposed so don't you worry. We'll make sure Kasey's taken real good care of," I joke.

"Stay the fuck away from my sister with your dick, Chavez."

"Woah, woah. I got a girl. It's not me you gotta worry about."

He barks out a laugh. "I better not have to worry about any of you assholes."

I meet Dominique's gaze in the rearview mirror and it clicks. He's not going for Kasey because of Aaron. Interesting. "Alright. Alright. You go get yours. I'm about to go get mine. Talk later, *cabrón*."

I hang up the call just as we pull up to Sarah's place. The lawn is packed with bodies, the streets lined with cars.

"Fuck, this is going to be a nightmare," I groan. How the hell are we going to find the girls in this mess?

Stepping inside, we're immediately overwhelmed by the crush of bodies, loud thumping music, and the strong smell of marijuana. "I'll check the living room and hallway. Go check the kitchen and we'll meet at the bottom of the stairs in ten," Roman grunts over the noise.

"I've got the back," Dominique adds, and we all part ways to see who can find our prey first.

I nod, eager to get this over with. Guys and girls are grinding against one another. Another couple is damn near fucking against a wall for everyone to see, the guy's hands down the girl's pants, and it takes zero imagination to know what he's doing.

I scan the heads around me, looking for Bibiana's raven black hair when I hear my name.

"Emilio!" Sarah squeals, launching herself at me. I stumble back a step before I steady myself and peel her arms from around my neck. Her smile falters at my expression. "Did you come to see me?" she asks, a thread of hope in her voice.

I sigh and shake my head. "You know I'm with Bibiana."

She harrumphs. "Then why are you here?" Sarah flicks her hair over her shoulder before folding her arms across her chest, a move I know she does to draw attention to her chest. Too bad for her I'm not even tempted to take a peek. My girl's got the only tits I'm interested in.

"I'm looking for Bibiana, Kasey, and Allie. Have you seen them?"

Her brows furrows. "Maybe." She hesitates.

"Sarah—" She doesn't miss the warning in my voice. I'm not here to play games.

"Urgh, fine. I think I saw them earlier getting a drink. Come on." She turns around, leaving me no choice but to follow as we make our way through to the crowded kitchen. "Do you want something?" she asks, reaching for a red cup and letting the dude manning the keg fill it for her.

"No," I bite out. "I'm not here to party. I'm grabbing the girls and then leaving."

Her lips press into a tight line. "It's only one drink," she says, holding the cup out to me. A guy crashes into her back and she stumbles forward, her drink spilling down my front. Sonova— My nostrils flare as I stare down at my now beer-soaked shirt.

"I am so sorry," she rushes to say. Sarah sets her now empty cup down and hands me a wad of paper towels. I blot at the mess but it's not going to make a lick of difference. The whole fucking cup caught me.

"Great. I'm going to smell like the beer the rest of the night." Maybe I can convince Bibiana to take a shower with me. I know Monique is keeping Luis for the night and she was going to stay the night at Allie's but maybe we can change that.

Sarah's eyes brighten. "I think I have one of your shirts." She looks away with a shrug. "I mean, if you want it back that is."

My brows pull together and I cock my head to the side, not sure if I believe her or if this is some game she's playing. I don't remember leaving clothes here, but I mean, I guess I could have left a beater or hoodie or something like that.

She rolls her eyes. "Don't act so suspicious. I'm pretty sure you left one here from one of the nights you stayed over. It's upstairs." She heads for the staircase and yet again, I'm forced to follow. But honestly, what choice do I have? While the prospect of convincing Bibiana to take a shower with me is promising, I don't want to wear Sarah's drink for the next thirty minutes or however long it takes for me to find her and then get home.

We make our way upstairs and I stand in the middle of her room as she rummages through her drawers. "Take off your shirt and you can throw it in there if you want." She points toward a laundry basket in the corner. "I'll wash it and bring it to school on Monday."

I hesitate and she huffs out a breath. "Emilio, you're being stupid. I get it. You're seeing someone."

Fine. I peel the shirt off, tossing it in the hamper before moving past her and stepping through the open doorway of her bathroom. I wet a rag and run it over my chest and abs to get off some of the lingering beer off before walking back out into her room.

"Shirt?" I ask.

She holds up a black shirt I vaguely recognize and saunters my way, a little extra swing in her step. And here we go. She places the shirt in my hand, but a second after I accept it, she tosses her arms around my neck and stares up at me, longing in her gaze. Fuck. Her eyes have that glazed look too that says she's probably had one too many drinks herself and is about to do something stupid.

"Sarah—" I warn.

"Come on, Emilio. Weren't we good together?" Her voice is breathy, more of her wannabe porn-star shit and I am not in the mood. "Why don't we have one last round together? For old time's sake," she purrs. "I'll make it good for you."

"I'm seeing someone," I remind her, grinding my teeth together. I hold myself back from shoving her off me which is exactly what I want to do, and instead grip her arms with near bruising force to keep her from climbing my body like I'm a goddamn tree. The feel of her hands on my chest makes me shiver, and not in a good way. I hate the press of her body against mine. It's just... wrong.

Despite my hold on her, she still leans up on tiptoe and presses her lips to my neck, her teeth grazing the column of my throat. "I don't mind sharing anymore," she whispers. "I miss you."

I've had enough. Fuck the shirt. Fuck this shit. I don't want her or anyone else that isn't my girl touching me.

"Sarah—" I growl, but the creak of the door stops me from finishing the sentence as my eyes meet twin pools of anguished blue. "Hey ma—"

She doesn't wait for me to finish. She bolts from the hallway, her slender legs taking her quickly from sight as I shove past Sarah and chase after her. "Bibiana, wait!" I shout after her, but she doesn't stop. Fuck.

I lose sight of her raven-colored hair in the sea of people when we make it to the main part of the house. Shit. Where is she?

I scan the crowd, calling out her name. Several heads turn in my direction—none of whom are her—but I don't give a fuck what people think. I need to find my girl. What she thinks happened didn't and I don't want her worried for even a second longer than she needs to be. Allie is the one who drove so she can't go far on her own. That's the one thing I've got going for me right now.

I pull out my phone, firing off a quick text message and praying she takes the time to read it.

Me: It's not what it looked like. Let me explain.

I stare at the screen for several seconds, willing her to respond.

She doesn't. Shirt still in my hand I throw it on over my head and scan the room again, spotting baby Henderson surrounded by a circle of seniors. Motherfucker. What is she thinking? I make a beeline for her and move to drag her away from her admirers. One of them steps forward to object—some asswipe I recognize from the school's basketball team—but it only takes a second for him to realize who the fuck I am, and he immediately backs off. "Sorry, man. I didn't realize Kasey was Devil property."

"She's not." Kasey tries to wriggle away but I tighten my grip. "But she is my friend's baby sister and she's fourteen. Which makes her too fucking young for you to get your dick wet with." He drops his head, a chastised look on his face. Good. These fuckers need to stop trying to rob fucking cradles.

"Emilio, knock it off," she snaps.

I ignore her, shoving her toward the front door with my hand on the center of her back. "I do not have time for your shit, Kasey. I need you to help me find Bibiana."

She stops struggling and whirls around to face me. "What did you do?" she asks, hands on her hips.

"Nothing." I bite out. "Sarah threw herself at me, but nothing happened. Bibiana doesn't know what she saw."

Her eyes narrow. "I swear to god if you—"

"I didn't do shit," I yell at her, but she doesn't look convinced, and goddamnit if she doesn't believe me how the hell am I going to convince Bibiana?

"Yo," I turn and find Dominique and Roman a few feet away. Allie beside them.

"Either of you seen Bibiana?" All three shake their heads as they move closer. Dominique shifts to Kasey's side, taking a protective stance beside her as his expression screams to every guy within range to back the fuck off.

"No. She was looking for the bathroom before Roman found me. It's been kinda long for that though," Allie says, and I rub the back of my neck.

"Would she have gone to your place?" I ask Kasey. Desperation bleeds into my voice. Where is she?

She shakes her head. "I don't think so."

"Fuck."

"Hey," Allie says, stepping closer. "What's going on? What happened?"

I run my hands through my hair. "Nothing, but Bibiana thinks something did. I just need to find her."

She reaches out and places a hand on my arm. "Take a breath. We will. Let me call her."

I nod, my gaze still scanning the room in case I catch sight of her. Allie dials her number, but then pulls the phone away from her ear to frown down at the screen. "What—"

"One sec. She sent me a text."

I move to peer over her shoulder as she reads it aloud.

Bibi: Catching a ride home. Sorry. I'll explain later.

I rush out the front door. Who the hell would she get a ride with? Everyone who's fucking trustworthy is right here with me. I don't want some random asshole trying to take advantage of her. If she's leaving though, then she has to be outside somewhere. I ask a few of the kids I recognize if they've seen her when I spot her curly hair in the dark cutting her way through the crowd. Relief floods through me. I take a step forward, and then notice that she's veered straight for the bright red car sitting in Kasey's driveway. One I know doesn't belong to either Henderson.

I squint. "You have got to be kidding me," I curse, heading toward them when the driver comes into view. He is someone I immediately recognize and someone I do not want anywhere near Bibiana right now. Not when she's pissed. Probably hurt over what she thinks she saw. Fucking Jae. Can't this guy just disappear or something?

"Bibiana!" I shout her name and she spins, her face red and splotchy in the moonlight, wet trails running down her cheeks as she stumbles a bit before regaining her footing. My chest tightens. Shit. I did this. "Mariposa, please. Talk to me." The endearment rolls off my tongue, but as soon as she hears it, she flinches as though struck.

I'm almost to her but she manages to swing open the car door, climbing inside and shutting it quickly behind her. I slam my palm against the glass and lift the door handle, but it's locked. "Momma, open the door." She won't look at me. I can tell from their mouths moving that she and the fucker inside are arguing about something, but I can't hear their words. I can feel her slipping through my fingers. If she leaves right now without talking to me, without hearing me out, I know deep down in my gut that we're done. I don't know how I know that, but it's a visceral feeling I can't shake.

I need her to open the door. Now.

THIRTY

Bibiana

A text message flashes across my screen.

Allie: Stay. I'll take you home if you don't want to see Emilio but you should hear him out. I don't think he did what you think he did.

My fingers fly over the illuminated screen as tears track down my face. Of course she would take his side.

Me: I know what I saw.

He had his shirt off, his hands holding her to him as she sucked on his neck like a goddamn vampire. So, no. I do not want to hear him out. I don't want to ever talk to him again. Urgh! I press the backs of my hands to my eyes.

Nothing can excuse what he did. What he was about to do. God, I am so stupid. I thought I meant more to him. I thought that the flirting and whatever at school was unintentional. Like maybe he didn't realize what it looked like. I tried to brush it off, but this, I can't ignore this, and god does that hurt. I thought—I thought maybe he wanted to build a life with me. That we could be a family—him, me and Luis. But I was wrong and now I feel sick. Nausea twists and turns in my gut as I buckle my seat belt.

"Can we leave?" I ask Jae, ignoring the look of concern on his face.

Emilio never cared about me. I was convenient. Easy. A heavy weight presses down on my chest as I realize just how insignificant I am to him. Was this all just a ploy to hurt me? Was any of these past few weeks real?

I shake my head, the alcohol making my head spin.

"Bibi—"

I groan and press my head against my seat. "I'm crying. I'm drunk. And my boyfriend or baby daddy or whatever the hell he is supposed to be was with another girl so for the love of God, can we please leave!" My voice is shrill in the car and I don't even care. I can't—my chest heaves and I begin to hyperventilate.

"Are you okay?"

No. I am not okay. I'm pretty sure that's obvious right now, but I don't say that.

"Open the door," Emilio shouts, knocking on the window, startling me as he tries to pry the door open with brute force. Good luck with that. "Mariposa, please. Talk to me."

My upper lip curls at that single word. I am not his butterfly. I am not his anything. I turn to face him and suck in a shaking breath. "Leave me alone!" I scream loud enough for him to hear me.

His hand is still holding the door handle as if he can stop the car from leaving. His nostrils flare and he gives one firm shake of his head. "We need to talk. You can't just run away from—"

"Fuck you, Emilio!" I flip him off. I don't care that it's childish. He deserves it. "Leave me the hell alone." Angry tears spill down my cheeks and I hate myself for them. Hate that I can't lock up my emotions right now. "Why can't I stop freaking crying," I complain out loud, and Jae squeezes my knee.

"It's okay," he says.

Emilio shouts, "Dammit, Bibiana. Nothing happened!"

I want to believe him. Believe he would never throw what we have away, but I know what I saw, and I refuse to let him make a fool out of me. How long has this been going on? Did he ever stop seeing her? Has he been fooling around with her behind my back this entire time?

"Drive Jae."

"Are you sure? If you need to talk to him—"

"Just drive!"

His face is tight with worry, but he nods and puts the car in reverse, backing out of Kasey's driveway.

"Bibi, please—" Emilio's voice cracks.

I can't look at him. Not when it feels like my entire world is crashing down around me. They say when you lose the one you love, your heart breaks. But it isn't only my heart that hurts. My chest aches, my breaths are ragged and shallow. I didn't realize just how much I cared about him before, but the weight of my feelings slam into me like a Mac truck and I feel like I'm going to have a panic attack if I have to look at him even a second longer.

Is this what he wanted? To hurt me? To see me fall apart? To know he owned my heart and then throw it away?

Emilio chases us out of the driveway, panic written all over his face. "Don't do this! It's a misunderstanding. A fucking misunderstanding," he shouts. But I'm done listening.

Jae peels down the street, finally putting some much-needed distance between us. I see Emilio come to a stop in the rearview mirror, arms at his sides and a hopeless expression on his face as he stands in the middle of the street. I stare at him as his figure gets smaller and smaller. The hole in my chest growing wider and wider.

We turn a corner, and as soon as he's out of sight, the tears come faster. Angry, hurt, confused sobs wrack my body, making my chest heave and my shoulders shake.

I bury my face in my hands, a keening sound escaping my lips. Jae pulls over on the side of the road and I hear him unbuckle both our seatbelts before shoving his seat back as far as it will go and dragging me into his lap. His arms wrap around me and he holds me tight in a fierce embrace. "It's going to be okay," he tells me, but I have no reason to believe him. No part of what happened tonight feels like it will ever be okay.

"You've been drinking, B. Things might look different in the morning," he tells me.

I don't bother responding. He wasn't there. He doesn't know anything.

I don't know how long we sit there on the side of the road, but eventually my sobs subside, leaving behind a gaping pit in my chest. "I'm sorry," I tell him when I can form words again. "I didn't mean to drag you into this. I just—"

"Don't apologize. I'm here. For whatever you need. I'll always be here, okay?"

I nod against his chest, taking a few precious seconds to pull myself together before I lift my head from his chest and climb over the center console, taking my seat again. I wipe the tears from my face and suck in a shuddering breath. Get it together, I tell myself and decide here and now that I will be fine. I've been through a lot. I'm strong. I'm independent. And I can do this on my own. I've already proven that. I don't need Emilio to be whole. Brick by brick I will put myself back together. I won't become my mother. I won't settle for a man who doesn't really love me.

THIRTY-ONE

Emilio

S he won't take my calls. I know she moved in with Jae, but I don't know where the fuck that even is. She picked Luis up this morning. Dominique called to let me know she showed up at his place, but I wasn't able to make it there fast enough to intercept her and Monique refused to tell him what time she was coming for me to plan ahead. Fuck. I should have just showed up at seven this morning and waited. That would have been the smart thing to do. The creeper-stalker thing too, but I could live with that.

The girls are locking down hard. Even Allie is vague-booking shit. Telling me to give Bibiana space. That she just needs time to think.

No, the fuck she doesn't because all she's doing is thinking about shit that never fucking happened. Giving her time and space right now is not going to help me in the least. It's only going to make shit worse.

"Take a breath," Allie says, handing me a cup of something warm. Cocoa by the looks of the mug. I accept the drink and take a sip, immediately recognizing the spiced flavor of Abuela's hot chocolate, but I barely taste it. Everything feels bland to my senses, my world a colorless haze of gray.

I take another drink, hoping the warmth will seep into my bones and calm me down, but it does nothing for me. My leg won't stop bouncing. My mind is racing a mile a minute trying to come up with a way to win my girl back. If I could just talk to her...

"Emilio?"

I look up from my cup.

"Whatever you're thinking, stop. It's not that bad." Allie says, dropping down into Roman's lap and leaning against him. We're all sitting in their living room—Dominique, Roman, Allie and I, as I try to come up with a plan, but so far, I've got nothing.

I scrape my bottom lip through my teeth and shake my head. "You don't know that. You didn't see the look on her face when she left—"

"She thinks you cheated. That this probably isn't the first time," Allies admits as if I don't know that already, but hearing it aloud pisses me right the fuck off.

"I didn't cheat!" I snap at her, shoving to my feet. "I never cheated. Not once."

Roman glowers at me. "Calm the fuck down and don't yell at her," he bites out.

Dominique's hand on my shoulder stops me from stepping closer and instead I sit back down, my shoulders slumping in defeat. "I didn't fucking cheat. I told you guys what happened. I wouldn't—"

"We know," Allie says. "And we believe you. Just... give her some time. Right now, she's hurt and—"

"She doesn't need to be. If she would just talk to me. Let me explain. I could fix this."

Allie nods her head, a solemn look in her dark brown eyes. "I know. But she asked for some space. You need to give her that. Let her realize her mistake on her own terms. Don't push her or you'll end up pushing her away. You have a visit with Luis tomorrow, right? It won't kill you to wait one more day to see her."

I tighten my jaw. *It might.*

I hate that I'm using the visit too. I want to see my boy. I have the right to. But I won't lie. I'm one hundred percent leveraging that against her as a way to make her see me. The only communication I've had from Bibiana since last night is a text saying she'll send me the address to Jae's tomorrow an hour before my scheduled time to pick up Luis. That was it. This wasn't even supposed to be our first one-on-one visit. I was going to hang out with her. With them. But I guess she's pissed enough to rush our timeline along. I should be happy about that. I get my boy. But, fuck. I want her too.

She won't even leave her phone on long enough for me to respond. I can't lose her. The thought alone has me feeling paralyzed. Helpless. There's this ache in my chest that won't subside. I don't want to be without her. She's...she's everything. I won't lose her. Not over something like this.

My palms are sweating. I'm picking up my kid from another dude's house. One who I'm sure is enjoying playing house with what is mine.

"Emilio, you need to calm down," Dominique, the voice of reason, says beside me in the passenger seat. Roman and Aaron are sitting in the back, the three of them having collectively decided I couldn't be trusted to handle this on my own. "If Bibiana sees you like this, no way in hell is she letting you leave with Luis."

My lip curls and I scowl at him, flicking on my turn signal as I take a left at the stop sign. "He's my kid," I remind them.

Dom snorts. "Like that fucking matters. Bibi is going to see you and go full on momma bear. Remember what happened the night you found out Luis was yours? She didn't cave to you then and she won't cave to you now. Take a breath. Chill."

I do as he instructs, but the tension riding me keeps me stiff. She's been avoiding my calls. Avoiding me. And now, picking my kid up like this, none of it sits well with me. We pull up to the address she gave me, and I immediately spot Jae's car. I figured he'd be here. It is the fucker's house after all, but she could have at least—I don't know—asked him to leave for a little bit.

I tighten my grip on the steering wheel for a second before I force myself to open the door and step outside. "Breathe," Aaron tells me. "You've got this." The walk to the front porch feels like I'm heading to a funeral, but I have a plan. I just have to keep my eye on the prize. I ramp myself up as if I'm about to step on the field. I've got this.

All I gotta do is explain what actually happened the other night. Make her listen. Once she knows, she'll understand. I get why she's hurt. Angry. Hell, if I thought she stepped out on me I'd be pissed too. But this is nothing. We can get past it. I'm sure of it. I take a deep breath. Stick to the plan.

I knock three times on the door before it swings open and it's Jae's face that greets me.

"Hey," he says in way of greeting and opens the door wider, taking me by surprise. I figured he'd posture or some shit. Try and knock me down a few pegs. He picked her up from the party. He saw what a mess she was. I'm sure she's told him what she thought happened, so I expected anger from him. Or maybe satisfaction. But I get none of that. Just mild resignation.

Despite the greeting, I shake my head. I don't want to go inside. I don't want to be anywhere near this fucker because I am two seconds from going off and slamming my fist into his face. *Breathe,* I remind myself. He can downplay whatever he'd like, but I know he wants my girl and I'm sure he'll use this situation to his advantage. If I were in his shoes, I would.

My worry from last night has morphed into righteous anger. I need someone to take it out on and unfortunately for me, it can't be him.

"Where's Bibiana?"

He sighs and disappears down the hallway leaving the door open for me to follow. I don't. But I can't stop myself from looking around, my eyes taking in the scattered toys and Bibiana's backpack near the door. She's made herself right at home.

A few seconds later she appears, Luis in her arms and a diaper bag hanging over her shoulder. My chest tightens when I see her. Her hair is pulled back into a ponytail and her face is bare, showcasing the dark circles under her eyes. She's beautiful, but those signs of exhaustion worry me.

"Can we talk?" I ask, itching to reach for her, but instead I shove my hands in my pockets and wait.

"Is it about Luis?" she asks, dodging the question with one of her own.

I shake my head. "No. It's about us."

"There isn't an us anymore, Emilio. I think it would be best if we kept our communication centered around our son." Her tone is clipped, without an ounce of emotion in it, but I don't miss the clenching of her jaw.

I bite the inside of my cheek and glance at Jae who is hovering a few steps away. I don't want to have this conversation with him watching, but I can't very well tell him to leave either. And despite what she wants, we're going to talk.

I shift my gaze back to Bibiana, careful to keep my tone calm, soothing even. I don't want to tick her off and I don't want to make a scene in front of Luis. I know he's little. Doesn't understand what we're saying all the time. But I remember my parents fighting in front of me as a kid. That isn't something I ever want to do in front of my son. "It isn't what you think. I didn't—"

"I know." Still holding my gaze, she shakes her head. "I know what happened. I know you didn't cheat on me."

"You do?" Relief crashes over me and my shoulders relax. I take a step forward about to reach for her when she leans away. My arms fall back to my sides. If she knows, then why is she still being like this? My heart squeezes in my chest. What am I missing?

"I talked to Allie. And Kasey. And Aaron." She sighs. "I didn't have much of a choice since they just kept calling and calling, but yeah, I heard about the beer. The shirt. That you pushed Sarah away. I know all of that."

If all that's true then—

"But," she takes a deep breath, "I still can't be with you. Not like that."

Wait. What? "Why the hell not?" I snap my teeth together to bite back the rest of my words, knowing I'll say something I'll regret.

Moisture pools in the corners of her eyes, but she blinks it away before holding her arms out to hand Luis to me, her movements stiff, almost robotic. I take him, careful to support his weight as she hands me his diaper bag. "Because the other night made me realize a few things I hadn't stopped to consider."

I flick my gaze between her and Luis and wait. He smiles, showcasing the two bottom teeth he has, and I take a second to properly greet him. "You ready to spend the day with your old man?" He gurgles and jabbers, swinging his arms and kicking his feet.

Bibiana remains quiet, so I decide to push.

"Like what?"

"I don't trust you."

Ouch. I mean, that much was already clear with how she reacted, but hearing it aloud is still like a knife to the gut.

"But—"

She raises a hand. "Let me finish."

I give her a stiff nod, clinging to my son like a lifeline.

Bibiana's chest rises and falls with her breaths and she turns to Jae for a moment. He gives her a nod of encourage and that alone makes my hackles rise. What is he encouraging her to do here, exactly?

"Luis needs to come first, always."

"He does."

"But he won't if we're fighting. I don't want to risk burning bridges with you. We're both young. A relationship would have never worked out between us. Not long-term."

"You don't know that," I bite out. She's refused to give this a real chance, fighting me every step of the way. She didn't want to get married. Didn't want to fucking date. I don't even know what to call what we've been doing, but even that was half-assed on her part.

But before I can say any of that she continues, "Seeing you with Sarah the other night made me hate you. It made me want to hurt you and the best way to do that is with him." She nods toward Luis. "I don't want to be that person. I don't ever want to use him against you or have him used against me. He isn't some bargaining chip and I hate myself for even considering it."

Air freezes in my lungs as her words hit their mark and my eyes narrow. She folds her arms across her chest and looks away. A single tear slips past her defenses and she hastily wipes it away.

"We can't afford to be at one another's throats. We can't feud and fight. This can't be messy. We have a child together and that's complicated enough. Trying to date, to be whatever it is that you want, it just makes an already complicated situation worse. I think for both our sakes, we need to focus on being co-parents. Not—not anything more."

I stand there, stunned. I expected her anger. Her fury and hatred even. But I was prepared to fight for her. To convince her of my innocence. Now, I don't know what to do. My mind is left reeling. She knows I didn't cheat but she still doesn't want me. I'm not worth the effort, I guess. Not worth her time. And that she even considered keeping Luis from me...

I bite the inside of my cheek harder until blood pools in my mouth, the metallic taste grounding me.

She clears her throat. "Everything you'll need should be in the bag, but if it isn't, call me."

I nod my head.

"He ate about thirty minutes ago so he should be okay for at least another hour."

I nod again.

"Oh, and he's happy and awake now but he usually takes his second nap around two, so you'll notice he'll start to get crabby. His *chupeta*"—pacifier— "is in the right-side pocket and his blanket is in the large compartment. He won't sleep without both of them."

I know all of this already, having picked most of it up during our time together, but I let her run through her list before she tells Luis goodbye.

"Alright. I guess we'll be on our way."

"Okay."

Fuck. Fine. This is not how I planned shit to go. I turn and take two steps towards the SUV when Bibi calls out, "Wait," and I freeze thinking maybe she's changed her mind. Maybe—

She rushes to me and gives Luis a quick kiss on the cheek, running her hand lovingly over his hair. "Okay." She seems to gather herself. "Have a great time together. And if you need—"

"Bibi..."

She pauses. "I know. I'm sorry. I'm not changing my mind. It's your day with him." She visibly swallows. "I know he's safe with you. Just ignore me."

"I'll bring him back at seven."

Another nod. "Okay. Thanks." She gives me a forced smile and this time when I turn to leave, she doesn't stop me.

Fuck. I wish she did.

THIRTY-TWO

Bibiana

Watching Emilio leave with Luis is torture. Not only because my heart is breaking or because it's hard sharing Luis, but also because any thoughts I had of the three of us being a family, a real family, have been shattered.

Hope—that one word means so much, and I now have none of it.

We're not a couple anymore. I don't know that we ever really were. What we are is co-parents. Two people who need to navigate parenting our child responsibly as a unit.

I watched the videos. Read the books. Listened to the podcasts about effective co-parenting. Anything I could get my hands on this weekend, I binged it. And the biggest take away from them all was how complicated having a romantic relationship with the other parent is. How detrimental it can be to your child's well-being if things don't work out. How it's safest and often best to just shelf any ideas of a romance and focus on your child's needs. So that's what I'm going to do.

Luis has to come first. Always.

I won't lie, I'm relieved Emilio didn't cheat. Relieved he wasn't hooking up with Sarah Draven or anyone else all this time behind my back. Truly, I am. But, this is for the best. Even if it sucks. Even if it feels like my insides are being ripped out of my chest. The pain will go away eventually, right? I mean, it has to. Isn't that how the saying goes? Everything gets better with time? That's all I need. More time.

School is strange the following week. Allie is still my friend. So are Kasey and Aaron, but things are noticeably different. I arrive to school on time as usual and take Luis with me to first period. Like the other days before, Dominique greets me once the bell rings and takes Luis for second since he has a non-schedule.

"Everything good?" he asks. And while innocent enough, it feels like a loaded question.

I force a smile past my lips. "Yeah. Great."

His dark brown eyes drill into me and I can see the word *liar* hanging in the air between us. Thankfully, he keeps it to himself.

"I'll see you at lunch."

I swallow hard and nod, wondering if maybe I should just keep Luis. This is awkward, to say the least. I don't want him to feel obligated to help me especially now that Emilio and I aren't well anything.

"I… umm… you don't have—"

He shakes his head. "Whatever is going on with you and E, that's between you two. It doesn't affect me helping out."

My shoulders sag. "Are you sure?"

He nods and without another word, turns and heads for the library, Luis safe and snug in his arms.

Kasey approaches me on the way to my next class, her expression more subdued than usual. "You doing okay?" she asks, linking her arm with mine. I wish people would stop asking me that.

"As good as can be expected," I tell her, which is the truth.

"You know, you don't have—"

I cut her off. "Yeah, I do. You know I do."

Her lips press into a tight line.

"Kasey, you know how he is with girls. They throw themselves at him every chance they get." And that fear, that doubt, isn't something I can make go away. It will eat at my self-confidence. It will tear at the threads of any relationship we attempt. I'm insecure and I know it. I look at these girls with their perfect looks, perfect bodies, and know I don't compare. Not when my stomach is soft, my skin loose and stretch marks streak across my skin. They're in their prime and I'm, well, not.

Her expression is tight, but she nods. "I know, and I know I've always given him hell for being a player but"—she hesitates—"he was at my house this weekend."

I frown. "What for?" I know he and Aaron are friends, but they don't strike me as close. The relationship between Aaron and the other guys seem to mainly exist because of Allie's influence and maybe Roman's acceptance, though I've never outright asked.

A shrug. "I don't really know to be honest. All the Devils came over and hung out for a bit before going to pick up Luis from you." She bites her bottom lip. "I wasn't supposed to be eavesdropping but...."

When she pauses, my chest tightens, almost like my body is bracing itself for her next words. The urge to shake her and make her tell me everything is whirling through me like a storm, but I force myself to inhale, take a deep breath, exhale. Let it go. It doesn't matter what was said. It doesn't matter if he's upset or relieved or anything. I made my decision. This is for the best.

I squeeze her arm. "It's okay. You don't have to tell me." My smile is forced, but I keep the expression until we reach the door to my next class. "I gotta go, but we'll talk later."

"Oh." Her nose scrunches. "Are you sure?"

"Yup. Don't worry about it."

I wave and go into class, counting my steps as I go. *This is for the best*, I remind myself for what feels like the one hundredth time. It has to be.

Lunch is weird, but what did I expect? Emilio takes Luis as soon as Dominique arrives, and I let him. It's what we agreed to. He isn't coming over every day anymore, so we agreed he could have Luis at lunch and during fourth. He's also picking him up twice a week on Tuesdays and Thursdays. We haven't worked up to overnights yet and I'm thankful for that. I don't know when or if I'll be ready for that step anytime soon, and like we'd agreed before everything unfolded, he's letting me set the pace. I get to make the big decisions and he's not pushing for more than I can give where Luis is concerned.

Dominique, Roman, and Emilio are on one side of the lunch table. Kasey and I on the other. With Aaron and Allie in the middle, acting as a divider between our two groups. The division doesn't go by unnoticed, and already people are starting to look and whisper.

"So, this Thursday," Kasey hedges, "You're sure you want—"

"Yes!" I say, hoping to cut her off before the boys overhear us. I lower my voice to keep our conversation private. "I need the job and I'm really grateful you were willing to talk to your aunt for me."

She smiles and nods her head, blond curls bouncing with the movement.

Kasey's aunt runs the Sun Valley Station, a local diner Allie works at and that Kasey sometimes helps with. Kasey doesn't need a job, nor does she particularly want one, so she was more than happy to put in a good word for me if it meant getting her out of picking up the vacant shifts. It's only two days a week—Thursdays when Luis is with Emilio, and then on Sundays. Monique has offered to watch him anytime I need the help and I gratefully accepted the offer, but I know I need to give Emilio the option first. If roles were reversed, I'd want the option of more time with my son before leaving him with a sitter, even if it was a friend. Co-parenting the right way. Right?

"Okay, then I guess just show up on time and you're all set. Allie works this week so she can show you the ropes."

"Sounds good."

A girl walks up to our table, a determined look on her face. She has a little extra swing in her step and her entire focus is zeroed in on Emilio. She reaches him and says something, but I can't make out the words. She laughs. I look away, but still track their movements in my peripheral. Emilio turns his head to look at me. I can't make out his facial expression but having Kasey close by means I don't have to.

"I think he's gauging your reaction," she whispers low enough for only me to hear.

I sigh hard and shrug. "I don't know why. He can do whatever he wants. He doesn't have to worry about my feelings." I force a smile and climb to my feet. "Thanks again for talking to your aunt."

"Don't thank me yet. I've helped out before and it's no walk in the park. Half the clientele are students and they're mostly assholes so, just try not to let anything get to you. Okay?"

Despite myself, I chance a glance back at Emilio. The girl is gone but he's staring at a small piece of paper in his hands, his expression serious. A phone number. Figures.

"No worries. I'm becoming a master at not letting things get to me."

THIRTY-THREE

Emilio

We've been *co-parenting*, as Bibiana likes to call it, for three weeks now. Torture is a more accurate term if you ask me. Football season is officially over now that we took state, so I don't have anything to occupy my free time with. I considered getting a job, but my brothers shut that idea down real quick. They want me focused on school and Luis. When I argued—because hell, we have bills and I'll be damned if I don't pay my way around here—they informed me Raul had a life insurance policy. Surprise, surprise. Guess the POS was good for something. I guess he and our mom set something up when things were still good between them, and Roberto's made it a point to keep up on the monthly premiums. That right there was thinking ahead.

There was a decent chunk of change there that the four of us decided to split five ways. One portion went to living expenses. It paid off the house and will cover the utilities for at least the next few months. The rest we each put into individual bank accounts for later use. I have no clue what Roberto or Antonio will do with theirs. I still don't really know what Roberto's plans are now that he's back stateside. But Sofia says she's saving for college. Smart girl. And I gave most of mine to Bibiana.

She fought me at first. Didn't want to take it. She said it was too much. But if you ask me, the ten grand I gave her wasn't enough. I had to remind her we agreed I'd pay child support. I wasn't there in the beginning and I didn't have much to give when she came back. This was the least I could do to make sure she and my boy are taken care of. It took some convincing, but when I threatened to have the janitor open her locker and leave it there, she finally took it.

I don't need the money. I have a full ride to Suncrest U. I can live here or in the dorms, it makes no difference to me, and my scholarship will cover my day-to-day expenses once school starts. I was worried about supporting Luis before, but this makes it easier, and if she needs more, I'll give it to her. I'd give that girl anything, even if all it does is make her more comfortable. She's still living with Jae and who the fuck knows how long that will be for, but I don't have a say in the matter. Even if I think I should. With any luck the money will help her get her own place sooner rather than later.

She got a job too. Part time at a local diner. I thought she might quit once I gave her the money, but she didn't, and every chance she gets to pick up a shift, she takes it, not that I can complain. It means more time with my boy, but I can see it wearing on her. She doesn't smile as much, and there are always dark circles under her eyes.

Because of school she works the closing shift and the diner is open till midnight most nights and then classes start at seven thirty. She isn't getting enough sleep. Isn't taking care of herself. And it grates on me that I can't be the one to take care of her.

I miss seeing her and Luis after school every day. And now, I have nothing but time on my hands to sit and dwell on how much I hate this arrangement.

"You wanna grab a bite to eat?" Antonio asks, poking his head in my room. "Roberto and I are taking Sofia to the station."

I shake my head. "Nah, man. I'm good. Not hungry." My stomach decides to call me a liar and rumble.

He frowns. "You sure?"

I nod again. "Yeah, man. I'm good." I'm not great company right now, and I don't need to dampen on my family's good mood. We got the call earlier from social services that they were closing Sofia's case. Roberto is old enough, responsible enough, and has his shit together as a retired vet to be trusted with the welfare of our baby sister. It's good news. I should be with them celebrating but I just—I can't get my mind in the right head space for it.

"Alright. Let us know if you change your mind." With that he leaves, and I do exactly what I've been doing this past week. Think. But no matter how much I analyze my problem, I still can't find a fucking solution. This isn't like a mathematical equation with only one answer. There are too many variables and my brain struggles to figure them all out, but three weeks is three weeks too long. Something needs to give.

My phone pings beside me and I check the screen. A somewhat familiar number flashes and against my better judgement, I answer it. "Hello."

"Hey, E—" A breathy voice says on the other end of the line.

I roll my eyes at the ceiling and throw myself down on my bed. "What do you want?"

There's a pause. "It's me. Kaitlyn."

"And?" I ask. Is her name supposed to mean something to me? I know at least four Kaitlyns. Five if you count Sofia's friend, but I'm pretty sure she isn't the one calling me. There's a different girl hitting me up damn near every day. At first I played along. I wanted to see if it made Bibiana jealous. I wanted to know if she cared. But all it took was the one time I caught hurt on her face for me to put an end to that. Only now, I can't get the girls to back off.

"So, I was thinking, umm, there's this party."

"Pass," I say and hang up the phone, dropping it on the comforter beside me. Rolling to my feet I head for the kitchen, ignoring the buzz of my phone as another call comes in. Leave a voicemail, or don't. Either way, I'm not answering and I'm not calling any of these chicks back.

I'm almost to the refrigerator when there's a knock at the door that stops me. It sounds again. You've got to be kicking me. They're showing up at my house now? This is going too far. I clench my teeth and storm to the door, jerking it open only to be greeted by the one asshole I definitely do not want to see. Not today. Not tomorrow. Not fucking ever.

"What are you doing here?" I bite out, hands fisted at my sides.

Jae stands there like the smug bastard he is. Dressed in black jeans, a white shirt so long it reaches mid-thigh, and a black beanie he glowers at me, almost like he's just as unhappy to see me as I am to see him.

I lean against the doorjamb with zero plans to welcome him inside. "Well?"

His lips tighten and a muscle jumps in his jaw. "I'm here for Bibiana," he says, and I fold my arms over my chest. Right. Because she would totally send this asshole to come find me.

I straighten. Wait. What if she did send him to find me? What if something happened? To her or to Luis. "What happened?" The words barely make it out of my mouth before I'm grabbing my keys off the counter and brushing past him.

He jogs to keep up. "Where are you going?" he asks, irritation in his voice.

"To Bibiana. What happened? Is she hurt? Is Luis—"

"No. They're both fine."

I pull up short. "Then why the fuck are you here?"

He exhales a harsh breath. "I'm here because she isn't and because someone needs to talk some goddamn sense into you."

I bark out a laugh. Oh. This is rich.

"Why the fuck do you care?" I swear it's like I can't catch a fucking break. All week I've had to watch my girl from a distance. I've had to pretend I'm fine with this situation when I'm anything but. I've had to watch her get out of this asshole's car every goddamn morning only to climb back into it at the end of the day. And he's here to what? Rub it in my face that Bibiana doesn't want me anymore? That she was pissed off about something I didn't even do and decided to make decisions that don't only affect her life, they affect mine. *Fuck.* This is bullshit.

"Fuck off. I have nothing to say to you." I turn to storm back to my front door.

His eyes narrow and he takes two steps forward, blocking my way and shoving his finger into my chest. It takes everything in me not to swing for his face. The guy has some fucking nerve showing up while he's moving in on what's mine. And no one can convince me that that isn't exactly what he's doing.

"Fuck me? Really. God, you're such a child. Grow the hell up, man."

My nostrils flare. "Get out of my way."

"Not until you hear me out."

"Why? Nothing you have to say means anything to me. Your opinions are lower than shit as far as I'm concerned, so go crawl back to whatever hole you came out of and leave me the hell alone. You already got the girl. What else could you possibly want from me?"

"God, are you hearing yourself? You're so fucking selfish."

"Excuse me?"

He advances on me. "You heard me. You're selfish. All you're thinking about is how this affects you. Woe is me. Poor Emilio didn't get the girl. How sad." He sneers. "Do you have any idea what Bibiana is dealing with right now?"

"Don't act like you care—"

"I don't. Not about you. But I care about her. I care about Luis."

I snort. "Right. You care so much that—"

"That I went out of my way to talk to the last person I want in their lives. The one person who can take them away from me. Yeah, asshole. That's how much I care, so shut the fuck up and listen."

My jaw snaps shut at his words. I bite the inside of my cheek until I taste blood and wait for him to say whatever it is he came here to say. I'm in no mood to deal with this guy, but he doesn't look like he's going to leave until he says his peace.

"That girl has been through hell, and you don't even know the half of it."

"But you do? Is that it?" I shake my head. If this is some twisted ploy to—

"Shut up! God. You are so goddamn arrogant. Are you too fucking proud to see what you're about to lose?"

My lip curls into a snarl. "I already lost her, or haven't you heard?" I cock my head to the side. What's this guy's end game? Is he here to gloat? Does this little chat earn him brownie points or some shit? So he can go back to tell my girl that he put me in my place. Is that it?

"I can't believe you're this dense. That girl *loves* you."

My heart skips a beat before kicking back into overdrive. I school my expression, refusing to let this fucker see just what hearing those words does to me. I pop my knuckles. Maybe I will punch him after all. If he thinks he can come over here and dangle that shit in my face—lie to me about something so important and get away with it. Nah. Not fucking happening, *cabrón*. Not today.

I'm about to tell him exactly how I feel about what he's doing, but he just keeps on talking, oblivious to the rage brewing inside me.

"You need to man up and fight for her."

"She told me to back off," I remind him, knowing full well he was eavesdropping when she and I spoke.

"*Porca puttana!*" he curses.

"What the hell does that mean?"

He glares at me. His eyes little more than slits. "*For fuck's sake*," he grinds out. "It's Italian."

"I don't know if anyone told you, but you're Asian."

He stares up at the sky as if answers are going to fall from it.

"젠장, happy?"

Whatever he said sounded like *jenjang*. "Cool, you speak Italian and Chinese. Bravo. Are we showing off now?"

His jaw flexes. "I'm not Chinese, asshole. I'm half Korean, half Italian. Not Asian. Not Chinese." He mutters something under his breath that is probably more swearing, not that I care. "Do you like being called Hispanic?"

My chest puffs up, but then I realize what he's doing. *Fucker*. "Point made."

He grunts.

"Look, I don't have all day and you're not exactly the company I want in my face right now so if you've got something else to say, get on with it."

He scowls and shakes his head. "I don't know why I'm wasting my time."

Cool. Leave then. I don't know why he's wasting his time either. I sure as hell didn't ask for him to come here. He looks like he's about to do exactly that, but then he hesitates.

"You know she had a baby brother?" he asks, and while no, I didn't, what does that have to do with anything?

"He died when he was a kid. She named Luis after him. His middle name."

My brows pull together. *Afonso.* I just figured it was a name she liked or maybe her dad's or something. I don't know. I never thought to ask. But thinking about it now, why didn't I know this?

"After her brother died, her dad left. Couldn't handle the grief, so he bailed."

My jaw locks. Seems we have that in common. Our parents take off when the going gets tough.

"And now, her mom has all but forgotten about her. She's so afraid to be alone again that she's put on rose-colored glasses and can't even see the monster she's throwing her daughter away for."

I suck in a breath. "Why are you telling me all this?" I'm not complaining. I want to know these things about Bibiana's life, but it grates on my nerves that he's known all these things about her and I never even had a clue. I know shit is strained with her mom. It's why she brings Luis to school. But I figured they'd work it out. Bibiana said they were close. Her mom had always been there for her. You'd think she'd snap out of trying to save her rapist boyfriend eventually or at least be a fucking parent.

"So you can get it through your thick head that in her mind, you're already fucking gone. It's always been a forgone conclusion." He tugs off his beanie and runs his hands through his hair, forgetting that it's tied back in a top knot and messing up whatever style he was going for. K-pop wannabe or some shit.

"You're not making any sense."

"Everyone leaves," he tells me. "Her brother died. Her dad left. He mom has all but abandoned her. Everyone leaves that girl eventually, whether by choice or circumstance. She might not admit it, but in the back of her mind, she knew you'd bail. That's why she jumped to the wrong conclusions. Why she pushed you away even after she knew the truth. She's just been waiting for you to leave and right now, you're proving her right."

I bite my lower lip and suck my teeth as a lead weight settles deep in my gut. My own baggage comes back to punch me in the face, and I realize I'm doing to Bibiana what I expected her to do to me all this time—give up.

My nostrils flare. "So you think she *wants* me to fight for her? Despite that being the exact opposite of what she told me she wanted."

"I know she wants you to fight for her. She's miserable. A shell of the girl she used to be."

We're both damaged. Broken beyond repair. Neither of us willing to trust the other enough to make this work but.... I stumble back a few steps and look around, for what, I'm not sure. I just—my brain is moving a mile a minute. Think, Emilio. Think. Everyone leaves. But, what if they didn't have to? What if we could be the missing piece to fill each other's broken spaces?

I've been going at this all wrong. Fuck what everyone else has been telling me. She never needed space. She needed me to push. To not stop pushing. But I did stop. I stopped for three fucking weeks and just left her alone. I did nothing to show her that I was still here, waiting. That I'd always be here.

"Where is she?" I whirl back around to face him, an idea already forming. "Where is she right now?"

Face drawn, he shakes his head. "I don't know but you need to think—"

"I've been thinking." That's all I ever do. I think about how this girl who owns my bleeding fucking heart doesn't want it. How I'm not good enough. How I'll never be good enough. But what if she doesn't see me like that? What if she doesn't think I'm worthless. Even if I am. *Fuck.* I scrub my hands over my face. How could I be so stupid? I've been angry, so goddamn angry that she could just give up on us like that. Throw me away like I meant nothing to her, but that wasn't what she was doing. She was protecting herself.

I need to change that. Convince her I'm not going to leave her. I'm not like everyone else. I'll stand with her if she'll have me. But shit. Will she have me? If I push, can I get her to change her mind? Or is it truly too late now. Three weeks might not sound like much, but it's felt like forever. Did I wait too long?

THIRTY-FOUR

Emilio

B ibiana doesn't go to work for another few hours. She's working the closing shift, which I only know because earlier this week she asked if I wanted Luis an extra day when she had to go in. I agreed right away. Obviously. But Jae said she wasn't home, and I'm not due to pick Luis up until six. That's still three hours away.

I pace my room as I wait, the minutes ticking by at a snail's pace when the distinct sounds of my brothers and sister returning greet me. They're laughing about something and it's a sound I'm not used to hearing here, in this house. At first, I tense, my body certain that the noise will draw unwanted attention, but then my mind catches up. Raul is gone. We're safe.

I let myself enjoy my baby sister's laughter. Listen to the ease and joy she has and take comfort in knowing she never has to worry about being hit again. Not here in her own home.

I want to hear my son's laughter here too. To have all of the ugly memories I have in this house replaced with new ones. Better ones.

The door to my bedroom opens, my oldest brother leaning in. "What are you doing?" Roberto asks, his tone gruff but not unwelcome. Having him home still feels weird. We were never very close and being overseas the last four years didn't help us get any closer, but I meant what I said when I told him we were good. I can tell he's trying. He goes out of his way to check on all three of us, and he's been great with Luis when I bring him over, really taking on the role of uncle. My hard exterior brother has a soft spot for my boy.

I look down at the football in my hands for a second longer before throwing it in a box. I've been wracking my brain all afternoon on how to show Bibiana that I'm different. That I can change. And this is one of the ways I plan to show her I'm ready to put her, put our family first. I know she's insecure. Has issues with other girls flirting with me and I don't know how to make that shit stop but, I sigh, I need to get the fuck over myself. This is the right move. I had a back-up plan for a reason and an educational scholarship is just a good as a football one and will take some of the attention off of me.

If I have any chance of winning my girl back, I need to put her and Luis first. They have to be my primary focus. Not football. I need to be sensible. Get a real job. Take care of them. And I can't do that and chase my dreams at the same time. I've had nothing but time to think about this. It has to be this way.

"Just packing up some junk," I say, tossing my cleats in next.

He considers me for a moment, and I try and ignore the way his stare makes me feel. Like I'm a problem he can't quite figure out. My brother is good at that, puzzling things together, assessing a situation and then responding in the manner he thinks is necessary. I'd blame it on the military, but a part of me remembers him always being like this. He sees too much that others don't.

"I never thought I'd hear you say anything football related was junk," he muses.

"We all have to grow up at some point, right? Isn't that why you came back home?" I don't need to look at him to know my words hit their mark.

"Do you love her?"

I take a deep breath and ignore the need to snap at him. Isn't it obvious? If I didn't love her, I wouldn't be this much of a fucking wreck. I wouldn't be packing up all my shit. Closing the door on all the things that matter most to me. And I sure as hell wouldn't be taking Jae's goddamn advice. "Yeah, man. I do."

"Do you love her more than you love being angry with her?"

"What the hell does that mean?" I'm not angry with her. Not anymore. I mean, I was, sure. But I get it now. I understand her damage, or at least I think I do.

"It's a yes or no question," he says.

"I'm not angry," I say with a huff.

He shakes his head. "Yeah, bro, you are. You've been angry for a few weeks now and all I see is you getting angrier by the day."

"Nah, man. You don't know—"

He raises a hand and starts ticking off the reasons he believes I'm angry. "You're mad she isn't giving you a chance. You're mad she's made opinions about you that you don't think are true. You're mad she's got your boy most of the time while you get visitation. You're mad—"

My blood boils over. "I'm not fucking mad." He raises a brow and I exhale a harsh breath. "I don't enjoy being angry with her. I don't want to be pissed off at the girl I care about." But he's right, I am. I'm so fucking angry, even as I'm miserable without her. Even as I convince myself that Jae has the right of it, that she's damaged too and that I have to fight for her because dammit, I want her to fucking fight for me too.

"Do you want to be angry at her for forcing you to sacrifice your dreams, too?"

"It's not that simple."

"Yeah, man, it is. If you give up on football, you're going to resent that girl. You might get her back, but it'll only be temporary. You'll sabotage it. Trust me. I know."

"Then what the hell do you suggest, huh?" How else do I show her that I'm in it for the long haul? I've been sitting here for hours and this is the best I've come up with. If Roberto is saying it isn't good enough, then fuck me, because I don't know what is.

He looks at me like he's trying to explain psychics to a toddler. I wait.

"Let the anger go. It's that simple."

I scowl. "I did. I am. I—"

"The past doesn't matter. The fact you didn't know about Luis for however many months, does not matter." I open my mouth to argue. We've moved past that, but he doesn't give me the chance. "The fact that she got upset and broke things off with you doesn't matter." I bite down on the inside of my cheek until I taste blood. "All that matters is whether or not you want to be with that girl bad enough to work for it." He watches me for a beat. "Whether or not you want to put in the work to raise your son as a unit and not a broken family."

I clench my jaw and look away. "You already know I do. I'm going to figure this out. I'm going to talk to her. Or try to. I don't want my kid growing up in a broken home like we did."

He nods and waits until I meet his gaze again. "Then you gotta let the anger go. You're hurt. I get it. But your hurt is making you angry and that shit will turn to bitterness in a heartbeat. You can't fix what's broken with you two if you're still broken on your own. Trust me, I would know." I almost ask how but can tell by the look on his face that whatever it is he's angry about, it isn't something he's ready to talk about.

"You want to go storm over there and win back your girl, I see it in your face but that isn't your best move right now."

"Then what is?"

"I cleaned out Dad's room and moved my stuff in there so my old room next to yours is empty now," he says, seemingly out of nowhere.

I frown. "Uh. Okay. Cool." I have no idea why he's telling me this. What does that have anything to do with what we were just talking about? Is he worried I'll give a fuck that he's claiming the bigger room? Not like I plan—my brother smacks me upside the head and scowls at me.

"What the hell, man?"

His scowl only darkens, and the soldier in him is definitely showing. He's standing stiff and straight with menace radiating from his pores. "Do you know *why* I spent all day yesterday clearing my stuff out of that room?" he hisses.

I rub at the back of my head, irritation at the forefront of my mind. "Because you're a selfish prick and wanted the master with a bigger closet and your own bathroom?"

He smirks. "That too. But *hermanito,* I cleaned out the room because Luis needs a bedroom, doesn't he?"

I jerk my gaze to him, scrutinizing his face for any sign that this is some sick joke. His face is dead serious.

I swallow hard. "You think he should have a room here, for when I have him?" I hedge, not entirely sure if I'm hearing him correctly. I mean, I only have him two, sometimes three days a week, and he usually sleeps with me in my room until Bibiana gets off her shift.

"No, stupid." Roberto huffs out a breath and levels me with a look that says *you're a complete moron*. "I think you should go get your girl and my nephew and move them both in here."

Emotion clogs my throat. His plan sounds way better than mine which consisted of some begging and most likely some yelling that she needed to, no, *had to* give me another shot. I mean, I was going to say it a hell of a lot better than that, but that was the gist of it. You're broken. I'm broken. I won't ever leave you. Let's be broken together. Okay. When I repeat it to myself in my head it sounds stupid as hell but this—

I'm not sure what to say, so I state the obvious in case Roberto is late on the pickup. "We, uh. We're not together. Luis's mom and me, I mean. She wants to co-parent. She doesn't want a romantic relationship." With me, at least. So what does moving her in accomplish, aside from getting to see my son every day which I am completely down for but...

He shrugs his shoulders. "She's family now. She shouldn't be living with some other guy who wants to play house with your kid when she can be here. When your son can be raised by both his parents. Together. Whatever your relationship status is, that's between you two. But I for one think my nephew and his mom should be surrounded by family. Don't you?"

I scrub my hand over my face, almost afraid to let the excitement rush in because yeah, they should be here. And put like that, there's no pressure. She doesn't have to be in a relationship with me to move in. We can be roommates. Yeah. She might go for that idea, right? And then maybe with time, she can see that I'm not such a fuck up. That I can be someone she can depend on.

Roberto steps further into the room and pulls the football out of the box, handing it back to me. "You don't have to give up on your dreams because you're a father," he tells me. "If anything, you have to fight harder for them now more than ever. Show Luis what hard work and determination gets you. And if you want to win back your girl"—he pauses—"then let go of all your pent-up anger and show her you at your best. The Emilio who fights for every yard, who smiles through his pain, and who gets up every fucking day and keeps going no matter how hard shit gets. That girl is looking for someone to weather the storm with her, be that person."

I suck on my bottom lip and shake my head. "But—"

"We're family," he says again. "We look out for each other. I know I fucked up when I left you and Antonio. Left Sofia. I should have stayed. Made sure you were all safe." He looks away, shame coloring his features. "I can't change our past. But I can change our futures. I can be here now, the way you need me."

I scrub my hand over my face and blink back the moisture in my eyes. "I don't blame you for escaping this hellhole," I tell him. We all do what we have to do to survive.

He considers me a moment, almost like he's weighing my words before he nods his head. "Appreciate it. But I still fucked up and I'll own that." He sighs. "I know you were going to go to the dorms after graduation, live on campus but this is your home. For however long you want to be here. For you, Bibiana, Luis. Family takes care of family. Alright?"

I nod. "Thanks, man."

"Don't thank me. Get off your ass and go get my nephew."

I look at the clock. It's only an hour before I'm supposed to pick up Luis. Fuck it. I'll take my chances and just hope Bibiana is home. This can't wait a minute longer.

THIRTY-FIVE

Emilio

Knocking on the door and waiting for her to answer has to be one of the most nerve-wracking experiences of my life. I've gone over what to say again and again in my head but when Bibiana opens the door, Luis propped on her hip and fast asleep, all of my carefully planned words escape me. God, she's so fucking beautiful. Her hair is thrown up in a tangle of curls. Dark smudges darken the skin beneath her eyes. She doesn't look to be wearing an ounce of makeup and still, I've never seen her look more beautiful.

"Hey," she says after a full minute passes of me just standing there, drinking her in. "You're here early." She tucks a few flyaway strands of hair behind her ear.

I look down at my sneakers, shoving my hands deep into my pockets to keep from reaching for her. A move I know she would not appreciate right now. "I was hoping we could talk."

Her mouth tightens. "I'm supposed to be getting ready for work."

"I can hold him while you do that. *Please.* I don't want to fight or anything. Just give me five minutes."

She bites her bottom lip but nods, opening the door wider and allowing me to step inside.

I catch sight of Jae in the living room and when he spots me his eyes widen, but he tilts his head in approval, stands up, and heads toward us. "I'm going to grab a coffee," he tells Bibiana. "Want anything?"

"Anything caffeinated," she says, and I know it's meant to be a joke, but hearing her request only confirms she's not getting enough rest. Between school, work, and Luis, she's running herself ragged.

"You've got it." He slips outside, leaving us alone in his house as Bibiana leads me down a hallway that I'm assuming goes to her room. Once inside she hands Luis to me, careful not to wake him before retrieving a makeup bag from her dresser and signaling me to follow her to another room. We make our way to the hallway bathroom where she drops her makeup on the counter and starts pulling out a series of products. I lean against the wall, content to hold Luis and watch as she gets ready. This feels oddly domestic. I like it. The ease and simplicity of it all.

"What did you want to talk about?" The words are casual, but I can see the stiff set of her shoulders like she's bracing herself against a coming storm and I don't want to be that. Something she has to weather.

I meet her bright blue gaze in the mirror and force myself to relax. To set my anger and my feelings aside and say these next words. Take this first step toward the future I want for the three of us.

"I wanted to apologize."

Her brows furrow, a leery expression on her face. "Okay." She doesn't sound convinced.

"I let chicks flirt with me, knowing it would upset you. I contributed to your insecurities and that shit isn't okay."

Her mouth makes a small "o" before she recovers and clears her throat. "Where is this coming from?"

I take a deep breath. "I was also hoping you'd consider something for me. For Luis." I hastily add on, because if there is anything I know about Bibiana, it is that she will always put our son first even before her own wants and needs.

She looks at me, her penetrating stare telling me to go on.

"I have an extra room at my place. I...I was hoping you'd move in. With me. Us. I mean. I live with my brothers—Roberto and Antonio. And my little sister Sofia. You'd like them."

She opens her mouth, but I rush on before she says no without hearing me out completely. I need her to see all the positives before focusing on the negatives.

"You don't want to give a relationship with me another shot. I understand why and I accept it. That isn't why I'm asking you to move in." Lie. It's a part of it, but not the main reason. Not all of it. Baby steps, I remind myself. "I'm not trying to trick you or any bullshit like that. I just..." I stare down at the top of Luis's head. If I look at her face, I'll lose my nerve because the thought of her saying no is soul-crushing. "I want to see my son every day. I want him to have a chance to get to know his uncles and his aunt. I want him surrounded by family where he'll be loved and cherished to the point he'll probably hate it as he gets older because we're going to smother him with so much damn love."

I pause to take a breath. "I know shit with your mom is strained. You have the world on your shoulders. You have school and Luis and now a job. I don't know how you're doing it. But I want to help carry the load. I want to do my part. Watch Luis while you do homework or go out with your friends and help in the mornings when you need to get ready for school because you deserve to graduate. I don't want you giving up on your dreams when you don't have to. My brothers and sister want to help too. If you'll let them. They want to be your family too. Not just Luis's."

The silence stretches between us and I'm almost afraid to look up.

"I don't have any dreams," she whispers.

I raise my eyes to hers, letting her see the sincerity in my own. "Then I want to stand beside you as you make some."

"You want me to move in with you?"

I nod. "No strings. We don't have to be together. You and Luis will have your own space. I just... I want to take care of you. Support you and Luis the way I should have been doing this whole time. That is, if you'll let me." Her lower lip trembles. "Shit. I didn't mean to upset you." *Fuck.* Is the thought of seeing me every day *that* awful?

"You didn't upset me. You..." She sniffs and wipes her tears with the backs of her hands. "That all sounds really great."

"It does." That's hard to believe because instead of looking happy, she looks like an absolute wreck. A beautiful disaster. God, I'm falling hard for this girl. She's strong and smart. Resilient. And braver then anyone I know. No wonder I don't fucking deserve her. But I will spend every fucking day of my life trying to. I won't let this girl down again. And if a relationship isn't in the cards for us, I guess I'll have to accept that. Maybe. Okay, no the fuck I won't, but I don't need to say that out loud.

Bibi's head bobs up and down. "Yeah. Okay. All I ever wanted for Luis was for him to have a family. To be loved, you know? To have people, more than just me or you, that he could rely on to have his back."

"He does. He has Roman and Allie, Dominique, Aaron, Kasey, my brothers and Sofia. We all want to help take care of him. Hell, Roman's mom has even been bugging me to bring him by, so he's got a grandma and grandpa too that are going to love the shit out of him."

Knowing I shouldn't, I reach out and cup her face, stroking my thumb along her cheek. "I will always do right by him. I will always put him first and I will always be there for you. No matter where we stand, no matter what you need, I will show up and I will be there. I promise you I will not abandon either of you, and I think moving in with me is the right move. For all of us."

"Okay." She smiles through her tears and I stomp down the impulse the kiss her. To seal the agreement with our mouths and show her just how great the two of us can be together if only we try. But we're not there yet.

"Yeah?"

She smiles. "Yeah."

"Yes!" I shout, startling Luis, who emits an angry cry. "Shit. Sorry, little man." I bounce him in my arms and manage to calm him down. He yawns once before closing his eyes again and shoving his face between my neck and shoulder.

"Can I help you pack your things?" I ask, eager to get this ball rolling.

She shakes her head, exhaling a strangled laugh. "Let's maybe slow down just a little. I can't move in with you right this minute."

I frown. I thought—

"I have to be at work in less than an hour. How about you come help me tomorrow and we'll go from there."

Oh. Yeah. Tomorrow is good too.

"I can do that." I kiss her cheek. It's quick and chaste, but her cheeks turn a beautiful shade of pink and I have to force myself not to stare. "We'll get out of your way so you can get ready and we'll talk more about this tomorrow."

Her smile widens, a wistful expression taking over her face. "Tomorrow."

THIRTY-SIX

Bibiana

"Bibi!" Antonio—Emilio's brother—calls my name, and I poke my head out of the bathroom door, toothbrush still in my mouth.

"What?" The word is garbled, but he gets the gist.

"You're going to be late. Let's get this show on the road." I groan and duck my head back inside the bathroom, glancing at my phone for the time. Shit. It's almost six. I am going to be late.

I spit the toothpaste in the sink, add a quick layer of gloss over my lips and grab a hair tie, hastily throwing my hair up as I make my way to the front door. Antonio waits for me, keys in hand and a smile on his face. "Ready?"

"Yes. Sorry."

He chuckles. "Don't apologize."

He opens the door for me and ushers me outside where Emilio has Luis in his arms as Roberto runs around the yard, Sofia right behind him as she tries to catch up and tag him, but he's too quick. Their laughter is infectious, and Luis waves his hands in the air, eager to join the fun.

"I'll be back," Antonio calls out and three heads turn our way. Emilio's eyes meet mine and a smile spreads over his face, nearly taking my breath away. He looks at me like I hang the moon and stars and I still can't understand why. He was right when he said moving in with him and his family was the right move for us. I haven't been living here long, but already it's like a weight has been lifted off my chest.

At first, I was nervous. I thought he was going to push for more than I was willing to give and I kept waiting for the moment when he would demand a relationship, but he never did.

I've been living with the Chavez family for almost a month now and not once has Emilio crossed the line of friendship. We have movie nights as a family and every Sunday we barbecue with our friends. Everyone comes over and we have carne asada and tortillas. Sofia helps me make the rice and beans, and the boys put together the salsa. It's a family affair, and something I look forward to every week.

When I don't work, Emilio and I put Luis to bed together. It's not usually a big deal, just a bedtime story and then we tuck him in my bed. I considered asking Mom for his crib, but I like having my boy snuggled up beside me. And on nights I do work, Emilio puts him to sleep in my room for me and lays with him until I get home, carefully slipping away as I take the spot he vacated.

Only lately, I haven't wanted him to go.

"Let's give Momma a kiss," Emilio says and my heart stutters, but then I realize he's leaning forward to allow Luis to get closer. My boy reaches out to smoosh my face in his tiny hands, giving me an open-mouthed and slobbery kiss on the nose as he tries to all but eat my face. "Thank you, *benzinho*," I tell him.

"Bibi!" Antonio calls again.

"I'll see you boys later," I tell Emilio. "Gotta run if I don't want to miss my ride."

Emilio snorts. "Antonio wouldn't leave you and you know it."

True, but still... I rush around the car and climb in the passenger seat, making sure to buckle my seat belt. My heart is full as I watch my family continue to play in the front yard, and I wonder not for the first time, if I gave in to my wants, would our lives be even better?

I slip in the back for my ten-minute break, my feet tired and my shoulders stiff. We're deader than dead, which should make my job easier, but it seems to only make the night drag on longer. At least when we're busy time flies by and the next thing I know, we're closing. When it's like this, all I can do is think, and right now I'm not sure thinking is what I should be doing.

"How's it going out there?" Allie asks, setting a stack of plates aside.

"Slow," I tell her, hopping up on the countertop to sit. "I'm taking my ten."

She wipes her hands with a towel and jumps on the counter opposite me. "Cool, I'll take mine too."

She tosses me an apple and I bite into it, swinging my legs back and forth in front of me. "How's living at the Chavez house going?" she asks with a small smirk.

"Fishing?" I ask her, because this question comes up near daily.

She shrugs. "Maybe. Can you blame me? It's been a month and I don't know, it's weird."

My brows furrow. "How is it weird?"

"Haven't you noticed that Emilio's been acting strange?"

I shrug my shoulders, not really sure what she's getting at. He seems like the same old Emilio to me.

"When was the last time a girl gave him her number?" Allie questions.

"I don't know. Probably yesterday." Which sucks but it's probably the truth.

"Nope. It's been at least three weeks."

My eyes narrow. "And you know that how?"

"Because the last time a girl gave him her number, he had Kasey copy it down and give it to every boy in the school. Kasey might have taken things a step further than Emilio intended by telling them all to send a dick pic to that number but—"

I snort and apple flies out of my nose. Ow. Gross. Ow.

"That is disgusting."

"Shut up. You're the one who made me laugh." I clean up my mess and set my apple aside. "Okay, keep going."

She quirks a brow. "Oh, never mind. You're not really interested anyway, right? It's not like you want Emilio or anything."

"Allie," I growl in warning.

She rolls her eyes. "Right. So anyway, its public knowledge now that if you give Emilio your number when he didn't ask for it, every guy at Sun Valley High is going to get it, including the freshman. Penelope Reese had to change her number because the dick pics would not end."

"Why would he—"

"Oh, and prom is next month."

"Really?" Prom wasn't really something I was keeping track of.

"Yep. He's been asked at least eight times that I know of. He's said no each time."

"He's probably just waiting for a better offer," I joke, even as my chest tightens. The thought of him going to prom with anyone else makes me sick to my stomach.

Now it's Allie's turn to snort. "You're kidding, right?"

I shrug. "What?"

"You know how he feels about you, B."

I shake my head. "It's not like that. We agreed—"

She huffs out a breath. "Did you though? Did you both agree, or did you decide?"

"We agreed," I say, but I'm not so sure now. "At least, I thought we agreed."

"You're not dating either," she reminds me.

"I don't have time to date. I have Luis and work and—"

"And Emilio?"

My cheeks heat. "Who is the father of my child and a really great co-parent."

"He is. But now that the dust has settled, are you still sure that's all you want him to be?"

"Yes. No. I don't know."

"Maybe now is the time to be a little daring. Spread your wings and take a chance." Emilio's words echo through my mind. *Spread your wings, mariposa. Fly.*

Things might not have turned out as planned when I first heard those words whispered in my ear, but maybe this is fate's way of telling me I need to do it again, take a chance. I got Luis out of the deal the first time around, and I wouldn't trade him for the world. Maybe...maybe it's time to reach for just a little more.

It's close to midnight when I make it home, having caught a ride with Allie. I creep inside the house, careful to keep my steps silent as I slip off my shoes and coat and leave them near the door. I wash my face and slip into my sleep shorts and tank that I left in the bathroom before making my way to my room.

Luis is curled up in the middle of my bed, Emilio beside him. As I slip inside, the soft glow from Luis's night light shows me that Emilio is fast asleep. I chew on my bottom lip before deciding to leave well enough alone for one night. I slip beneath the covers, curling around my son as my feet accidentally brush up against Emilio's.

His eyes jerk open. Dark brown pools meet my own and a small smile curls his lips before he's forced to stifle a yawn. "How long was I out?" he whispers.

"I just got home, so probably not long."

He nods and turns to sit up, but I reach out and wrap my fingers around his hand before he has the chance to. He frowns, a look of confusion on his face as his eyes flick from my hand to my face. "Stay," I whisper.

His frown deepens and he hesitates.

"Please."

He nods and slips back beneath the covers, facing me with Luis between us. We stare at one another for several minutes, the silence between us heavy, but neither of us brave enough to break it.

I wrap one arm around Luis, Emilio following suit, his arm carefully covering my own. I close my eyes and force myself to relax. To not overthink this moment and for once to just let it be.

THIRTY-SEVEN

Bibiana

I wake up to a heavy weight in my face and shift my body, attempting to dislodge whatever it is that's trying to smother me. A baby giggle greets me and the next thing I know Luis is sitting up, letting me breathe for a quick second before he decides to body slam my face again.

Ompf.

"Hey, little man," Emilio's sleep heavy voice cuts through my own early morning fog. "We gotta be nice to Momma." Luis giggles again, content to use me as a cushion before shoving his face between my breasts, his way of demanding to be fed.

I groan and roll to my side, tugging my top down to expose my breast without even realizing what I'm doing. Emilio sucks in a breath and my eyes jump to his right as Luis latches on and decides to be extra sweet with a quick scrape of his teeth—the only two he has—to remind me I kept him waiting. I bite down on my bottom lip and glare at him. "Bite Momma again and she might just cut you off," I warn.

He ignores me, of course. Almost a year old now, he's decided to become a boob barnacle every chance he gets. "Sorry," I say sheepishly. "I wasn't thinking when—"

Emilio cuts me off. "You don't have to hide, you know?"

My cheeks heat. "I know." But I have been. Whenever Luis has needed to be fed, I've slipped into my room for privacy. Not because I feel like I need it, but because... Well, I don't know why. But nursing him with Emilio present has always felt intimate in a way I can't quite describe.

"How was work?" he asks, casually changing the subject.

"Long. Slow."

"How'd you sleep?"

I yawn but manage to push through a grin. "Good. But not as long as I'd have liked," I complain. Luis likes to wake up around seven, so without looking at the clock I know it must be around that time.

"Why don't I—"

"Bibi!" Sofia bursts through the door without a care in the world as any middle-schooler would do. "Is he awake."

I chuckle. "Yes, he's awake."

She flicks her gaze to Emilio and raises a single brow. "Why are you in here?"

"Because I'm spending time hanging with my boy," Emilio says smoothly.

Sofia doesn't look convinced. "Did you sleep in here?"

The next thing I know Roberto and Antonio are poking their heads in the door too. "Hey have you seen—*oh.*" Both brothers pause. I turn away, my cheeks heating as I pray they can't all see my tits on display.

"Sorry. We were just looking for—"

Emilio waves. "Right here."

"Right," Antonio says.

'What do you want?" A thread of annoyance filters into Emilio's voice.

"Nothing. Sofia come on. Let's—"

"But I want the baby," she whines.

"Right. Yeah. Grab Luis."

Hearing his name, he rears back, releasing my breast to peer over my shoulder. Seeing his aunt, he lunges for her, crawling over my body and forcing her to make a quick grab for him. "Guess I've been replaced."

"You two, uh... catch up on some sleep. We'll take care of Luis, here," Antonio says.

The three of them leave and the door closes behind them, leaving Emilio and I alone in my bed. I turn to face him, his eyes caught on my breast when I realize I never pulled my shirt back up. "Oh, my god." I rush to cover myself and he snaps out of it.

"Shit. I'm sorry. I didn't mean—"

"No, it's fine. My fault."

We both burst into a fit of laughter as I realize just how stupid this is. It's not like he hasn't seen my boobs before. When I finally get myself under control, my chest is heaving. I wipe the moisture from my eyes and turn to find Emilio staring at me, a wide grin on his face.

"What?" I ask, my heart suddenly loud in my ears.

He shifts closer, closing some of the gap left behind now that Luis is playing with his aunt and uncles. "You still tired?" he asks.

I lick my lips, his eyes tracking the movement.

Spread your wings, Bibi. I tell myself. *Fly.*

To him, I just shake my head. "No. You?"

"No."

The next thing I know, he's closed the distance, his hand cupping my cheek and his eyes boring into mine, giving me every opportunity to pull away. I swallow hard and reach out a tentative hand to trace the line of his jaw. He shudders beneath my touch. "I've missed you." The words slip past my defenses and I freeze, waiting to see what he says, but he says nothing. Instead, his lips press against mine and I melt against him before I realize that I must have the absolute worst morning breath and tear myself away.

"Shit. Did I read that wrong?"

"No. No. Umm..." I jump out of bed. "Wait right there." I rush to the hallway bathroom, brush my teeth faster than I've ever brushed my teeth in my life, and then hurry back to my room, closing the door behind me. My back is pressed against the door, my chest rising and falling as I'm treated to an unobstructed view of Emilio now that he's no longer hidden by the covers. He's sitting against the headboard, the blankets pooled at his waist and his chest bare, showcasing his tattoo.

"You okay?" he asks, worry evident in his voice. "I can go. I mean, I know you said stay but..."

I shake my head and climb back onto the bed, sitting on my knees and facing him. "I don't want you to go."

His shoulders relax. "What do you want?" There is so much unspoken between us, so much left unsaid, but this time instead of letting fear or doubt get in my way, I tell him the truth.

"Everything."

The word barely passes my lips when he's on me. He presses me back against the bed, his body flush with mine and the fact he's only wearing boxer briefs becomes apparent when his hard length presses against my core. I gasp, my back arching off the bed.

"Are you okay? Is this okay?" he asks me, his lips nipping at the column of my neck.

"God, yes," I hiss, clinging to him.

He pulls back and I make a sound of protest in the back of my throat, reaching for him, but he doesn't give. "What is this, *mariposa?*" That single word unravels me.

"I don't know."

He pulls away, sitting back on his knees. I push up on my hands as his dark brown gaze meets mine and he hides none of what he's feeling. All his want, his need, are stamped across his face. But there's something else, a vulnerability I'm not used to seeing.

"I don't want this to be nothing," he says. "If this is just some itch—"

"It's not," I rush to say.

"Then what is it? I need some information here, so I don't go out of my mind." He leans forward, pressing his forehead against mine. "If we go down this road, I don't think I could give you up again. It was damn near impossible the first time. I..." He releases a shaking breath. "No hesitation. No doubts. We do this, we're both all in. One hundred percent."

Is that what I want? Before the question forms completely in my mind, I know it is.

"I'm all in," I whisper, a smile spreading across my face.

"Yeah?"

"Yeah."

"Yes! God, yes!" he shouts. I laugh, falling back to the bed as he towers over me once again. "I am never letting you go again, Bibiana Sousa. Never. "

I bite my bottom lip. "I think I'm okay with that."

He kisses me, his teeth biting at my lips and I open for him, his mouth devouring mine in a hungry kiss before he murmurs, "You brushed your teeth."

I laugh. He moves to pull away again, but I wrap my arms and legs around him, grinding against his length. "You're fine. Keep kissing me."

He groans and does as I ask, his mouth hot against my own.

He takes his time kissing me as his hands roam over my body as though he's trying to commit me to memory. His thumbs hook into the edge of my sleep shorts and panties and I loosen my legs, allowing him to tug them off and toss them to the ground. His fingers trail between my thighs and his thumb finds my clit, stroking me in slow circles that make my pussy clench with need.

God, it feels so good.

He stops just as the pressure begins to build and I cry out in frustration, but he only chuckles.

"Patience," he whispers, his hands sliding up my torso and beneath the hem of my tank. My breathing shudders. He peels the fabric from my skin, baring me to his hungry gaze, and I instinctively wrap my arms around my middle.

"Nah uh. No hiding," he says, tugging my arms free. I wait for his disgust, but the open want in his gaze never changes. He bends at the waist, placing a kiss between my breasts before moving his mouth to kiss one hip bone and then the other.

"Emilio—"

"Shh... relax for me." His gaze is heavy with desire, but it's attentive too, like he wants to make sure I'm okay. And I am. I close my eyes, letting my head fall back as he settles himself between my legs. His hands press my thighs open and I fight the urge to clamp them shut, but I let his eyes drink their fill. "So fucking beautiful, and all mine."

Slowly, he slides a finger inside me, his lips latching on to the sensitive bundle of nerves above my opening at the same time. I gasp and moan his name, unable to hold still as he finger fucks me and sucks on my clit. The pressure builds inside me almost like I'm running a race, and within minutes I'm reaching toward the finish line. What he's doing feels amazing, but I want more. I want him.

I'm already on the edge, my release hovering right there, but I want him buried inside me when I get there. "Emilio, please." Mistaking my words, he increases his pace adding a second finger and I clench around the intrusion. "I need... you... inside me." I gasp and he pulls back to look at me, his fingers still buried in my core.

"I want you to come with me," I tell him, and a savage grin spreads across his face before a flash of irritation has him pulling away entirely.

"One minute."

Still clad in his black boxer briefs he leaves the room only to come back seconds later with a small foil packet in his hands. My shoulders relax and he returns to my side, dropping the boxers and rolling the condom onto his length. I lick my lips.

"You ready for me?"

I nod. So damn ready.

He grabs my hips, pressing me deeper into the mattress as he guides himself to my center, his movements excruciatingly slow. His eyes search mine like he's waiting for some sort of permission, so I nod letting him know I'm not changing my mind.

His body shakes with need as he enters me and I thrust my hips forward, forcing him in deeper. He groans before sinking the rest of the way in and then we just stay like that for several seconds, both of our chests heaving as we savor the feeling of one another.

He kisses my mouth, nibbling at my lips and nipping at my jaw and neck. "I'm going to fuck you, Bibiana. I'm going to show you just how much I've missed you."

"Yes," I moan because God, I want that.

He withdraws his cock only to slam back into me and I cry out. He smiles before his hand comes up to cover my mouth, smothering my cry of pleasure. "Gonna make my brothers think I'm hurting you," he warns.

Oh, my God, I completely forget we are not alone in the house. And they just heard... I groan again, only this time for an entirely different reason.

He chuckles. "Don't be quiet on my account," he says. "I like making you scream."

He keeps his hand pressed over my mouth as his thrusts quicken, his hand muffling my sounds. "That's it, *mariposa.* You like that don't you?" He bites my shoulder and my release slams into me, my pussy convulsing around his cock. He grunts but keeps going, his thrusts coming harder, faster. His kisses grow more aggressive and his hand slips from my mouth to wrap around my throat in a possessive hold.

The fingers of his other hand dig into my hips as he thrusts into me with savage strokes. My sex clenches around him and he grits his teeth, a second orgasm already building inside me. His fingers find my clit, and he rubs quick circles over me, sending me closer to release. Without warning he dips his head, his mouth capturing one taught nipple between his teeth and I sail over the edge, a second orgasm crashing through me like a hurricane.

He doesn't slow his pace, his thrusts erratic as he bites my breasts, my neck, whatever his mouth can find. My hands roam over his back, my nails digging into his skin. It only seems to spur him on. I wrap my legs around his waist, my hands clinging to his shoulders. God, it feels so good.

I can feel the moment he gets close, when his body stiffens, and he thrusts into me one more time before his entire body quakes above me.

He collapses to the bed, shifting his weight at the last second so as not to crush me.

We both lie there, skin slick with sweat, breathing heavily and staring at the ceiling. After a few seconds pass, he rolls to his feet, disposes of the condom, and then climbs back onto the bed beside me and tugs me into his arms.

"I missed you," he says against my hair, and a feeling of contentment sweeps through me.

"I missed you too."

He takes a deep breath, his nose buried in my hair as he says, "You going to marry me this time?"

I choke on a laugh and try to turn to see his face. He's kidding, right?

I catch a smirk and know right away he's just messing with me, so I say, "Nope."

He pretends to be wounded, a mock crestfallen expression on his face. "Fine. Fine. But you'll date me, right? Be my girl?"

I bite my lip. "Yeah. I'll be your girl."

He squeezes me again. "About fucking time. And we're making this Faceplace or Tikgram or whatever the fuck they call it official."

I laugh. "You're not even on social media."

"Don't care. I'll download all the damn apps just to let everyone out there know that Bibiana Sousa is *mine*."

Need More?

Be sure to *order your copy of Cruel Devil, book 3 in the Devils of Sun Valley High series.*

https://hi.switchy.io/Cruel-Devil

And turn the page for a sneak peak of the book. Dominique & Kasey are explosive!

Cruel Devil

Dominique Price is good-looking, arrogant, a football-God,
and my brother's best friend.
He hates me.
He wants me.
But he can never have me.
Everything comes so easy for him.
I refuse to be just another game for him to win.

Go to https://hi.switchy.io/Cruel-Devil
to binge-read your copy or Cruel Devil.

THIRTY-EIGHT

Kasey

T his year will make me or break me. Personally, I'm hoping for the former. But, as I sit in the back seat of my mother's SUV, I have a feeling it's going to be the latter. There's this sense of foreboding thrumming through me as I look up at the impeccably manicured lawns and twin pillars that decorate where I'll be living this next school year. All one hundred and eighty days of it, plus winter and spring breaks. I'm going to hate every minute.

I'm very much aware that there isn't a seventeen-year-old out there who wouldn't kill to leave the nest a little bit early. And trust me when I say I'm not feeling like my life is about to take a turn for the worse just because I'm moving out at the ripe old age of seventeen. What does have me feeling this way is the fact that I'm joining a sorority. Not by choice, I might add.

Sorority life isn't my scene. And no, I don't have any firsthand experience with sororities, and yes, I'm absolutely judging them based on what I've seen on TV, but let's be real, if you knew anything about me, you'd agree that me and the perfect plastics I see walking in and out of the houses on sorority row aren't a match made in heaven.

When I applied for Sun Valley High's running start program —a program that allows me to attend college courses and earn both college credits and the final credits I'll need for my high school diploma, I thought, *this is exactly what I need.* An escape from the stupid drama that is high school life where I never really fit in. It's hard to relate to the people at school when all they can talk about is how Suzie made out with Jason behind Ruby's back and other stupid nonsense, like who is asking who to senior prom.

Meanwhile, my best friends have all graduated and are planning their weddings and being moms and doing real-life things that matter. It makes it hard to relate to high-school life. Hearing the gossip and then seeing all the back-stabby antics, it's not what I'm interested in. And don't even get me started on the boys.

They're so incredibly stupid in high school. The catcalling and fuck-boy flirting. Urgh. You'd think they'd find a better pickup line than, "You must be an angel, because you look like you just fell from heaven."

Barf.

The guys I go to school with have zero game. Not that I'd be interested in anyone at Sun Valley High anyway. I almost wish I was. It'd make seeing a certain broody asshole on the regular a hell of a lot easier.

Both of us attending Suncrest U isn't going to help, but with any luck I won't see him any more than I have to. Suncrest University is his turf, and here he reigns supreme, not that I'm surprised. Dominique Price and his best friends ran the halls at Sun Valley High as the school's football gods, so of course their reputations would follow them to college as they continue to dominate on and off the field. I used to hate those three for what they put my brother through, but now we're all friends. Hell, more like family. But I don't need people realizing we know each other, especially with the unwanted attention that will bring, so I'd like to keep our association under wraps.

And since I'm in college now, Mom decided it was the perfect time to accept an out-of-state promotion and force me to join Kappa Mu—her alma mater. Guess that makes me a legacy.

Yay.

Not.

The alternative was moving with her—so not happening. The prospect of uprooting my entire life to move halfway across the country holds zero appeal, even if the alternative is, well, this.

"Ready to braid hair and paint your nails bubblegum pink?" my brother—Aaron—asks from the front seat.

I roll my eyes and flip him the bird. "Ha. Ha. You're so funny."

He turns to glance at me, pushing the blond hair from his face to give me a wink. "Don't worry, sis. They'll leave you alone once they realize what a prickly personality you have."

I lunge forward to smack him but he swings open the passenger side door, stepping out, just in time to avoid my swipe.

"Kasey!" my mother admonishes me.

"What? He started it," I tell her as I unbuckle to follow him. Despite the early hour, the house is already buzzing with activity—what looks to be a party in full swing. Girls in all manner of summer wear are flitting about, socializing, drinking whatever is in those red Solo cups—and let's be honest, it's not water—and carrying boxes, doing exactly what I'm here to do. Move in.

I wrinkle my nose and glance at my mom as she slings her oversized purse over her shoulder and moves to join Aaron and me on the sidewalk. "Not too late to change your mind?" Aaron mutters under his breath. "You know you wanna."

I elbow him in the ribs. "Are we telling jokes now?"

When mom concocted this grand idea of me joining her former sorority, Aaron, being the protective big brother he is, was nice enough to offer me the spare room at his place. An offer I was quick to decline.

Under normal circumstances, I'd consider it. We were never very close growing up given the four-year age gap between us, but Aaron has always looked out for me. Most brothers would balk at the idea of living with their baby sister after they moved out, but Aaron genuinely wouldn't mind. He's pretty chill about stuff like that.

The problem isn't living with my brother. It's living with my brother's very hot, very broody, drives-me-insane, asshole of a roommate—Dominique Price. On the best of days, we tolerate one another. On the worst, well, things can be openly hostile.

"I'll pass on living with the devil and take door number two, please," I tell him, and he chuckles.

"Dom isn't that bad."

I snort. "Are we talking about the same person, here?" Dominique Price very much is that bad. He gets under my skin in a way no one else can, and the pull he has over me, urgh. I hate it. Sometimes so much so that I think I hate *him*. When we're in the same room, I want to kiss him and punch him in the same breath. That he makes me question my own sanity is infuriating.

Aaron gives me a light-hearted shove. "Alright, sis, have it your way. But don't come crying to me when you realize the grass isn't greener on the other side."

A gust of wind blows my hair into my face and I hastily push my blond curls out of my eyes. "I won't," I assure him. "The grass on your side is already dead and yellow so the bar is set pretty low."

He smiles, his eyes scanning past me, and I turn to see a familiar black Escalade roll up beside my mother's car. The broody asshole I just mentioned parks his overpriced SUV and three doors open, letting out Dom, Roman, and Emilio. Somebody please shoot me now.

"What are they doing here?" I groan.

Aaron throws his arm over my shoulder and pulls me into a side embrace. "They're being good friends and helping you move into your new place." The fact that he genuinely believes that should be concerning, but I know better.

"Whose idea was this?" I ask.

Already their presence is drawing curious looks from some of the girls. It won't take long for them to realize who they are. God dammit, he is such an asshole. It would have been bad enough if he came on his own, but bringing Roman and Emilio is taking it one step too far.

"Dom's," Aaron confirms what I suspected and my mother being the weirdo she is, gushes.

"Isn't that so sweet of them, Kasey? It makes me so happy to know you'll have such a great support system here. Makes me feel so much better about my baby girl going to college." She sighs, the smile on her face wistful as she turns back to the house. If I grind my teeth any harder I'm liable to break a tooth. She cannot be serious right now.

"Yep. Soooo sweet," I tell her while giving Dominique my most murderous glare. Does he shake in fear like he should? Of course not. Instead he smirks like the cruel bastard he is and heads right for me, Roman and Emilio right on his heels.

I'm going to make him regret this. I cannot believe he'd set me up like this.

The guys do that guy handshake bro hug thing as if they didn't all see each other a few hours ago, then Dom turns his full attention on me and I have to force my expression to remain impassive. Age has only worked to sharpen his features, making him even more striking than the boy I met my freshman year of high school three years ago. With his hair tightly braided away from his face, his sharp jawline and full lips stand out in stark relief, and I can't decide if I want to kiss him or punch him—a frequent struggle of mine, so I do what I'm best at and just antagonize him.

"Are you so desperate for female attention that you have to drop in on the girls of Kappa Mu for a little bit of an ego stroke?" I smile in satisfaction when his dark brown eyes narrow.

Dominique has this edge to him that's difficult to describe. He's both regal and rugged; the juxtaposition between the two is likely what makes women flock to him. He has two thin slashes in his right brow that somehow take him from attractive to dangerous, and after graduation he filled out to a full six-foot-five, stacked with all the muscles you'd expect a division one athlete to have. The effect he has on people is hard to miss.

When he scowls the way he is doing right now, he's damn near terrifying to behold. But when he smiles, a real smile that doesn't hold an ounce of malice—and mind you those are rare—his entire face lights up and for a second it's like standing in the sun after months of nothing but rain. God, I hate him.

"I don't need an ego stroke. Not a single woman here can hold my interest," he says, his eyes boring into mine and waiting for a reaction. One I refuse to deliver. *Asshole.* Of course he'd say something like that. Dominique hasn't dated, like seriously dated, for as long as I've known him. He gets around, I'm sure. What football player doesn't when you have an entire fan club of jersey chasers? But the only girl I've seen him with more than once is Tamara Vinzent. I haven't had the pleasure of meeting her yet, but she's his date to any event or function that requires one. I don't really understand their relationship, and for my own sanity, I try not to think about it too much, but somehow she's outlasted everyone else and has managed to sink some form of a hold into Dominique where no others before her have succeeded.

When Dominique realizes I'm not going to respond, the corner of his mouth curls into his signature cruel smile. "You worried someone will catch my attention?" He scans the growing crowd. "Not really my type, but maybe I can—"

"Yo, Baby Henderson," Emilio says, cutting Dominique off from whatever he was about to say and cutting through the growing tension in the air. "You gonna show us the new digs? Introduce us to your new lady friends?" He winks, and if I didn't know him better, I'd think he was serious. But Emilio is head over heels in love with his girlfriend, one of my best friends, so I know this is for show and he's just helping me out. The softy. Too bad his little act of kindness won't keep him safe if he and the others don't get the hell out of here before anyone realizes the school's star quarterback, wide receiver, and cornerback just showed up.

I shake my head. "Hard no. You three need to leave."

Roman smirks and Emilio clutches his heart as though I just wounded him. "Baby Hen—"

"Stop calling me that and go home or I'm going to tell Bibi about your big surprise," I warn.

He sucks in a sharp breath. "You wouldn't. You love me?" He meant it as a statement but it comes out more as a question.

"Wanna bet?" Because today is day one of campus life for me and I'm not going to let these three muck it up.

Emilio backs away, hands raised in the air. "You win. I'll stay in the car." He turns and jogs back to Dom's Escalade. One down. Two more to go.

I turn to Roman and raise a single brow. "You too, mister."

"You don't have anything you can use against me," he says, his voice filled with confidence he should not be feeling right now. Doesn't he know me? I have something on virtually everyone. It's little sister 101. You always find the dirt and horde it to later get your way.

I prop one hand on my hip. "I don't?" I press a finger to my lips as though thinking before letting a wide smile spread across my face. "Hey, Aaron, did I ever tell you about the time Roman and Allie went to Silverdale?"

Roman's eyes widen briefly before his brows draw together. "How do you—"

I pull my phone from my back pocket. "Allie sent me pictures from that weekend. You two were so cute together. The couples—"

Roman jerks forward, pressing his palm over my mouth. His dark brown eyes fill with a mix of disbelief and fury. "Not. Another. Word," he growls. If he were anybody else, I might be worried by the threat in his voice, but despite his rough exterior, Roman is a big ole softie and his fiancé is one of my other best friends. He wouldn't hurt a hair on my head. She loves me. He loves her. Therefore, I win. So instead of pushing his hand away or trying to say anything, I wait for him to realize what I already know.

It takes only a handful of seconds.

"Fine. Don't say anything else. I'll go chill with E. Deal?"

I nod and he slowly releases me, hesitating for just a second to make sure I'll keep my mouth shut before he turns, slaps Dom on the shoulder with a muttered, "You're on your own, man," and joins Emilio in the car.

"Damn, sis, remind me not to get on your bad side," Aaron says, as if I haven't used this exact same tactic on him before.

"Got anything on this one?" He nods toward Dominique, who raises a brow of his own, expression smug because, no, I have nothing I can use against him to make him do anything he doesn't want to do and he knows it.

God, I hate him sometimes.

Go to https://hi.switchy.io/Cruel-Devil *to binge-read your copy or Cruel Devil.*

And for more Emilio & Bibiana, head to https://BookHip.com/WRLRFP to download a free bonus scene

About the Author

Daniela Romero is a USA Today and Wall Street Journal bestselling author. She enjoys writing steamy, new-adult and paranormal romance that delivers an emotional roller coaster sure to take your breath away.

Her books feature a diverse cast of characters with rich and vibrant cultures in an effort to effectively portray the world we all live in. One that is so beautifully colorful.

Daniela is a Bay Area native though she currently lives in Washington State with her sarcastic husband and their three tiny terrors.

In her free time, Daniela enjoys frequent naps, binge reading her favorite romance books, and is known to crochet while watching television because her ADHD brain can never do just one thing at a time.

Stop by her website to find all the fun and unique ways you can stalk her. And while you're there you can check out some free bonus scenes from your favorite books, learn about her Patreon, order signed copies of her books, and swoon over her gorgeous alternative cover editions.

www.daniela-romero.com
You can join her newsletter by visiting
https://hi.switchy.io/VIP

Acknowledgments

This book was a struggle. 2020 was a rough year for many of us and 2021 has decided to give 2020 a run for its money.

My grandmother passed away on the first of the year and writing has been really difficult. Deadlines have been missed and emotionally, I just haven't been in a great head space. To the readers I let down, I'm incredibly sorry. Hopefully Emilio was worth the wait. I really wanted to do him and Bibiana justice. I really wanted to show a glimpse of the struggles young moms experience. Not only as single mothers but as women who are grappling with the profound changes our bodies go through. Hopefully I captured that honestly.

Thank you to Lisa and Cynthia for helping me push through this book and coming in at the final hour to help me polish it and make Savage Devil shine. I couldn't have done this without you.

And thank you to my wonderful children for putting up with Mom being a zombie night after night due to too many sleepless nights spent writing.

On a personal note, I would be incredibly grateful if you took a moment to leave an honest review for the book when you are done reading. Reviews are like giving your favorite author a hug and sometimes we could really use a hugs.

xoxo

Daniela Romero

9 781953 264039